A WINTE

A Winter's Tale

Adam Chandler

HEADLINE
Liaison

First published in 1996
by HEADLINE BOOK PUBLISHING

A HEADLINE LIAISON paperback

10 9 8 7 6 5 4 3 2 1

ISBN 0 7472 5424 9

Typeset at The Spartan Press Ltd,
Lymington, Hants

Printed and bound in Great Britain by
Cox & Wyman Ltd, Reading, Berks

HEADLINE BOOK PUBLISHING
A division of Hodder Headline PLC
338 Euston Road
London NW1 3BH

A Winter's
Tale

Chapter One

As the curtain rose and came down again for the ninth time, before the applause had even abated and the house lights gone up, Rachel Franklin felt his hand roaming in the back of her dress.

'Nine months I've been waiting for this. You promised,' her leading man, Robert Grosvenor, said, gripping one of the cheeks of her behind through the tight red material of her dress.

The whole cast stood in a long line at the front of the stage, arms linked in unity following their final triumphant performance of *Crossed Wires*. His arm had been around her waist before dropping lower with a studied casualness Rachel could see coming from a mile off. The curtain had gone successively up and down, individual bows were taken, and then, when they were in the long line, his hand had meandered towards her behind.

Rachel kept her smile fixed at the curtain for a few more seconds in case they got one more call, but when she was certain they would not, her beam faded and she glowered at him.

'You could at least wait until we're off stage. I thought you were going to do it during my last speech the way you kept looking at me,' she said. 'At least let me get out of costume.'

'Oh no. In costume,' he whined. 'That's part of the deal.'

Rachel sighed. During the first week of rehearsal and in a fit of temper, she had irrationally promised Robert

Grosvenor the chance to have his way with her if the play ran for its full nine months. 'If this thing runs for the full nine, I'll personally let you screw me on the closing night. While I'm still in costume,' she recalled saying to him, the recollection now somewhat woeful.

The costume was a close-fitting red cocktail dress transformed into lurid fetish wear by the costume designer and requiring all the effort and skill of Rachel's dresser Terri to get her into it in the short time between her penultimate scene and the play's climax. 'I take it you won't need *my* help to get out of it later,' Terri had whispered in the wings as Rachel stepped out into her final scene. Not much got past Terri.

Crossed Wires, a knockabout farce with a nineties media edge, had played its full run in the Mercury Theatre in London's West End to above average houses as well as getting a favourable critical reception. Rachel played Antonia Ford, a ruthless careerist with a turbulent personal life who gets her come-uppance in the end, although the play's conclusion was generally happy for everyone involved. It was almost a reprise of a role Rachel had played in a television sitcom lasting only one series and she could usually feel the audience rooting for her as she played the bitchiness for laughs.

Now, it was over. Apart from a promise made months ago to a frisky actor. A pledge made at a time when she herself was in the first flush of attraction to him – a fascination that had withered the more she got to know him. For Robert Grosvenor's part, his attraction to her seemed to remain constant, occupying a level of casual prurience. Not that he wasn't attractive. Of course he was attractive. He was an actor. It made him both attractive and unattractive at the same time. The familiar paradox.

Robert was leading her gleefully off, ignoring the odd bit of applause or kind word from the stage management and heading towards the dressing rooms. Rachel felt practically pulled along, still dazed with the elation of performance and the let-down feeling of it all being over. It had been a good closing night, which she supposed it should have been after such a long run. Rachel shuddered at the memory of the rehearsals, where things were bad, the final dress, where it got worse, and the previews, where it was terrible. It was nice to go out on a good show, especially as many of her friends who had attended the first night or the early part of the run had returned that night.

'Your place or mine?' Robert Grosvenor giggled nervously through his nose and clenched teeth. The rest of the cast called him Mutley behind his back.

Rachel wondered what the now departed character of Antonia Ford would say, still fresh in her like a fledgling ghost. It occurred to her that the best way to handle this was to stay in character.

'Yours, darling,' she said, gripping his behind firmly and giving it a pinch.

They dashed up some stairs, her arm brushing some ropes holding the flies in place, tied off on a handrail. The further they got from the stage, the gloomier the light became. Another thing dawned on Rachel. Robert's character was quite attractive in a villainous way. It would make perfect sense for the two characters to consummate their antagonistic relationship, the lack of such resolution on stage being the motor driving the play forward.

Somewhere in the part of her that was not quite Rachel Franklin and not quite Antonia Ford, she found a reserve of desire spurred on by the euphoria of performance. In one sense, she realised, *Crossed Wires* was not quite over.

Robert's dressing room was packed up much as her own was, a few carrier bags and a box resting by the chair in front of the mirror, stark without its personal trivia. A bouquet and a bottle of champagne in a bucket sat on the counter, a card from the director laying next to it. From her own dressing room earlier that evening, Rachel had sent

Terri scuttling around the theatre delivering parting gifts to the rest of the cast.

Rachel bolted the door and looked at Robert. His hair had been severely cut for the part and she had listened to him fume about it for the first three weeks after they opened. She knew he was worried about losing his hair but she thought the cut took the requisite five years off his true age and made him appear passably in his late twenties. His light blue eyes sparkled like wet glass and the gaunt face was accentuated by the make-up. He smiled and it became a cheeky leer of anticipation, his eyes travelling over her and then coming to rest on the hem of her skirt.

The bottom of the short dress clung to her thighs, pushing her legs together. The fishnet stockings were heavier than normal, exaggerated for the stage. In Rachel's final scene, her character had been duped into attending a formal event dressed inappropriately, a sort of farcical equivalent of her trousers falling down. She had extracted maximum laughs from the funny walk the snugness of the dress forced her to take on.

Robert approached her and she let her back rest against the door, putting her hands on his hips. They wouldn't have long she knew and she felt more urgent than she had expected to when the moment came. His body was warm against hers and she fell into synchronisation with him, feeling her own passion find the same sharp rhythm.

Looking over his shoulder as he nuzzled her neck, Rachel regarded the over made-up face loooking back at her from the mirror. It was the most make-up she had worn on stage in a long time, the final scene demanding it. The lipstick was a deeper red than she would have worn herself, her black hair slicked closer to her head than she would have liked. It made her look like a mercenary, heavily-applied blusher hiding the natural light tone of her skin and transforming her small and pretty face into an intimidating façade. From behind the mask, her eyes looked out, large hazel rounds that gave a warmth and funniness no amount of greasy armour could hide.

The dress was tight like a pelt and his hands stroked the fabric, sending a tingle through her real skin beneath. The taut material held Rachel in check and the swell of anticipation made her feel as though she would literally burst at the seams. Locked in a kiss that had come suddenly and was hard and desperate, Rachel felt his hands lifting her behind, sizing and weighing the pert cheeks, attempting to separate them from the clench of the dress.

Robert's fingers toyed with the hemline, lighting on the heavy net of the stockings. He slipped his fingers under the dress and worked it up her thighs and over her hips, almost peeling it. Bunched around her waist, it revealed the suspender belt and sheer red knickers Rachel had worn to enable her to take on the sleek sexiness of her character. Every night, as she paraded around in the final scene, the crotch of the tiny panties pulled tightly into her lips and her pubic hair sprouted over the top. Moving about the stage in them caused a delicious rub between her legs and now, in the authentic hunger for sex, she realised just how tight they were and how severe the elastic felt on her.

With the dress up, he could get at more of her behind. The panties made a small V across her cheeks and his hands caressed the soft, slightly warm and slightly sweaty flesh of her buttocks. With a finger, he scratched at her knickers from where they led away from her behind and down onto the underside of her sex. She groaned as the friction increased, the static crackle audible. Rachel moved her leg to one side, opening herself to him as she put her toes to the floor. She raised herself and leaned against his body to allow it more access to hers.

Outside the dressing room, there were the bustling sounds of happy people, people who sounded like they had been let out of school for the summer. They know what we're doing in here, Rachel thought. She leaned on Robert's shoulder and let him continue to caress the base of her sex through her knickers. When he slipped his fingers under the fabric, she was shocked at how different it felt and she squeezed him tightly, pushing her head into his shoulder. His movements were urgent in the damp recesses of her sex as he toyed along the join of her lips and occasionally dipped through the wet outer folds.

Robert pulled away from her, glanced at her for a second and then fell to his knees. He pulled her knickers off quickly, Rachel lifting each foot and then kicking off the high heels. He stood and kissed her, his hand between their bodies, tickling her pubic hair. Rachel searched his mouth with her own, flicking her tongue at him, running it along the ridge of his top teeth and then pushing it further in.

There was a hefty thump on the door and they both froze, Robert looking up and over his shoulder. The handle turned and the door was pushed against the lock. Neither of them were breathing. He looked at her and shrugged. No one could get in or would dare to try, but the interruption gave the added beat to their excitement, a small glitch after which they quickly found the groove again, Robert continuing his fervid kisses.

'We don't have long,' she whispered in his ear, trying to encourage him along.

She looked around the room, trying to decide what she wanted to do. Her eyes came to rest on the high-backed chair in front of the mirror, naked bulbs shining brightly around its perimeter. What would Antonia Ford do? she asked herself.

Without a word, she broke away and led him by the hand to the mirror. Apart from the champagne and roses, all that was left on the counter were the minimum of accoutrements required to take off his make-up. Rachel picked the chair up and span it with the grace of a dancer so its back faced the mirror. While he looked at her smiling, Rachel stood on the chair. Holding the back, she carefully came down into a squatting position, enjoying the feel of opening herself to him so rudely and relishing the surprised look on his face.

He ran his hand along her taut buttocks and fiddled with her sex, which felt as though it were hanging low and heavy, burdened with desire. She watched his face in the mirror as he set to unfastening his trousers. Rachel could not see his groin from where she squatted on the chair, but his expression was enough, his face impatient and anxious for her.

'Take off your shirt,' she said, wanting to see his torso as he stood behind her and plied her with himself.

Robert pulled it over his head, not bothering with the cuffs or many buttons beyond the first two. The musculature of his chest was lightly defined under a smattering of dark hair, nipples like small bullets, tiny and brown. One of his hands disappeared from view and she watched the muscles in his upper arm flex as he worked on himself, his eyes half-closed. It occurred to her that she had no idea how large he was and what it would be like when he entered her from such an unusual angle.

The head of his cock grazed the underside of her sex and Rachel was conscious of her own juices lapping onto him. She arched her back and pushed her sex at him, her feet on tip-toes and her knees resting lightly on the back of the chair. She was glad of the table and mirror in front of her, preventing her from toppling forwards and enabling her to watch herself – and him.

From somewhere underneath her, his cock came and pressed through her outer lips. It was precise and certain, the angle of his cock strange as it breached her. She gripped the chair and arched her back, looking at the strain in her neck muscles as they were displayed in the mirror. Rachel could sense the size and shape of him as the wide ridge of his glans pried her inner lips apart and he entered in earnest.

Rachel concentrated on keeping her eyes open, wanting to see his expression and her own as he entered her. It was tempting to fall into the reflex action of closing her eyes, but her determination was strong. It was a look of surprise, she thought, as her face seemed to light up beneath the heavy covering of make-up. Mostly, it was her eyes which seemed to brim over with something other than tears. One of his feet was on the bottom bar of the chair, steadying it, and both his hands rested on her hips at the top of her behind.

It was a welcome and solid intrusion and she groaned when she felt the head of his cock skim over the front wall of her vagina, touching the sensitive spot hidden deep within her. With it in her as far as it would go, he began to make the gentlest of thrusts, barely enough to rock her forwards. Rachel flexed her muscles around his shaft and felt the small reverberations in her swollen clitoris. Tenderly she moved her rear from side to side, grinding herself lightly onto him, the feel of her sex soft, hot and wet over his erect member. Their movements were careful and surprisingly restrained given the previous tenor of their desire, as though they were slow dancing with each other. It was a carefully calculated and eagerly anticipated release of tension for both of them.

Rachel gripped the chair hard with her left hand while she used the right to feather tentatively over her clitoris, the position exciting and precarious at the same time. Her orgasm was close and she eased the pressure on her bud, not wanting to succumb to the climax too soon. Looking at him in the mirror, Rachel watched the movements of his upper body, seeing echoes of the efforts he made as his groin ground against her tight backside and his cock worked itself in the slick channel between her legs.

The dress held her tight, pulling her in at the hips and pushing her chest out, the bra shoving her breasts together and up. Sweat ran down her face and over the make-up, the exertion visible on her face. Rachel was lost in character, dressed and painted to be someone else and yet somewhere in the midst of it all, she found a sense of who she was and why she was doing it. Her own emotions filtered through the intensity of the moment and she felt herself tipping over the edge, the balance of her passion as delicate as the position she held her body in.

Robert gripped her tightly and shoved harder, his orgasm imminent. Rachel felt the muscles in her legs quiver, the stockings and suspender belt pulled over them like tight chord. The pressure built through her, both in her muscles and in the feelings of passion, ready to flow over and extinguish the last of her character, leaving only Rachel Franklin in its wake.

When she came, it tore down the façade. It welled up in her and she groaned, holding in her breath for a moment before letting it escape as a scratchy gasp that started in the back of her throat. For several long moments, she was conscious only of herself, not of Robert, his character or hers. It was a painful and personal moment, intense and self-revealing. Her muscles were in spasm, all the way down her back and along her legs. The centre of all the activity was between her legs, her sex shimmering and pulling. The sensations made her sag forwards, her shoulders heavy and her neck loosening with each burst of pleasure.

Robert's shout brought her back to earth and his movements lost their order and rhythm as he was dragged along by the power of his own orgasm. He cried out and Rachel caught a glimpse of his face, the contorted wrench that blurred the lines between agony and release. In her sex, pulsing into her vagina in warm spurts, she felt the results of his exertion.

They did not move for several moments, Rachel gazing at her reflection, face sweating and body heaving.

'Rachel,' he said to her as she straightened her dress.

She put her finger to his lips. 'See you at the party,' she said, climbing down off the chair.

Chapter Two

Rachel already felt tired as she entered the private room above Cogito for the end of run party. Certainly, she was physically tired but knew the over-activity in her brain meant sleep was still a long way off. When Rachel did finally sleep, she would awake and it would be the day after, all the excitement of the closing night already dissipated as she set to pondering if a month or two off had been such a good idea after all. Still, she thought, all that would be for tomorrow, whenever it came. Rachel tried to ignore such nagging feelings of anticipation and concentrated instead on looking suitably happy for the party.

Cogito was a private club in Soho, not quite as exalted as the Garrick or the Groucho, but plush in a lived-in way nonetheless. Much of the fabric covering the many easy chairs dotted around the warren-like ground floor reminded her of draylon from cinema seats. Leather-surfaced side tables and portraits abounded, but the majority of the membership of Cogito were too young and trendy to be reined in by such seriousness, most times running amok through the place like children having a party while their parents were away for the weekend. The rationale for holding the party there was that the play had poked fun at the very people who *would* frequent such a place and, ironically, had been written, directed and largely performed by people who *did* frequent the place. It was the sort of self-satisfied cannibalism people of a certain age but un-certain confidence enjoyed. Even at twenty-six, Rachel was painfully aware of being on the cusp of one generation, ready to move on to the next.

The large function room was on the third floor and could easily be mistaken for the state room of an embassy, comfortably accommodating dignitaries and diplomats. Instead, there was an unruly mix of cast, stage crew and assorted friends. The party was already swinging and no one noticed her as she stood in the doorway. Rachel's tryst with Robert Grosvenor had delayed her arrival and she spent longer than normal in her dressing room, wiping away Antonia Ford. She declined Robert's offer of a shared taxi, pleased that he seemed nonplussed by her refusal. He knew not to cling, she thought.

Every year it was the same. Whatever Rachel was doing currently, it always seemed to be the best thing she had ever done. Then something else came along and it felt even better. Doing rep was better than drama school. The first two West End shows were better than rep. Even the drab English film, quickly followed into oblivion by another, a misfiring screwball comedy, had seemed good – to Rachel at least. The part of Eliza in *Pygmalion*, filmed specially for television, and then six episodes of a television sitcom, they seemed to be the best she had done. Finally, or just most recently, there had been *Crossed Wires*. Every year *was* the same, but only to a point. A point Rachel felt she had reached.

Rachel's agent continually told her she had a gift for comedy, a rare gift that should be used to its fullest at every opportunity. The problem with a gift, something bestowed rather than learned as Rachel was fond of pointing out, was that it didn't really grow, it just stayed the same. People didn't get funnier, they just got older. Funny came naturally to her, emanating from a part of her over which she had no conscious control. Rachel could no more stop it than she could stop breathing. At best, she could hold it in until she turned blue and sputtered it out, gasping. Rachel was ready for something different.

'Rachel,' said a deep voice, drawing out both syllables of her name.

Rachel looked up to see Nikki Price cutting through the party goers with a beaming grin and a heft of the shoulder. She was stout with short blonde hair, orange lipstick and over made-up eyes. Rachel's cheekbones rose into a smile similar to Nikki's, as inside her heart sank and she wondered how a tabloid gossip columnist had made it into the party.

'Nikki,' Rachel said, sounding excited.

'You usually make a bigger entrance than that, darling,' Nikki was saying as they presented their cheeks to each other for pecking. 'You looked so forlorn standing at the door.'

'Just a bit glazed. You know what performing's like,' Rachel said.

There was a sharp glint in Nikki's eyes. Rachel and Nikki had been at drama school together and although it troubled her to feel so negative about another human being, Rachel thought Nikki was an appalling actress. It was an opinion about Nikki not unique to Rachel. Most people, teachers and staff, had thought so, some more openly than others and, half way through drama school, Nikki gave it up and left. After a job on the *Daily Star* and then the *Sun*, she had freelanced in magazines for a while but was now back with the tabloids, writing a gossip column on show business, spelled showbiz. As harsh as the two k's in her name, Nikki brought the same level of passion to everything, love and hate alike. Rachel's strongest memory of Nikki, of her whole time at drama school, was sitting dumbfounded with all the other students as, during an improvisation exercise, Nikki talked fondly to a chair and then railed furiously against it for ignoring her. It had been a performance worthy of the slow build of De Niro.

'Good show,' Nikki said.

'Was that a statement or a question? Were you there?' Rachel asked.

'I wish I could have been. It's Saturday night. I have to do the rounds of restaurants and clubs, looking for drunk pop stars or misbehaving footballers. Are you here on your own?' Nikki asked, peering inquisitively over Rachel's shoulder as though someone might suddenly have appeared.

'I'm meeting Oliver here,' Rachel replied evenly.

'Are you two moved in together yet?' Nikki asked.

Rachel regarded Nikki with a cool gaze.

'Off the record, promise,' Nikki said.

Rachel laughed. 'You should call your column that.'

'It's just that I heard a rumour about you and Damien Todd,' Nikki said.

'He's a baby,' Rachel said, snorting.

'He's twenty-two, not twelve. Besides, Oliver must be pushing fifty, so that could make you his daughter.'

'Don't let Oliver hear you say that,' Rachel said.

'Actress ditches sugar daddy for wild-child soap star toyboy,' Nikki said, actually sounding impressed with it.

'How come I never hear rumours about you?' Rachel asked.

'We have a secret code of honour, gossip columnists, not to rat on each other. You're changing the subject, Rachel. You and Damien Todd, true?'

'I've never even met him. I'm here with Oliver, if I can find him.'

'I saw him earlier snorting round a barman like he'd found truffles,' Nikki said.

'You can be such a cow, Nikki.'

Her worst friend and best enemy smiled. 'I just tell it like I see it. I've got to go to Stringfellows now,' Nikki said, tapping her hand on her mouth and miming a yawn.

As she was about to walk away, Rachel touched her arm. 'I don't want to read next week that I'm marrying Damien Todd, Nikki. Don't hurt me or Oliver like that.'

Nikki said nothing. In an instant, she was gone.

Lifting a wine glass from a tray as it glided past her, Rachel made for the bar. Oliver was normally to be found in the place most suited to holding court. People nodded or smiled at her and she returned compliments like tennis balls, but they all knew each other so well that the proceedings had the feeling of a wake rather than a party.

At the small bar in a corner, on a high stool and with three people around him, Oliver Kelton was venting. Forty-eight and a successful actor since the sixties, he had been the contemporary of people like Bates, Stamp, Finney and Caine. He was striking to look at, even from across a room. His dark hair touched his ears and the back of his neck in gentle waves and his skin was pleasantly powdery, pink in a baby's bottom way with bones underneath it as prominent as tent poles. Through the late-sixties and early-seventies, he was the resident angry young man. As the seventies became the eighties and Oliver moved into his thirties, he took his place among the lost generation, in touch with his own feelings and out of step with everyone else's. Now, when he chose to work, he was generally cast as avuncular and childless. Too much himself to become anyone else, Oliver was typecast as himself. On and off the stage and screen, he was too tutored to fit in anywhere with precision, gliding from situation to situation, playing the father figure to any willing adoptee.

Rachel did not recognise the three men around him. Two of them she knew by type, which was to say they were young, cute and well-built. Oliver had more success with that type than Rachel normally managed. A few months after they began seeing each other, Oliver told her of what he described as his 'passions'. Despite the lofty Greek manner in which he couched his explanation, Oliver's 'passions' essentially meant any fresh-faced man in his early twenties who didn't want to get too involved. Rachel had listened to his well-mannered explanation, expecting her temperature to rise, for her to begin shouting and then storm out of the room. None of that happened. It was hard to explain, bizarre even, but through his passions, she had more in common with Oliver than any other man she had been with.

The third man she did not recognise at all. He was tall, thin and had grey hair with a beard to match. He stood listening intently, his neck cricked as though stiff with anxiety. Rachel approached the group, the rhythm and resonance of Oliver's voice familiar as it produced an anecdote.

'Darling,' Oliver said when he saw her, the word perfectly natural and unforced on his lips.

He stood and kissed her, whispering congratulations in her ear. A few words of private praise from him was worth ten times more than public shows of adulation.

'This is Blake Jordan,' Oliver said, politely but definitely ignoring the other two men who seemed content to fade into the middle distance, hovering on the edge of a new group.

The name was familiar. It fitted into place. He was an American producer who had a musical running on Broadway at that moment. Not in the same corporate league as a Cameron Mackintosh or a Lloyd Webber, he was still an important producer. His name was mentioned from time to time in *Variety*. As they shook hands, she wondered if he had been at the show. He looked more like a music teacher in a provincial school than the last of the impresarios.

'Loved the show. Loved you,' Blake Jordan said in clipped New York vowels.

'Thank you. I think we went out on a pretty good one,' she replied.

'I was in one of Blake's first plays in, oh, nineteen-seventy-one,' Oliver said.

Blake Jordan was still focused on her.

'*Pygmalion* was on PBS earlier this year. I watched every show. Very good,' he said.

'More compliments, please. Keep them coming.' Rachel tried to remember the name of the musical running on Broadway so she could say something equally admiring.

'Have Oliver bring you to New York sometime and I'll guide you round some shows,' Blake said.

'Well, I'm a big girl, Mr Jordan, and sometimes I'm allowed out on my own.'

Blake Jordan seemed confused, as though she had just started talking in a foreign language. Oliver was shooting her a sharp glance as though he wanted to shake his head vigorously at her. Rachel let the awkwardness build for a second or two, just like comic timing, and then broke it with a broad smile.

'How long are you in London for?' she asked him, feeling everyone breathe out with relief.

'Just a few more days. Oliver tells me you've been in a couple of movies?'

Rachel made an embarrassed face. She leaned forward and whispered as though telling him a secret. 'They weren't the best things I've ever done.' She wished it could have been a secret, how bad they were.

'A friend of mine at NBC says they're looking at your show with a view to buying it,' Blake said.

'The sitcom?' Rachel asked, surprised.

'Sitcom. I love that,' Blake said.

It dawned on her. He was feeling her out for something. A familiar sensation came over Rachel, one of wishing she could rewind and reenter the scene, calculate her answers to fit what it was he wanted. Why should I? she thought. It always happened the same way. If Blake Jordan didn't like her native state, then so be it. She was paid to act on stage, not off it, she thought stubbornly.

'Will you be seeing any other shows while you're here?' Rachel asked.

'I've seen most, and the ones I haven't, I don't really want to, but I have to,' Blake said.

'It's not like the old days,' Oliver said.

'You should have seen the play Oliver was in. The clothes were bad enough,' Blake said and they all laughed, Oliver pouting slightly as he did.

Somebody Rachel didn't know called Blake's name from across the room and waved at him.

'Excuse me,' Blake said. 'Good to have met you.'

'What was all that about?' Rachel asked when he had gone, the two young men now dissolved completely into the fizzing crowd.

Oliver shrugged. 'I didn't even know he was in town until this afternoon. He called me wanting a ticket and I got him one, which was no mean feat. Miriam was running the box office when I was here seven years ago in one of Harold's.'

'He could've had Daddy's ticket,' Rachel said.

'You didn't really expect him to be here?' Oliver asked.

'He didn't make it to any of the run, not even my birthday. He probably called Mummy and made some excuse.'

'I'm not complaining, but it surprises me your mother refuses to come to the end of a run, or at least the party afterwards,' he said.

'It makes her nervous. I'm sure she thinks she's in the way, like she wants me to enjoy it without her being around. Besides, this is far too late for her.'

'Tell the old cow she would be in the way,' Oliver said brightly.

'I'll kick you if you don't behave,' she warned.

A champagne cork popped. People laughed. All around her, members of what, for the past nine months, had been her surrogate family, were disengaging from each other. They were all leaving home in their own ways, many wondering what they would be doing next, where they would be going. Everyone was too polite or politic to ask. Some already had work lined up and were, mentally at least, more or less there already. Others had nowhere to go and clung onto the last moments of the current job.

It was different for Rachel. She had turned work down. It made her feel guilty when there were so many others who could not find a job. Still, she reasoned, her refusal was someone else's chance. After nine months of *Crossed Wires* she felt genuinely in need of a break. Another West End show had been on offer and Rachel could have gone straight into it. What troubled her most about the role was the way it seemed to be little more than a rewrite of the one in *Crossed Wires*, which in turn was an outgrowth of her television role and even, she thought, Eliza Doolittle. Perhaps it was time to have a pause and then do something people weren't expecting.

Many actors, she knew, could not countenance such a prospect and would be nervously fidgeting, waiting for their agent to call after only a day of inactivity. Rachel had worked almost continuously since leaving drama school. The promise of a rest was inviting, even if she did feel apprehensive about her ability to deal with it, even in the most simple of ways such as filling the time during the day.

'I wonder what he wanted?' Rachel said distantly, as she and Oliver looked at Blake Jordan, hunched and listening to the director of *Crossed Wires*.

'If it's anything, we'll find out. You were late arriving,' he said.

'I had a promise to keep, you know that,' she said.

He stroked her behind discreetly. 'Mr Grosvenor is rather delicious, although somewhat to seed now. You should have seen his Romeo.'

'Nikki Price was grubbing around me earlier,' Rachel said.

'Ah the price of justice is eternal publicity,' Oliver said.

Rachel looked at him quizzically, wondering where the quote came from.

'Bennett,' he said, as though reading her thought.

'Alan?'

'Arnold, actually.'

'We can't all have your education, dear.'

'Thank god. If you did, you might all see what a phoney I am,' Oliver said, the lines in his forehead creasing more deeply as he smiled. He seemed slightly tipsy to Rachel. 'What did Ms Price want?'

'What she always wants, Ollie. A story. Enough random facts to make a significant connection. She should have been a statistician, the bitch.'

'Tempers run so deep between the two of you. What exactly did she say?'

Rachel thought about Nikki and her smug, self-righteous belief of being on some sort of mission. For a second or two, it riled Rachel and she could feel invective building up. Then, she realised the best manner with which to deal with Nikki was the same method she had always adopted – to let it go.

'Nothing important, Ollie. If it was, we'd know about it already.'

'Do you want to come to my house for breakfast tomorrow?' he asked. 'A sort of, day one of the great Rachel Franklin "Darling, I'm resting," phase? I'd like to help you usher it in. Bottle of champagne, something like that.'

'Sounds wonderful. What time?'

'Ten. No, wait,' Oliver said and scanned the room with obvious glee, letting his eyes fall to rest on a man carrying a tray, short blond hair razored close on the back of his head and a cute fringe that sloped up at the same angle as his snubbed nose. Very sexy and very Ollie. 'Better make it nearer to eleven. Who or what are you up to for the rest of the evening?' he asked.

'I haven't decided yet,' Rachel said.

'I think that's not true,' he said, knowingly.

'Maybe you're right,' she said, winking at him.

Chapter Three

Rachel was along Shaftesbury Avenue, around Piccadilly Circus and at the hotel in a matter of minutes. It was two-thirty in the morning and London was still alive and in the throes of a Saturday night. She strode across reception boldly, rode the elevator to the fourth floor, making one quick, paranoid check that she had not been followed by any prying journalists or snap-happy paparazzi. Rachel knocked on the door and, almost immediately, as though her arrival had been anxiously anticipated, it was opened.

Damien Todd was twenty-two. With an unruly mop of reddish-brown Beatles hair that touched his eyebrows and extended into sideburns, he was a naughtier version of what Oliver might have been in the sixties. He never looked very smart; lots of faded jeans and untucked baggy T-shirts hanging loosely over his wiry frame. Underneath the clothes, however, was a different matter. Always well-scrubbed, his lithe body was fresh and sexy to both the touch and the taste.

Where he could have easily been a model for the rakish Calvin Klein campaign or the lead singer with a band, instead he played Paul Watson, the laddish London character in a soap opera called *Oakwood*, set in a Birmingham shopping mall. Because he was young, good-looking and a well-paid cast member of an established soap opera, there was inevitable tabloid interest in his private life, linking him, often rightly and more often wrongly, with various women. Rachel did not ask and he did not tell, the only effect on their relationship being the extra discretion required to avoid unwanted media attention. There was something alluring about their lust on the run liaison despite the logistics it often entailed.

They stole a quick kiss in the doorway before shuffling across the threshold with all the awkwardness and ardour of a five-and-half-month-old relationship.

'Have you been waiting long?' she asked.

'I didn't get off set until nine and I was here a bit after midnight.'

On the cabinet next to the television, there were a few empty bottles of beer. Damien wore a bright orange T-shirt with navy blue sleeves and a pair of long and loose gray shorts that just hid his kneecaps. She tossed her coat onto one of the beds.

'You look like one of those kids that ride skateboards under the Festival Hall,' she said, struck by how young he looked.

'These are my comfortable clothes for when I've had a shower.' His voice had a suburban accent, the hard edged cockney grit he used on television not in evidence. 'When you wear someone else's clothes all day, you need a break. You should see some of the stuff wardrobe have been coming up with for me. How did it go?' he asked her.

'We went out on a high. The party was a bit flat but that made me feel less guilty about slipping away.'

They were silent for a moment. Usually, there were conversations but tonight they were silent in anticipation. Over the previous five or so months, Rachel had snatched the odd evening with him and they had spent a few cautious afternoons together. Being driven underground meant that most of their encounters were fairly frank and honest in their orientation towards sex.

Rachel made the first move. She held him by the hips, the material of his shirt was velvety and felt-like to the touch. Pushing her body against his, she resumed the earlier kiss, pressing her lips onto his small, pouting mouth. His hands touched her, stroking her back and behind, running up her side and round to her shoulderblade. Between her fingers, his hair felt damp from the shower and his skin soft, recently bathed. Rachel held his face in her hands and stared into the green shine of his eyes. He looked back at her with a lissom smile and she pulled him close, wanting to smother him.

Giving his pert behind a quick squeeze, she lifted his shirt up over his head. There was something so appetisingly normal about his body, not too scrawny and not muscled beyond the absurd. He could have been any number of boys from her school days, before she arrived at drama school and found everyone suddenly got too pretty by far. Damien's chest had just a sprinkle of hair and his nipples were small fleshy rounds, a thin slit-like line in their tips and mottled skin surrounding them. Around his neck, he wore a short leather thong with a small silver charm attached to it and on his wrist was a bracelet of well-worn yellow chord. His ear was pierced and he wore a tiny red-gold sleeper in it. Even when naked, Damien kept the thong and the bracelet on. Rachel loved seeing him clothed, looking at the necklace and the chord, knowing what they looked like on his nude body.

Rachel bit at his collarbone and ran her tongue over the few hairs. She leaned down and kissed the middle of his chest, moving from right to left so she could plant a kiss on each nipple. He sighed when she settled on one and began to mouth it wetly. Damien's hand held the back of her head in a gentle grip and he groaned. He was a mass of sensitive extremities and Rachel had a wide range of possibilities when it came to exciting him, Damien always ready to try something new. She kissed his torso and his hips, letting her tongue trail across his belly. Damien did not have a stomach, more of a nice white belly with a button that protruded ever so slightly and which made him giggle and fidget when she licked it.

From the hem of his shorts, up to his navel, a tiny gunpowder trail of hair ran. The shorts were extended at front and Rachel doubted he was wearing any underpants. She would find out soon enough. Puckering her lips and worrying the line of skin above the waistband, Rachel fell to one knee and slipped her hands up the back of the shorts. The skin beneath was smooth and hairless, his legs were more muscular than the rest of him. She explored a little further up, the first rounded area of his behind starting as a gentle curve. As she moved her hand further still, she found no fabric blocking her path and was able to use a hand over each cheek of his warm rear. One day, she thought, I'll put him over my knee and give his cute behind a good slap. She kissed harder at his navel. Rachel inched the shorts down just enough to reveal the border of his chestnut brown pubic hair, the flanks of his belly grooving into the triangle of his pubis. She left the shorts clinging to his hips, exposing just a fraction of his behind and the dark mat of his pubic hair.

Rachel stood and turned her back to him. Without words or directions from her, he ran the zipper from the middle of her back down to the base of her spine. He lifted the straps forward off her shoulders and Rachel shook the top half off. She wore no bra and it was good to stand with her firm breasts free. He was close enough for her to be able to feel his body heat when she pushed the dress to her ankles. Rachel stepped out of it and kicked off her shoes. Turning, she faced him in only her sheer white knickers. His hips were gorgeously narrow, his erection distending the shorts. It was difficult to choose a place to start.

Damien's body was warm from the pleasant heat of the hotel room while Rachel's skin was still chilled slightly from the walk to the hotel from the party. A glow came over her as she went from one temperature to another, getting hotter all the time. She put her arms round his waist and hugged him, Damien's pendant touching the upper curve of her breasts. The lightest trace of alcohol on his breath mingled with the wine on her own. He was pressing his groin insistently against her, his cock hard in the softness of her flesh. Rachel pulled him tight, squashing her breasts to his chest and his erection into the ever-dampening area of her sex. She put her hands in his shorts and, as she kneeled down, pulled them over his legs, revealing him before her.

On her knees, Rachel stared for a few moments, as though fascinated. Damien's compact, tawny frame made his cock appear abnormally large. His scrotum lifted his balls high into him and his long shaft stood out at an angle, the foreskin partially back. Rachel held one of his balls between a thumb and forefinger, rolling it in her grip. She exerted enough pressure to make him yelp and then released him, cupping both the delicate stones soothingly in her hand. With delicate and teasing fingers, she fondled the shaft of his cock from where it emerged at the base to just under the head, stopping short just before the wide ridge of his glans. She repeated the action several times, using light fingers on the heavy member. In her hold, his cock was a little spongy but the hardness soon spread as though from the inside to the outside, until he was fully erect, his foreskin almost all the way back. Rachel pulled on his cock and watched the skin roll back as his phallus blossomed, glinting in the lamplight as his desire revealed itself in fluid form.

Rachel stood and quickly walked him backwards to one of the armchairs, his cock swaying from side to side in time with his leather necklace. She pushed him back over the chair so his spine was arched, his rear on the edge of the seat and his open legs dangling off each arm. When she knelt in between his legs, all she could see was his erect cock, the tightly stretched skin of his belly and the underside of his ribcage, heavy with excited breaths.

Damien's body stiffened at the first touch from the tip of Rachel's tongue. She held his cock upright so it almost towered over her from the position of their bodies, and she eased the skin back until the darkened purple of his glans was on display. She tucked her tongue into the intimate join of his glans beneath his phallus, wetting him and then batting at him with her tongue. The muscles of his legs tightened and the arch in his back became more pronounced. She held him perfectly still and let her breath waft over him. Rachel wanted him to feel how close she was to him, but was not ready to swallow him into the welcoming depths of her mouth at that moment. She ran her tongue along the heavy blue vein embedded on the bottom of his shaft, slicking the way first and then applying pressure, letting the smooth skin feel the roughness of her tongue's surface. She made several long passes over him, flicking at the head of his cock and sending disproportionate reverberations through his body.

When Rachel closed her mouth over the head of Damien's cock, he let out a sigh of deep-seated contentment and moved his rear about on the cushion, settling himself. She smoothed her tongue on the underside of his cock, letting herself become accustomed to its presence in her mouth. Raising herself up on her knees so she was at a more suitable height, Rachel took more of him into her, feeling the tip of his member touch the uppermost cavity of her mouth. She closed her lips and sucked to give a vacuum sensation to him and he throbbed each time she drew on him. The small drop of fluid which had been at the end of his cock was now salty and thick on her tongue, savory desire that washed through her. While she held the base of his shaft in her hand and sucked tightly on his cock, she let her other hand roam over the tight and hairless skin of his abdomen.

Damien's tumescent member strained from the touch of Rachel's mouth. Every stroke edged him closer to orgasm, a liberation she would not grant him until she was ready. At times, her head moved rapidly up and down, feeding herself on him forcefully and making her lips tingle. Then she would slow until her tongue was no more than an agonising pulse against him. He called her name, groaned, growled and fidgeted on the armchair. When she removed him from her mouth, Rachel had smothered his orgasm twice, stopping him painfully short and as a result, his cock seemed abnormally large and inflated, shining from the attention she had given it.

Rachel's knickers were sopping in the crotch and she was eager to get out of them. She wanted to feel in her sex what she had felt in her mouth. When he finally toppled over, she wanted him to be inside her. Rachel stood up and removed her panties as Damien watched with his head raised, a lewd grin on his face. As she clambered onto him, he readjusted the position of his body so she could squat over his lap with her knees planted wide in either side of his now closed legs. She pinched his nipples, hard, and leaned forwards to kiss him. Damien was sweating and his face was flushed. Carefully, Rachel wiped the sweat from his brow and then wriggled her behind suggestively against his groin.

She had spent so long pleasuring him that when his finger touched the engorged lips of her sex, Rachel gave a shocked hiss as the tension in her shifted and took on a new direction, now focused on her rather than him. Resting a hand on either arm of the chair, Rachel raised herself up by several inches to allow him freer access to her. His movements were quick and precise, his finger sliding into the sleek strait between her legs. She felt oily and warm, her sex weltering from the sudden attention. His thumb found her clitoris, the tight nodule that held the key to everything, offering a way out of the excruciating grip desire exerted on her. The passion and the energy were storing themselves up in her, building until they would burst through her. This time, it was his turn to deny her and as Rachel was about to flutter into the liberation of an orgasm, his fingers were abruptly gone.

Damien held his cock upright with both hands and guided the angle of his shaft as Rachel sat down onto it. The head of his cock nestled itself in the outer folds of her sex, the tip boldly pressing at the quivering entrance to her. It ached in a way that was painful and yet absolutely necessary. The strain came at exactly the same time as his cock passed through the entrance of her vagina, pushing her apart and entering the elongated and dewy passage. Rachel sank down firmly, feeling it travel up her, invading her and filling her. She cried out and her muscles trembled around him, the intensity of the moment of ingress almost dangerous in its potency.

Her body came to rest against his and she paused, letting her breathing become more ordered and spending a moment taking it all in. His body, young and firm; his cock, large and bone-like, embedded in her. Rachel thought about riding his frame, using him to bring herself relief and to watch him beneath her, twitching and contorting with the exquisite torture of climax. She reached behind herself, feeling their sticky join and his balls pressed tightly between the combination of his closed legs and her backside. His cock throbbed in her, widening for a second and then the resistance of her muscles translated into pleasurable sensations which started in her sex and flowed on throughout the rest of her.

Rachel used her knees on the seat of the armchair and her hands on his arms as pivots from which to rock herself over Damien's prone body. He reached for a bottle of beer from one of several in the ice bucket on the side table. He took a quick swig and leered at her before holding the cold glass of the bottle between the sweaty cleft of her breasts. She shrieked and laughed throatily. He ran the bottle down her body until its bottom lighted on the upper regions of her sex. He held it there for a moment, rolling the cold brown glass from side to side, brushing near her clitoris with it. It was ice-cold in the heated mix of their bodies and Rachel writhed, unable to get away from it. Damien took one more swallow, fed her one and then dumped it back in the ice bucket.

After only the minimum of tentative movements, Rachel found the speed and depth that suited them both. It was fast and hard, directed to a common and quick climax. She rode him, using herself on him, grazing skin against skin, the path smoothed by the milky juices of her vagina. They both made a noise, grunts and yelps that were intimate in a strange and aggressive way, a wordless language communicating desire, clearly and accurately. Damien's cock pulsed so deeply in her it was like a rumbling at her very centre. The previously waylaid orgasms were evident in both of their movements, the short and snatching severity of them.

She reared up and then down time after time until it became hypnotic and beyond her own conscious control. Her mind was giddy, thoughts flowing free of their normal coordinates, unshackled by the most repetitive and driven of physical acts. Rachel drove down harder, using their bodies as a way of freeing their minds. She was no longer a character in a play or at the end of a run or at the party afterwards or even with Damien in the hotel room. The tempo increased even more but the basic meter of their hard coupling underpinned it. The first crack came and the prospect of orgasm crept through like a distant light.

Under her, Damien's body was sweaty and twitching. His nipples were hard and pointing up, his chest rising and falling, the soft skin of his belly forming into a concave from the excitement and the pressure of keeping it in check. His eyes were closed and his face had a strange look on it, almost smug in the satisfaction that his climax was almost upon him. The long drawn-out act was nearing its close and he lay there apparently ready for it to carry him off with aching release. The sight of him, all of him, and the feel of him in her, the forces of her lunges dazing her clitoris, sent Rachel into the final assault on him.

The muscles of her anus and legs burned from the exertion. Rachel put the last of her energy into it, using adrenalin and excitement to push her on. She pumped down onto his cock, feeling it plunder into her up to the hilt. She imagined the quiver it would give when he let himself go in her, spraying himself inside her with long jets. Her mind focused on orgasm, his and hers, and she roared as it prepared to spill over.

Damien's eyes were open and he was staring at her intently, almost looking through her. He reached an arm out to his side and there was a sluicing sound, and then Rachel saw he had a small rounded pellet of partly melted ice in his hand. She carried on moving and hollered when he inserted the cold pebble into her behind. It felt impossibly round to be passing through such a tiny orifice but it slipped in easily, the freezing sensation almost indistinguishable from heat. Her reaction of shock and surprise was enough to finish Damien.

It was familiar and she relished it. He lifted his shoulders, his nose twitched, followed by his mouth as his breathing halted momentarily and then he bawled out some incomprehensible word as his whole body convulsed. She felt his semen run warm and deep in her, gushing from him. He steadied himself by pushing his hands on her body, as though trying to get away from her. He unloaded himself in a desperate and vulnerable frenzy, Rachel aloft him and, for a few more seconds at least, in control of his supple young body.

Rachel quickly followed where Damien had just been, wanting to use the last echoes of his pleasure to fuel her own. The ice tingled in her behind and a thin trail of water left her and trickled onto the underside of her sex. Her rear was hot and cold at once, caught between the pleasurable mix of temperatures. In a swift spasm, Rachel banished her mind and thought left her in favour of sensations that seemed only physical, wired directly into the fibre of who she was. The orgasm shook her roughly, the muscles of her vagina and stomach thrashing violently in tight contractions. It found a voice and she let out a cry, his name somewhere in it. Rachel continued to buck on him for as long as he could bear it, her orgasm providing the energy which, finally, began to taper off.

Damien let out a contented sigh as she lifted herself off his slowly deflating cock. Once again, his eyes were shut and the endearingly vain and smug expression had returned, like a naughty boy at rest.

With a speed that took him by surprise, Rachel dipped her hand in the ice bucket and came out with a cube at least twice the size of the one that was still melting in her. She ignored his laughter and begs for mercy as she worked a cruel hand under his backside and found the entrance she was looking for.

Chapter Four

'So what did you get up to?' Oliver asked Rachel as she sat at the table, looking out of the window of his flat in Covent Garden. It was almost eleven on Sunday morning, but Covent Garden was already crowded with tourists trying to avoid crowds of tourists.

'Nothing that you didn't, I shouldn't wonder,' she replied briskly.

Oliver set a large plate of wholemeal toast in the centre of the table, next to a pot of espresso and a bottle of champagne languishing in a bucket of ice. Oliver baked the bread himself and the coffee was freshly ground.

'And that's as much as you'll tell me of your wild night?' Oliver asked. 'You can look out for the details of mine in my memoirs.'

'You'll never write them, Ollie,' she said.

'Wait and see. A lot of people will be petrified.'

'Will we be hearing about all the skeletons then?' she asked.

'It's the closets, not the skeletons, they should be worried about. I take it your little soap bubble has yet to burst?' he asked, carefully placing espresso cups on flat saucers.

'It *will* burst if Nikki Price gets her claws on the story,' she said.

Oliver poured the coffee and set the pot down with a dainty hand. 'Ah, the price of everything and the value of nothing. Don't worry about her. Will I get to meet the enigmatic Damien or should I just tune in one evening?

31

Bring him over and I'll cook for the three of us.'

Rachel sipped the strong black liquid and nibbled at the corner of a dry slice of toast, uncertain how she felt about dinner with Damien and Ollie. Oliver's flat was furnished with oddments pushed together in a way that really shouldn't have worked but did, if only for its lack of guile. Almost nothing in his flat matched anything else, every piece of furniture, ornament or houseware was an original in its own right. It was the same as Oliver's cooking, ingredients thrown cheerfully into a pan and coming out in an exotic and charming mix. She was not certain how Damien Todd would fit into such a recipe, the stage school brat versus the solidly trained and well-rounded actor.

'Are you missing the company already?' Oliver asked, referring to the imaginary kin of *Crossed Wires*.

'It was only a play,' she said.

'But nine months is a long time. I've had a marriage that didn't last as long,' he said.

'What do you want to do today?' she asked.

He thought. 'Perhaps we could go to the Tate, fight with all the tourists to get a look at the Turner prize, unless you're not feeling up to it.'

'No, that's fine.'

'When is your mother back in town?' he asked.

'Why?' she said suspiciously, pausing with her cup.

'After you left last night, Blake Jordan cornered me. He was drunker and his tongue was looser, even if his shoulders weren't.'

Rachel had put her cup down, pushed the plate aside and was leaning towards Oliver.

'Why didn't you tell me sooner?' she asked, a tinge of impatience in her voice.

'I couldn't have told you much sooner. I wanted you to at least sit down and have some coffee, food even,' he said, regarding her barely touched toast. 'I know once I tell you this, you won't sit down or eat for the rest of the day.'

'Well? Tell me. What did he want?'

'He's putting on a production next year and he's interested in you for the lead.'

'A London production?' she asked.

'Broadway,' he said, in a tone almost reverential.

Familiar feelings flooded her. Someone wanted her. It flattered her far too readily but it was always good to be sought out when she had known the despondency of being the seeker. Somebody wanted her for a part. They think I'm the right person. The first rush of adrenalin washed over her, drowning out anything so practical as what the prospect might actually entail or that it was the first day of her self-imposed rest period. The wave subsided and questions were left in its wake like pebbles.

'Blake Jordan puts on musicals. Singing and dancing. A Broadway musical,' she said, tasting it like a poison pill, her voice trailing off along with her enthusiasm. Oliver's broad grin distracted her.

'My first ever agent said to me, "When you deal with producers or directors, grin outside and groan inside, because you never know". When Blake told me he was interested in you for a part, my heart sank too, like yours just did. Of course, I was polite. It's not a musical, Rachel. It's a Broadway play. A serious Broadway play.'

'Who by?' she asked.

'Carl Milken.'

'Isn't he—'

'No,' Oliver interrupted. 'He's very much alive and well. Hasn't written a damn thing in fifteen years apart from that novel. Now he's back and very much alive.'

Milken was the Arthur Miller of his day, serious family dramas that took in all the concerns of a Tennessee Williams or Eugene O'Neill play and inserted them into the very centre of the issues and debates of the time he wrote in. Rachel didn't know very much more than that about him and what she did was mostly based on reputation.

'Why me?' she asked.

'Why not? You can hack a role like that. More than just hack, darling.'

'I know that. I mean, how did they stumble across me as a possible lead?'

'Just like Blake said last night when he was laying on the charm. He saw you on PBS and in the flesh last night. He told me Carl Milken was in London back in May and he came and saw you, while he was still writing the play.'

'What's it called?'

'*A Winter's Tale*,' Oliver replied.

Rachel looked at him. 'Shakespeare?'

'No, not the definite article. *A Winter's Tale*. Even Carl wouldn't want to better the bard.'

'Did Blake tell you anything about the play?'

'Well, it's all hush-hush. Not many people know Carl's writing it.'

'I'll probably have to do an American accent,' she said, getting ahead of herself.

Oliver paused. 'It sounded interesting. As far as I could gather, and we were both quite tight by this stage, it's a two act play centring around a childless woman's disintegrating relationship with her husband in the first act and then the grown-up experiences of the woman's foundling daughter in the second act, both parts played by the same actress.'

'How old are the women meant to be?' she asked.

'I don't know. I got the impression Blake didn't want to let on too much, and that he shouldn't even have told me what he did. I told him he'd have to spread the news eventually, if he actually wants people to act in it and, moreover, people to come and see it. Milken was always so secretive about his work, like you weren't meant to see it.'

'Who's going to direct it?' she asked.

'Milken's going to do it himself,' he replied.

Rachel made a sceptical face.

'I know,' Oliver said. 'I usually prefer the writer not to be involved. Dead is ideal.'

'I read the play of his that's like *Death of a Salesman*.'

'*Small People*.'

'Good speeches, if you're a man,' Rachel said wryly.

'Carl hasn't produced the greatest heroines of our time,' Oliver said a little sadly. 'Have some toast.'

She ignored him. 'Why couldn't Blake Jordan have approached me himself?' she asked.

'He's old-fashioned and shy,' Oliver said.

'Christ, that's no excuse. He's a producer, Ollie.'

'Blake and Carl Milken go back a way, Blake and I have some kind of history, so I suppose it seemed logical to sound you out via me, the linchpin as ever,' he said with a dramatic sigh and smile.

Rachel remembered the bashful way Blake Jordan had paid her compliments the previous night, the hunched shoulders and the badly mobilised neck and head. He wouldn't get away with a posture like that at her old drama school.

'Tell me I should feel more excited than this,' she said.

'You have to feel whatever you feel, darling. It's hard sometimes to formulate opinions when a lot of the information is so new. It would be both a challenge and a change.'

'So they're genuinely interested in me?'

Oliver nodded.

'What happens next?' she asked.

'Blake will be back in New York tomorrow. If you consent, he'll talk to Carl and send me a draft of the play, although God knows what it will be like. He wants you to look at it and if you're still keen, he'd like you to go over and meet with him and Carl, do some reading.'

'An audition you mean?'

Oliver nodded once again.

'What should I do?' she said into the room, hoping the answer would come back to her in an echo of her own voice.

It was Oliver's well-articulated and wonderfully bass tone that filled the kitchen. 'Let him send the material. You've really nothing to lose. Use the intervening time to think about it. Talk to your agent and to your mother.'

Rachel was still reeling from the end of *Crossed Wires*, full of mixed feelings about it. Had it been a good play or just totally bad and predictable? Should she have taken time off at all, turning down another play in the process? The idea of just slipping into another typecast Rachel Franklin role looked appealing suddenly, especially in the face of Broadway, Blake Jordan and Carl Milken. It sparked the most elaborate of fears and fantasies. A serious role, a high quality production, acclaim and a sense of achievement. Failing, being reviled, not being ready for a heavyweight role yet. The twins of good and evil, success and failure, plagued her instantly, balancing one on each of her shoulders. It was disquieting to wonder if she really were capable of making the fantasy into reality.

Oliver stood and began clearing the table, seeming to know food would be out of the question for the next two or three hours at least.

On her shoulders, she felt the generous weight of his hands, kneading the flesh and rolling it around on her collarbone.

'Let's go look at art,' Oliver said.

Lost in the world of the possible, Rachel barely heard him.

Chapter 5

Rachel sat on the square mat in the middle of the living room floor. She was cross-legged, the heel of her left foot tucked under herself and the side of the right one resting on the join of calf and thigh. Her yoga teacher called it a perfect posture. Rachel was able to manage a half-lotus and her flexibility was gradually increasing to where she might one day be able to accomplish a full one. Earlier in the day, she had given her voice its first really good stretch since Saturday. Rachel ran through some exercises for her diction and vowels, never tiring of trying to get it just right. The day before, she had been to see a voice coach who had given her some advice and some tapes to help her with an American accent. In short, Rachel was getting ahead of herself.

Spread out on the floor in front of her, the torn polythene DHL bag nearby, was the material from Blake Jordan. There were times when Rachel was superstitious about having full sight of something she might be appearing in, worried that it would enable her to graft too many preconceptions onto it. What she had in front of her was a work in progress. There was a typed synopsis, three pages in all, which went into some detail. Then, there were several scenes from the play, two of which were long speeches from the mother and the daughter. Handwritten notes and corrections filled the wide margins of the page. It was intriguing to have only part of the story, but she was also aware of the dangers. I could do this, she thought, imagining the challenge of playing two roles, doing the accents, getting the thread of each character and, of course, doing it all on Broadway.

The cordless phone by her side trilled, breaking the reverie of first night glory that sang so loudly in her head.

'Hello,' she said.

Damien's voice whistled through the cavern of the mobile phone network, his words cut off by crackle.

'It's me,' were the words which finally came out.

'Where are you?' Rachel asked, shouting.

'At the end of your road,' he replied, the line abruptly clearing.

'I thought you were supposed to be in Birmingham,' she said.

'My only scene this week was cut. I thought I'd surprise you.'

'Why didn't you just come and ring on the bell?' she asked.

'We had some photographers sniffing round outside the studios yesterday. I wanted to make sure the coast was clear.'

Rachel sighed. She would have to talk with Nikki Price about the situation. It had to stop. Rachel couldn't imagine who, apart from Nikki, would be seriously interested in who Damien was seeing. In truth, she could understand why Damien generated such interest. On screen, as a rogue in the fashion trade, he had three women on the go, including a mother and daughter. The press were desperate to blur the lines between Damien and his character, Paul. Of course, Damien was wayward, Rachel knew that, had been there herself. He was young and good-looking, so why shouldn't he? Rachel wondered how Nikki and the rest of the celebrity gossips would react if they knew in about six months time, according to Damien's highly secret story biography, his character was going to turn out gay.

She stood and went to the living room window which looked out onto the garden.

'The back looks okay. Come up the alley behind the house and I'll let you in the garden gate.'

Rachel waited a moment and then scampered down the garden, barefoot and in her cat suit, the stone path freezing under her feet. Damien was at the solid gate, more like a door, when she opened it. He wore a baseball hat and sunglasses. Giving him a long kiss, she took his hand and they ran up the garden path together, Rachel glad to be back in the comforting warmth of the house.

'What've you been doing?' he asked, looking her up and down.

'Just some yoga and a few voice exercises. They teach you that at drama school.'

Rachel liked to chide Damien who had gone from stage school to the background of a few childrens' shows and on into several small speaking parts before ending up a soap star. Damien had no training that would have been considered classical. It was a route which Rachel herself could have followed, if her father had not been so insistent that she finish her 'A' Levels, which she did before going on to drama school.

Damien looked at the papers spread around the mat. 'So, is this the famous Broadway play?' he asked, stooping to look and still wearing his sunglasses.

Rachel bent and tidied the papers quickly, stuffing them into the plastic bag, not wanting him to see them. She put the polythene envelope on the dining room table and threw her arms around Damien, letting her weight rest on him. Pushing her hands into his jacket, Rachel felt the fleecy warmth of the hooded sweatshirt he wore beneath it. He was layered against the cold and Rachel felt comparatively naked, covered only by the thin cotton film of the cat suit which clung to her and revealed in perfect detail the shape of the body beneath it. The yoga and voice exercises had made her feel loose and limber and as she kissed Damien, she began to feel excited by his presence.

Removing Damien's glasses, Rachel pushed his coat off his shoulders, still kissing him as she did. She paused, breaking contact with his mouth, to lift the first layer off, the grey hooded top. Beneath that, a plain wihite T-shirt. Finally, a vest with a basketball net printed on it. Rachel left him in his jeans and went to pull the curtains. Pushing herself against his bare chest, Rachel rubbed the lycra of the suit over his skin, her breasts taut against the satin-like fabric, nipples pointing through. Damien's jeans were baggy over his firm behind and Rachel hooked a finger through one of the belt loops, letting her hand hang there as they kissed. She made small sighing noises through her nose and they mingled with the sounds their joined mouths made, the rest of the house suddenly quiet around them.

Rachel held his forearms and sat on the mat, taking him down with her. They sat facing each other for a few moments. Without speaking, he got to his knees and leaned forwards, pushing her onto her back. He leaned over and kissed her while his hand caressed the side of her body. Damien kissed at the bare patch of skin on the join of her breastbone and collarbone. Gently, he positioned himself between her legs and Rachel let them fall open so he could push his groin against hers. When he was nestled against her, she wrapped her legs around waist, clinging to him tightly. Rachel could feel his erection pushing insistently into the soft and warm area of her sex.

As Damien knelt up, Rachel lay back and kept her legs around him, feeling like she were hanging off him, stretching her spine luxuriantly. His hands followed the line of her torso, her flat stomach and full breasts. Rachel lifted a shoulder at a time, allowing him to peel the suit down, removing the only thing that stood between him and her flesh. He worked it over her breasts and left it around her middle while he fondled them, weighing each in a hand and pressing her nipples with his thumbs as if they were buttons. Her body settled into a state of relaxation suffused with the first indicative energy of anticipation.

Pulling slowly, Damien brought the fabric over her stomach and to her waist, making it ride low on her hips and revealing the border of her pubic hair. With her legs gripping him, it was easy for Damien to slide the suit over her bottom. As the shining cotton came away from her sex, it felt damp and the air around her was chill even in the warmth of the living room. She released her legs and dropped her behind to the floor. Damien gave a quick tug and she was naked on the mat in front of him, he poised like an animal about to leap, bare-chested and still in his jeans.

Damien bent and kissed her stomach and then moved his face around, keeping himself an inch or so clear of her skin, as though sniffing at her. Rachel wriggled on the floor, knowing her damp sex would be giving off a sensual musk. He kissed her pubic hair and his legs felt surprisingly hard and pointed on the fleshy mound beneath. Inside, she felt muscles stirring and the juices flowing like a torrent in her sex. It would have been nice to have reached down and slipped in a finger of her own, to let it probe around the outer edges of her sex before dipping it in. Instead, she stroked his head for a second and then released it, putting her hand behind her head, her legs drooping open on the mat, wondering when Damien's mouth would make contact with her desperate sex.

She did not have to wait for long. Rachel gasped loudly when she felt his mouth on her. He was kissing her sex with a wide open mouth, feeding on the puffed flesh. She felt his tongue make a long, exaggerated slide along her crease, as though savouring some precious morsel. Rachel arched her back and tensed her musles when his tongue breached her outer lips, finding its way in between them. No sooner had it been there than it was gone. He moved his mouth over her clitoris, making it undulate. Damien flicked at it with his tongue, accentuating the tiny centre of her desire which it represented. It was as though all the feeling in her body, the desire for release, were focused into the small nodule.

Damien found a rhythm and pace that synchronised itself with her own and Rachel squirmed under his eager mouth. Her body twisted and she felt her muscles flutter between slack and tight as she neared a climax. His tongue mixed the wetness of his mouth with that of her sex, until she was a mass of swishing flesh as he used his mouth over her sex. Rachel raised her head and looked at him crouched over her, the bony bumps of his spine arcing down his back, the rear of his jeans only just visible. His head was bobbing and his hands were resting on the floor.

The sight of him, half-naked and making so much effort for her, sent Rachel over the edge. She dropped her head back onto the floor and moved it from side to side as orgasm surged through her. The climax emitted from her in a series of guttural sounds, Damien tenderly lapping at the sensitive tract of flesh around her clitoris. The first violent wave eased off and from deep inside of her came a sigh of contentment as she reached down and held his head, easing him away from her, her thighs trembling in an echo of her orgasm.

Almost immediately, Damien was standing. He kicked off his clumpy black walking shoes and fiddled with his belt. The baggy jeans fell heavily to his ankles and he stepped out of them, hopping from foot to foot to remove his thick socks. The underwear went next, tight white cotton clinging to his narrow hips. Damien stood over her, naked, his cock erect and hanging heavily away from his body. He gripped himself and Rachel watched his shaft swell under his hold. Slowly, he pulled back his foreskin and Rachel could see from his expression the effort he was making to force blood into himself, the tendons of his neck standing proud and his head shaking slightly. Towering over her, he continued to manipulate himself, teasing his cock to its full capacity. Rachel lay and watched, savouring the sight of a sexy young man readying himself for her.

Damien knelt down and moved his body on top of hers, his frame covering her as they nuzzled at each other, lips brushing ardently. He played with her hair and looked hard into her eyes, words seemingly somewhere below the surface. Rachel wondered what he might want to say to her, a little afraid at what it could be. Whatever it was, Rachel smothered it with the resumption of their kiss, rubbing her hands over his back and stretching down to his firm behind. Along the line of her sex, she could feel the heavy bearing down of his swollen shaft. She reached down between their bodies and he raised himself so she could fondle him. While Rachel held his cock, Damien moved his body so that the tip of his phallus caressed the lips of her vagina, which was wet and still reverberating from the recent orgasm.

Rachel opened her knees wide and used her own hand to guide him inside her. She put one hand on his chest and with the other she gripped the middle of his shaft and angled him towards her. He brought the lower half of his body gently down and the tip of his cock pressed through her outer lips. Rachel pressed his chest with her free hand, putting a brake on him as he rested against the opening of her vagina. He flexed his body and pushed with a slight impatience. Rachel smiled at him and met the push. The precise instant of his entry into her would be profound, altering the moment for her. Bracing herself, she felt ready to yield to him for a short while. Rachel released the grip from his cock and let her other hand fall away from his chest. Holding his hips, one hand either side of him, Rachel felt the soft warmth of the skin and as he moved, so her hands went with him, pulling him into her. Rachel gave a cry and then he was inside her.

After the intensity of his first entry, Rachel was held in the grip of powerful feelings as he insinuated the rest of himself in her. Her breathing became laboured as she came to accommodate him. It was pleasurable and also aching, the way he opened her with the width of his cock and filled her with its length. It seemed almost incomprehensible at that moment that once he had entered her, it would only be the beginning. Then he would move himself in and out of her with a slowly building enthusiasm until they would both be left senselesss.

Their dewy pubic hair made contact and Damien let some more of his weight rest on her. Rachel enjoyed the match of their bodies, she firm and supple while Damien was neither bulky nor skinny, pleasingly masculine without the need for overdone musculature. Settling herself on the mat, she rippled the muscles of her vagina around him while stroking his lower back. Carefully, he began to move himself back and forth, so slowly that Rachel was conscious of the skin of his cock rubbing against the walls of her vagina. His movements were unhurried and confident, as though he could sense the effect of his action on her. He felt large inside her and Rachel wondered how long he would be able to restrain himself before letting go. Damien's shaft throbbed like the beat of a heart and the momentary expansion it caused in her sex made her grunt appreciatively.

Damien's relaxed and calculated plundering of her continued for several minutes and each passing moment made Rachel feel more a part of him and what he was doing to her. Sometimes, he rocked from side to side or made a circular motion with his backside and Rachel was shocked at how much it changed the feelings inside her. All of the variety, the experimentation and the languorous manner served to highlight the fervour when he eventually picked up a familiar tempo and direction.

The slowness and the tenderness were replaced with speed and ruthlessness. It was what she wanted and her sex tingled to life, her clitoris buffeted about and agonisingly stimulated by his thrusting. Both of them breathed heavily, and, at times, irregularly, unable to keep up with the frantic demands of two bodies combined. The noises they made built up and sounded loud in the room, their bodies perspiring and their muscles exerting feverishly. Rachel's back was wet against the rubber square of her yoga mat and Damien's body was hot, raising the temperature even further.

Damien was driving into her with a speed that seemed to surprise even him and he was looking at her as though in shock at who he was and what he was doing to her. They both seemed to be staring at each other and Rachel was wide-eyed, looking at him as if it were the very first time they had made love. Somewhere in the middle of his torso, around his stomach, it was as though a muscle had given way and his motions became extreme, struggling towards something possibly unattainable. Rachel responded with encouraging movements and sounds, wanting his orgasm as much as her own. Damien continued to lunge at her, his body now flailing about hers as though lost even to himself.

Rachel clenched his cock as tightly as she could, exerting pressure on him with her vagina each time he was fully in her. Damien called out in a long gasp and his body became momentarily tense, the outer shell of him frozen while the core of himself pumped fluid towards its goal. Rachel heard the triumphant cry and then felt his ejaculation as he pumped back and forth, emptying hot semen into her. Rachel was caught between two poles of desire, not sure if she should carry on enjoying the feel of Damien coming deep into her or to try and reach another climax of her own. Taking Damien's energetic part of the experience, she integrated it into her own thoughts and feelings as she closed her eyes and focused on her tingling clitoris and the pounding it was receiving.

Image and feeling were aligned perfectly, Rachel able to see in her mind the image of Damien lashing about on her as he came and the feeling in her clitoris of being about to explode in a deliciously controlled manner. Rachel managed a quick and heated orgasm that followed largely in the wake of Damien's. He kept his own movements going, even as his orgasm receded, providing her with the final momentum she required as she gripped him tight and let her whole body become one sensitive quiver beneath him.

They went to bed and Rachel left him dozing as she went to shower. In the living room, she retrieved what little there was of *A Winter's Tale* from the table and returned to the mat, realising as she looked at the words in front of her that the play had not been off her mind for a single moment.

Chapter Six

It was a chill, cloudless day and Rachel decided to walk into the centre of town from Waterloo. Most times, she would get the tube to Leicester Square, in a rush to be somewhere. Now, she ambled over Hungerford footbridge, feeling it vibrate under her feet as trains shunted past her on their way in and out of Charing Cross. To her right was the city, sharply defined in the noon sun. In front of her, at the end of the bridge, Villiers Street sloped upwards into Strand. Beyond it was her favourite destination, the West End.

Rachel wore only the minimum of makeup, her face washed over with just moisturiser, like a canvas prepared to take paint. Her hair was concealed beneath a beret, her eyes hidden by Revo sunglasses. Against the icy breeze, she wore a long wool coat with a dense herringbone pattern and dark blue trousers in soft cashmere which tapered to the heel. Generally, Rachel did not get recognised much in the street and when it did happen, it was a fleeting recognition as though she were an old school friend or a face out of place. She doubted anyone would recognise her at that moment, wrapped up and disguised more than normal because she was afraid Nikki Price had got the scent about her and Damien.

Convincing herself about a role took three steps. It began with her current lover and she decided that was Oliver, not having thought too much about his status in her life until then. Oliver was clear on where he stood concerning the part – she should do it. The second step was her agent, Liz

Benton. That would be Rachel's task for the morning, to use Liz as a sounding board, test the idea on her and see how it felt. The steps to comfort increased in size and the biggest, her mother, would be left to last. At what point in the manufactured steps Rachel herself became sure, she had no way of telling. Mostly, she sought approval and advice and doubted she would really have bounced the idea off the people close to her if she had not already decided herself at some level.

On the Strand, Rachel almost made an unconscious right turn towards the Mercury Theatre. She could not resist a glance towards Aldwych before heading off for Charing Cross Road. Her name, which had rested next to Robert Grosvenor's in red neon for nine months as though on a wedding invitation, was nowhere to be seen. A small tinge of Antonia Ford came back to her. Midway through the run, there had been talk of filming it for television, an exciting prospect at the time. Now, even so soon after it was over, the thought of it made her shiver more than the gust from Trafalgar Square.

Liz Benton kept an office in the low numbers of Charing Cross Road, the view from the second floor window made up of a stark wall and a lump of the National Portrait Gallery. The hallway and stairs were narrow and warm, the carpet loose on some of the runners. In the small reception area, signed photographs and posters were fixed to one wall like a gallery. Rachel was near to the bottom and to the right, one of the most recent of a long line of actors represented by Liz Benton. Luke, her assistant, sat behind the desk flicking buttons on the tiny antiquated switchboard, his big hands clumsy on minuscule switches. He smiled politely at her and Rachel made her way through the open door of Liz's office. She dumped her coat, beret and glasses in an unruly pile on a worn sofa where they lay like a representation of herself.

As usual, Liz was working the phone, receiver pressed to

her ear with one hand, pen and cigarette in the other. She laughed and talked sharply, business never far from the surface. In her late-fifties with salon-red hair, a thin face and her ever-present pearl earrings, Liz was a fearsome agent, one Rachel was glad to have on her side of the table. Liz picked up a can of Pepsi Max and took a swig as she listened. The youthful can looked incongruous in her old hands and Rachel knew that under the table her feet would be clad in the battered Addidas trainers Liz wore around the office. It was the only scuffed thing about Liz Benton, who always dressed floral and flowing, looking like a lady about to slip out and drink her pre-ordered gin and tonic in the interval. Rachel had watched her hold court in Joe Allen's, trainers replaced by heels, Pepsi Max by bordeaux, as directors, producers and writers, young and old, were pulled into line.

'Luke, no more calls, doll face,' Liz called when she had put the receiver back into its cradle.

Liz's office was straight out of a private eye movie; Philip Marlowe relocated in theatreland and Liz in the centre of it all, the vamp who also ran the show. Through the tightly closed windows, sounds of London at lunch filtered in.

'I thought you were resting? It's only been three days and already you're here to see me?' Liz asked with her usual emphasis on the word 'you'.

'I was coming into town anyway and I thought I'd stop by,' Rachel said.

'I see. You're not here to chide me for missing the party?'

'Of course not,' Rachel smiled.

'Tea?' Liz asked.

Rachel nodded and Liz called polite instructions to Luke, as though persuading an errant son to help out.

'The other night, at the party, I met Blake Jordan,' Rachel said.

'Ah,' Liz replied. 'I thought I saw him last week at Le Caprice. He had his back to me, so I couldn't be sure.'

'Do you know him?'

'Not really. Years ago, I spent five minutes talking to him before he pointed out very politely that he wasn't actually Stephen Sondheim. I'd spent the whole time burbling on about *A Little Night Music*.'

Rachel drew in a sharp, sympathetic breath and Liz took a reflective drink from her can.

'Oliver knows him. After the party, well, after I left the party, he told Ollie he was interested in me for a part,' Rachel paused. 'On Broadway.'

'I get the feeling you're more surprised about it than I am. I could see you high kicking on Broadway like a regular Shirley Maclaine.'

'That's the point. He's not interested in me for a musical. He wants me for a serious part.'

Rachel waited to see if Liz would miss a beat, if there would be a flicker in her eye which gave away her true feelings. There was neither a flicker nor a pause. Liz spoke immediately.

'What part?' she asked.

'It's a new play by Carl Milken called *A Winter's Tale*.'

'I didn't think Carl Milken was writing anymore. He hasn't had anything on Broadway for at least ten years although some of his stuff is mainstay regional rep. A comeback would be pretty big news. Who's directing?'

'Milken's going to do it himself.'

While Rachel spent some time outlining what little she knew, embellishing it from time to time, Liz sat back in her chair and listened. Liz was smoking a cigarette grandly, drawing in sharply and releasing the smoke in a silent plume.

'So the play isn't finished?' she asked.

'No. The stuff Blake Jordan sent was very sketchy. I was surprised Milken would let it out like that. He sent it to Oliver and wants to hear something from us by the end of the week. I would have asked him to deal with you, but things happened so quickly and I didn't know about half of it,' Rachel said, feeling guilty.

'I think you can handle a role like this and I think it's a good time in your career to be doing it. Milken's not meant to be easy to work with, but, that said, he's got quality stamped all over him and you'd be crazy not to at least look at it. They will want you to read, I assume?'

'I'll have to audition for it in New York,' Rachel said.

'That's fair enough, I suppose, although if it were another London production like *Crossed Wires*, I think I'd want them just to offer you the part outright, but this is different.'

'It certainly is,' Rachel said.

There was a moment's silence while Liz considered things. Rachel waited, knowing that Liz would never categorically say she should or shouldn't do a part. Rachel knew Liz well enough to read any negative feelings and she was receiving none at that moment. Her relationship with Liz was somewhere on the borders of sisterly and maternal. Liz was like an insurance policy, a safety net onto which Rachel could fall. As well as handling the financial side, which Rachel would have detested, she was there as a bedrock of support. In the midst of all the good and bad advice she received from friends and enemies around her, Rachel found Liz to be the least judgemental, always on her side and ready to hear Rachel's doubts.

'Liz,' she said, surprised at how tentative the word sounded, like a whisper into a dark room. 'Do you think this part is really going to be too much for me?'

'What did you say to me before you did your series on the telly?' Liz asked.

'The same thing,' Rachel replied.

'And before Eliza?' she asked, becoming more stern.

'The same thing.'

'Now,' Liz said, 'before you went into *Crossed Wires*, what did you ask me?'

Rachel tried to remember the conversation. Liz filled in the gap.

'Nothing. You didn't say anything, Rachel. When you were considering going straight from *Wires* into the other play, you didn't ask me anything either. Maybe doing this thing with Milken will be like a wake-up call, help you shake off some of the complacency. I can see you're hungry for the part already, just don't make it too obvious to them. When are they thinking of opening it?'

'Blake mentioned February.'

'Doesn't give them much time. How long is the run?'

'It's too vague for me, but I wouldn't want to commit beyond four months, not after this last nine month run. It won't clash with anything because I've got nothing planned,' Rachel said.

'If it did, we could move it round.'

'There was one other thing,' Rachel said.

'What's that?' Liz asked.

'Mummy gets back from Oxford late tomorrow and I'm going to see her Friday morning,' Rachel said.

'No,' Liz said.

'Please,' Rachel whined winningly.

'I was the one who told her about the break you were supposed to be taking, which I am still sure she thinks was my fault. Now you want me to be the one to tell her you're not really taking a break, you just might be away in America for six months. No,' Liz repeated.

Rachel pulled an elastic face. 'Go on, Liz. You've known her longer than me. Call her late tomorrow. She likes to hear these things from you first. It makes her feel involved.'

Liz shook her head. 'I'll give her a call.'

'You're a star,' Rachel said.

'Hopefully, darling, you're the star,' Liz said.

Chapter Seven

'You know, I was thinking about this late last night, and it seems to me what Milken has done is cross *The Winter's Tale* with *Silas Marner*, the George Eliot book.'

Oliver was sitting on the winged armchair in his living room, the furniture pushed back to clear a space, and Rachel sitting in it, looking up at him as if she were a disciple. Oliver was dressed impeccably in what he had already told Rachel was a combination of Paul Smith and Commes Des Garçon. The previous year, Oliver had done some runway modelling, partaking in the vogue for using celebrities as models. 'If Malkovich and Hopper can do it, why not me?' he would say, recalling it.

'You really think it's like *Silas Marner*? I'm not familiar with it,' Rachel said. With Oliver, she felt no need to pretend she had read it.

Oliver nodded wisely. 'Definitely. All that lost and found child stuff. In *Marner* the child is called Eppie and Carl has opted to call his foundling Effie. And, this intrigues me more than it really should, both *Marner* and *The Winter's Tale* have gaps of sixteen years in them, just like Carl has.'

'I wish the gap was bigger. I'm going to have to play an eighteen-year-old American girl.'

'I'm sure you're fishing for some sort of encouraging comment in there, dear, but I can't quite tell what it is. Let's concentrate on the material,' he said, tapping the papers on his lap.

Rachel had never worked with Oliver. It was unnerving

53

at first, to read through the speeches she intended to do at the audition, conscious of his watchful eye and the movement of his pen on the pad he rested on his knee. They had both agreed it would be silly to do the material to death, but it would be equally silly to ignore it, given it was in their possession. They were both also in agreement, largely unspoken, that while the basic concept and structure of the play were a bit too pat, if interesting, the Milken touch would be the thing that eventually lifted it.

In Act One, Rachel would be Jennifer Thorn, a childless woman living in a remote cabin in the Pacific Northwest, shared with an increasingly estranged husband. There were hints of a woman wrongly accused of a crime, the suspicion never more than vague and, more importantly, there seemed to be the strong possibility she was on the verge of murdering her husband. The first act ended with Jennifer Thorn finding the baby Effie. The second act opened with the sounds of aggressive lovemaking coming from a darkened stage. The lights would go up to reveal what the audience would eventually come to realise was the grown-up Effie and her boyfriend. The second act was less complete but Rachel could see how it would slowly reveal the fates of her adopted parents and her own feelings of detachment and isolation as an orphan with no real sense of her own origins. There was little to the play beyond its words, the skeleton of the piece bearing almost no stage directions. It wouldn't take a great deal of blocking to establish who went where, not least because there were only two people on the stage. The outside world was represented by television and radio.

'Although a lot of this, most of this, in fact, seems quite bleak, I think there is scope for you to have enormous fun as an actress. The dialogue is as good as it ever was,' Oliver said. 'I heard Milken referred to once as Pinter without the pause. An American with irony. They'll stuff him when he croaks.'

'It just seems too easy to fall into a yin-yang thing with

the mother and daughter, to play it obviously, like they were twins or something. I keep thinking the obvious. It's all very obvious,' Rachel said.

Oliver thought for a moment. 'That's part of Milken's style. He takes something obvious and shoves it right under your nose. In *Small People*, that family looks like pure Americana and yet by the end of it, you can hardly believe how far you've travelled. It opens and closes with the same short scene around a dinner table and uses exactly the same dialogue. At the start it seems anodyne, yet when the scene plays again at the end, it sears off your skin. He's not in the business of writing a jolly farce about a cable telly station.'

'It's the isolation of it that's all so striking. I don't know what he's been doing for the last fifteen years, but he seems to know what it is to be alone,' Rachel said. 'For the mother, especially, I keep trying to hold onto the thread I've got for her and let everything else drain away until it's the only thing left. Do you really think she pushes her husband off that mountain side?'

'Ask him when you meet him,' Oliver said.

The meeting, a more neutral term than audition, had been set for less than a week's time in New York. Oliver had offered to make arrangements for her and she had agreed, glad not to have to deal with booking things in the midst of her preparation. Rachel had never been to New York, whereas Oliver had practically lived there for a year. She felt a degree of guilt at letting him arrange everything when she had so steadfastly refused his offer of accompaniment, but she thought he understood her need to go alone.

'Let's look at the bits you're going to do for the mother. Your accent is very convincing by the way, nothing like the horrible National accents every time they do a Williams.'

Rachel remained seated on the floor and they proceeded to run through the mother and then the daughter a few times. Alternating the two in quick succession helped her find the similarity and the difference. Gradually, Milken's words felt easier in her mouth, as though they might have been her own. Towards the end, the words became much less his or her own and started to belong to the character. If she got the part, much of Rachel's effort would be directed to creating a character in whose subconscious she could lay the foundations upon which such words could be built. Every part involved taking the words from the playwright and giving them back to the character, using herself as a go-between.

'Are you sure you don't mind staying here while I run off to New York?' Rachel asked when they were done.

'I would have been a marvellous guide,' he replied, 'but that might have been off-putting.'

'As long as you're not upset.'

He smiled. 'I might go and visit my apartment in Prague, see what sort of state Simon left it in. Last time I was there, I netted the most delicious boy at Ruzyne. I'd barely left the plane. Those pretty Slav faces almost make up for all that bloody Mozart.'

Rachel stood and went to sit astride Oliver, her knees planting themselves into the seat of the armchair. 'You're going to end up in real trouble one day,' she said, stroking his hands.

'I already might have,' he said wickedly.

'Thanks for arranging things. I hate all of that,' she said.

Rachel kissed him and nestled herself tentatively into his lap to see if he would be hard, amid all his talk about Slav boys. He was. Not wanting to let him spoil the moment by filling it with words, she kept her mouth on his, prolonging the kiss and moving her behind suggestively about on his lap. The hardness grew until it was a protrusion, too prominent and obvious for him to hide it behind a lot of blathering.

He was about to say something, Rachel could tell, but she was too quick for him. In an instant, she was on her knees, kissing the hard bulge in his soft cashmere trousers. Rachel gripped his thighs just above his knee, feeling the tendons tighten. When she glanced up at him, his eyes were closed. Rachel wondered where, in his mind, he was and who he was with. She knew what he wanted.

Rachel unclasped the top of Oliver's trousers and slid the zip down, listening to the tearing sound it made. When the front of his trousers were splayed open, the swelling at the front of his brilliant white underwear seemed massive. Oliver was larger than most of the men Rachel had been with. Apart from that, there was also something about his age which permeated their encounters, imbuing them with a gravitas. Partly, it was the experience; he had been with many more people than she had and, therefore, she imagined the variety and quality of his experiences to be much greater than her own. It wasn't just his age because it was easy for her to imagine him at twenty, just as lofty and grandiloquent as he was now. Photographs of him taken in the sixties had hinted as much. Rachel let her thoughts seep away into desire.

She decided to work his trousers and underwear down only a short way, wanting to get at him quickly. His shaft was wide and heavy, dense somehow. Even flaccid, Oliver was pendulous and oppressive, his balls solid rounds in the wrinkled sac of his scrotum. Rachel moved them around in her fingers, feeling them roll and retract towards his body with each passing moment of increasing hardness. The tip of his cock was brutish and blunt, the eye in the head long and broad. As she eased his foreskin back, she looked into the slit and recalled the times she had watched with fascination as thick white spurts left him with great force.

The glans revealed, a deep red that was almost maroon, Rachel settled her mouth over the head of his cock. There was a strong, savory taste of sex to him and she used her tongue on the underside of his phallus, feeling the wrinkled knot where his foreskin was stretched. Rachel moved more upright on her knees so she was at a higher angle above him.

She braced herself with a swallow and when her mouth was lubricated enough, she opened it wide and dropped her head onto his pulsing shaft. It filled her whole mouth and she did not stop until she had the tip of it at the back of her throat and her lips in his pubic hair. Rachel managed to hold the position for a few seconds, encouraged by his gasps, before she had to pull herself off, carefully letting her lips graze the full length of his member as she did. Rachel teased him a few more times, swallowing him up and feeling his cock move in her mouth and his whole body squirm.

Rachel set to work on him in earnest, eager to bring him to a sudden and unexpected orgasm. He was a solid presence in the wet softness of her mouth, his hands resting on the arms of the chair and twitching in the periphery of her vision as she titillated him with tickling caresses of her lips and tongue. She made the swollen bulb at the top of his cock into a shining wet mass of sensitive nerve endings, lubricating the skin and sliding her mouth over it. Rachel used her mouth like a loose sheath, not sucking but rather just feathering him. When she did exert pressure by closing her lips on him, he made a seething noise and pushed his back against the chair.

Oliver started to buck his hips up and down and Rachel met the movements with equal force, pulling the hot head of his cock into her mouth and flicking frantically at its underside with the tip of her tongue. When his body gave a jerk which seemed involuntary, Rachel knew he was close and she concentrated on the most sensitive part of him with the most deft part of herself. She could taste him all through her, pervading all of her senses. He jerked once again and then held himself stiff as though his spine had straightened and then locked. His rear lifted off the armchair as his heels dug into the carpet.

Oliver was noisy when he came. He shouted, a shocked and exasperated sound that started in his throat and was so uncontrolled and raspy compared to his normally sonorous tone. The noises became shorter and tighter, fighting their way out of his chest and then rushing from his mouth and nose all at once as a snort. He grabbed each arm of the chair, digging his fingers in, yelling and rocking back and forth.

In several quick spurts, Oliver came in her mouth. Rachel kept herself closed on him, encouraging him. She was more conscious of the fluid's heat than its taste. It was thick and she let it collect in her mouth in a hot pool. When he had shot his last into her, she waited a moment and then let him withdraw from her mouth. She took in a small gasp of air and then swallowed his semen in a single gulp, the taste bitter and yet exciting at the same time.

Rachel stayed kneeling with her head resting in his lap for over a quarter of an hour, almost falling asleep under the careful ministrations of his hand through her hair. When she did slip for a moment, she found herself in a hazy half-world, isolated except for the thread of the characters she was already assimilating into her unconscious mind.

Chapter Eight

Rachel walked along the high street in Richmond, away from her own house and towards Kew, where her mother lived. It was nine-forty in the morning, the air icy and the sun a distant lamp in the sky. Shops were just coming to life and a large number of the people walking in the same direction as her hurried towards the station, carrying briefcases and wearing top coats over their business attire. As a girl growing up in Kew, Rachel had often come to Richmond and frittered away time with friends, surprised by the number of faces she saw that were familiar from television. It seemed to be an enclave of minor celebrities garnished with the odd superstar. She could still remember the first time she had seen Mick Jagger and the way her brain had been phased by the experience and the attempt to integrate him into the context of something as ordinary as a clothes shop. Now, she supposed, she formed part of the scenery in Richmond, somebody people saw and wondered where she was from.

Since seven that morning, Rachel had been up and walking around the house, still preoccupied by the work she had done with Oliver. In the space of only a few days, the idea of *A Winter's Tale* had become the lens through which she viewed everything else. Somewhere inside her, she believed, were the resources with which she would find the thread of the play and the two characterisations it required. Normally, she would find some aspect of a character that touched on something in her and then let the two develop their own unique energy, she acting merely as a guide. *A Winter's Tale*, with the mother and the foundling child, created a kind of schizophrenia, where Rachel oscillated between the two characters, knowing that to crack the parts was not as simple as playing them as opposites. When developing a character, everything that happened, no matter how unconnected, suddenly seemed to go right to the centre of the part and to be speaking directly to her like a guiding voice. Watching a science documentary, she had found herself wondering what kind of mother one of the women would have made.

Rachel crossed the main road leading into London. Almost a motorway, it felt like a border between Richmond and Kew, her and her mother. Walking towards the pagoda, she crossed another road, made a right turn into a side road and was home. Back to the first place she had known as home and would always think of as such. From Kew to Richmond was not so far to have moved in any sense, geographical or emotional. As she stood at the door of her mother's house, Rachel realised she knew lots about what it was like to be a daughter, but wondered if she could draw on resources that chimed so deeply in her. Rachel let herself in with the key her mother insisted she keep, certain it would one day aid Rachel in saving her from a siege of some sort.

'Mum,' Rachel called out into the hollow of the house as she stood in the hall.

'I'm upstairs. Be down in a moment,' came the muffled reply.

Rachel walked into the front room which had always caught the best of the early winter sun. The floor was polished oak and there were several display bookcases and two glass-fronted cabinets filled with various family ornaments. Several Turneresque landscapes were affixed to the deep red walls and a gothic gun-metal light fitting hung ponderously from the ceiling. The comfortable furniture was Laura Ashley and the uncomfortable was antique. On the long and wide shelf Rachel's father had fitted into one of the alcoves a year before he moved out was a collection of framed photographs. Rachel went and stood in front of them.

Susan Franklin, Rachel's mother, was the most dramatic woman never to have been on the professional stage. She had come from a passably well-off family, an only child like Rachel, but she had been treated as a drudge by her parents. The outer reaches of Rachel's family on her mother's side were pictorially represented by frames pushed concertedly to the back of the forest-like collection. Pride of place, many times over, was reserved for Rachel herself. Pictures of her as a child, as a girl and as a young woman. Next to a picture of Rachel in a school production of *Harlequinade* was one of her mother in an amateur production of *The Importance of Being Earnest*, a play she had been in three years before Rachel had even been born.

In the photographic collection, there used to be several pictures of Daddy, all of which had disappeared during the separation and divorce. Lately, several years ago in fact, a single picture of Maurice Franklin had returned. Rachel had only once heard her mother regretfully recollect how there were rumours of a transfer to Wimbledon for their amateur *Importance* which never transpired. Whatever had happened years before Rachel's birth, her mother never did any more acting. Rachel picked up the photograph of her mother in costume and wondered what had been said between her and her father, that particular time and all the other times. What ultimate imbalance of words had ultimately pulled them apart? Rachel put the photograph down. There were no pictures of her mother and father occupying the same frame.

'Oh, darling, you must be feeling terrible. You've seen the paper, of course. I would have called but you should have been laying in. I don't normally buy the paper, of course, but the man in the shop told me, the one who had the operation last year. Oh, Rachel.'

In the flesh, Susan Franklin was still a presence with which to be reckoned, the sort other women half-consciously measured themselves against, whether positively or negatively. A year away from sixty, her face was a slowly shifting effusion of drama, empathy and outrage. Her still voluptuous lips were ever pursed to make a response or, more usually, to interrupt. Rachel's friends from school had been afraid of the fiery-haired woman, unable to understand her eccentricity and her pro-tectiveness towards her only child. It was the same thing which made Oliver so wary of her. What her mother wanted for her, a successful career and a settled relation-ship, were, Rachel believed, incompatible, but most of her mother's considerable energies were directed to the realisa-tion of the paradox.

'What are you talking about?' Rachel asked.

'You haven't seen it?'

'No. Obviously not,' Rachel replied patiently, rattled that the normal formalities of greeting following a period of separation had been abandoned.

Her mother led her into the kitchen and Rachel saw the opened tabloid on the table, Nikki Price's face beaming from the top of her column and a third of the page dominated by a picture of Rachel and Damien kissing at her garden gate, she in her cat suit, he in his dark glasses and hat, both of them clearly recognisable. It was a medium quality photograph which had obviously been taken with a long, concealed lens.

'Fuck,' was all Rachel could manage.

'Quite,' said her mother.

Rachel scanned through the text, such as it was.

'All the times she's been here,' her mother said, refer-ring to Nikki. 'The nights she sat at this table and ate dinner with you and I. I never trusted her. Eyes everywhere, like she was casing the joint. I've a mind to call her.'

Rachel held her hand up, indicating her need for a moment of silence. What was Nikki up to? Rachel's first instinct was to call Damien, but that might make things worse. Oliver would be unlikely to see it and even if he did, it would not worry him. Actually, she thought, it wouldn't really worry Damien that much, so why should she let it upset her? Like a bad review, she disconnected herself from it, let it go, and felt better immediately. She threw the paper to one side in a dismissive action.

'How was Oxford?' she asked, brightening a little, outwardly at least.

'Fine. Fine. What's Lizzie telling me about a part? I thought you were going to be resting? You turned down a part so you could rest, not that it would have been the right part in any case.'

Rachel sat at the table. 'I thought Daddy was going to come to the closing night.'

'I thought he would have too. If I hadn't been in Oxford, been there to whip him into it, I expect he would have. When did he ever,' she appended wistfully.

Susan married Maurice Franklin when she was young and waited a while before having Rachel. In the period before Rachel was born, her mother's family money and then inheritance had funded several of her father's more exotic business ventures. Treasure hunting, a boat restoring company, talk of buying a guest house. The list went on. When it was decided to have Rachel, Susan insisted Maurice settle down into a more regular job, using his qualifications. To his credit, he did, getting a job selling software for the subsidiary of a US computer company. Currently, he ran his own successful consulting business and Rachel's mother believed that forcing him to settle had been right because he ended up doing what he had always wanted – to work for himself. He lived with his new wife, three year's Rachel's senior, or, more pointedly, thirty years Susan's junior.

'I tried calling him at home and work, but all I got were machines,' Rachel said.

'I used to get the same, dear, when we were still married. He promised me he would be there for your last night. I'll get on to him about it, don't you mind it. Let's not talk about him. Tell me about the part Lizzie was on about.'

'I've got the chance for a serious role in a new play by Carl Milken, opening next year. He's going to direct it and Blake Jordan is producing,' Rachel said.

Her mother looked at her but did not speak. The older woman's silence tripped her the same way it had since she was a teenager and by the time Rachel realised that her mother knew more than she was letting on, it was too late.

'You have to go to New York for the audition, don't you?' her mother asked.

Rachel should have known better. Her mother and Lizzie were too conspiratorial. She would go to New York for the audition whatever her mother or anyone else said. Her mother would not, she knew, under any circumstances, try and stop her doing so. Yet, that was what made the situation so important. It went far beyond the binary simplicities of yes/no, approval/disapproval. It affected the spirit with which the thing was entered into.

'What's it about?' her mother asked.

'It's called *A Winter's Tale*. It's a two-act play, almost two connected plays and I play a different role in each. A mother in the first and her adopted grown-up daughter in the second.'

Her mother nodded and Rachel took it as a cue to go on and explain more about the play.

'When would you have to audition?'

'They want to see me next week, if possible,' Rachel said.

'Do you want me to come with you?'

Rachel hesitated. 'I'd like to go on my own.'

'To New York?'

'Mum, I'll be fine.'

'You want this part badly, don't you? Lizzie thinks you do,' her mother said, holding her with a strong gaze.

Rachel nodded. Her mother reached out, squeezed Rachel's arm and smiled. The spirit was good.

'What does Oliver think of all this?' her mother asked, managing to use his name as though it were a foreign word, unfamiliar to her lips.

'He thinks it's great and he's been really wonderful. We spent some time together yesterday going through the stuff and he's been coaching me, sort of. I've never seen that side of his craft before.'

'And him?' her mother said, nodding to the discarded paper and not even bothering to use Damien's name.

'Damien's happy for me,' she said.

'Do you think it's really wise, keeping these two on the go like you are? You'll end up hurt, like you always do.'

'You've been saying that for three months now, Mum. Yesterday, probably because you've been such a gloom harbinger, I was trying to think of ways Ollie might be able to hurt me and I couldn't really come up with any. We're both happy with the way things are.'

'Surely you don't trust that one?' she said, nodding at the paper again, as though everything tabloid stood for Damien.

'Trust is not really part of that situation, Mum.'

'You should hear yourself. You're going to tell me I'm old-fashioned in a minute. In the sixties, I was almost the age you are now and believe me, all that freedom usually meant we were still left holding the babies.'

'You are old-fashioned. You just have to let me go my own way, Mum.'

'I've never prevented you doing that, but you shouldn't prevent me having an opinion. Look at the trail of actors and directors you've left behind you and I bet you thought none of them would be able to hurt you either, but plenty of them did.'

'What's brought this on? Are you upset over the piece in the paper?'

The older woman did not speak, her nails trailing the surface of the table. 'I know you think I interfere—'

'I don't, Mum, I—'

'Well, I want to interfere just once more. Wait here,' her mother said, rising from the table.

A minute or so later, she reentered the kitchen and laid a postcard down on the table as though she were trumping the situation with it. On the front of the card was a photograph of a shop, a gleaming gold cup and saucer with steam rising from them painted onto each window. The sign above the shop read *Cup of Joe* and the word 'of' was written on a cup similar to the ones painted on the window. Rachel turned it over and read the short message, noting that it was addressed to her at her mother's house.

Rachel,
It's been a long itme. If you ever want to talk, you can call or write me at the address below. If you're passing, drop by for a cup of coffee. I'm always here (I own the place).
Best,
Gary Tate

The address was Portsmouth, New Hampshire. The American stamp was faintly postmarked and Rachel squinted to read it.

'February?' Rachel asked. 'It's December now. Were you ever thinking of giving me this?'

'I'll be honest with you, Rachel, I don't know. February didn't seem like the right time.'

'And now does?' Rachel asked, feeling more tense than angry.

Ten years earlier, Gary Tate had for a short moment in time filled her mind in a way nothing or no one since had quite managed. Gary's mother worked for the US parent of the same computer corporation as Rachel's father. They worked on a transatlantic project together and a week in England on business for Gary's mother was soon decided to be spun out into a three week holiday for her family.

Rachel had seen Gary Tate three months before she actually met him. His mother had sent over a local newspaper carrying a picture on the back page of a smiling Gary in American football garb. From the moment she saw the picture, Rachel became transfixed by it. The paper was put into an overstuffed drawer in the front room and Rachel made frequent trips there, quietly sliding the drawer open and staring at the picture, uncertain exactly what drew her there. The solid jaw and cheekbones hinted at good Ivy League breeding, monogrammed cardigans and houses in the Hamptons, but they were things a sixteen-year-old Rachel knew nothing of. Rachel could not vocalise her thoughts about the boy in the picture even if she had been willing to do so. Words failed her and she was left with the vagaries of feelings, at times so strong and so confusing she would lay in bed and do things she couldn't imagine other, nicer girls did.

One night, over dinner, her father cheerfully announced Gary's mother would be in England on business and was bringing her husband and son with her. Immediately, Rachel's appetite was gone and her stomach felt hollow. In the space of a few sentences, Rachel's mother was suggesting the visitors could stay with them and her father was amiably agreeing. Rachel sat and listened, unable to comprehend that the picture would come to life and be in their house in just over a month's time. She feigned polite interest, while inside she was a frenzy of almost electrical intensity.

'I would have given it to you at the time, but you were only just getting over Michael, and there was the pressure over the play, my row with Daddy,' her mother was saying through the haze of Rachel's memory.

Rachel looked at her mother and felt a bit teary. She held

the card and tried to calm herself. Holding the card was like finding something lost for a long time and not realising until the moment of recovery how much it had really meant, how much she had missed it. Rachel knew the card had sparked the old electricity, a literal shock that was throwing her judgement off course and regressing her straight back to where she had been ten years earlier. And yet, it was such a deliciously comforting direction in which to travel.

'After they went home early, you and Daddy barely mentioned them again. I never expected to hear. Not after all this time,' Rachel said.

'You were only sixteen then. Twenty is a lot older for a boy at that age. I sensed you were attracted to him, even if your father didn't.' Her mother raised her eyes. 'Your father and I were both too wrapped up in ourselves and our own problems, too bloody selfish as usual.'

Gary and his parents should have been in England for twenty-one days but as it turned out, they stayed for only ten of them. Rachel was shy and awkward around them and, for the first few days, Gary and his father palled around in a sort of boy's club Rachel felt she could not break into. Over the weekend, when everyone went to Kew Gardens, the boundaries began to dissolve. The aloof manner Gary had shown for the first few days went and they were soon hanging back from their parents or off in front of them, wanting to be alone. He was a grown-up compared to her, but Rachel found him easy to talk to and by the end of the long day in Kew, silences had become meaningful between them.

That night, her legs still glowing from the day of walking, Rachel had lain awake and willed him to get up and go downstairs. Over an hour passed and nothing happened, the house silent with the slumber of the two families. Rachel got up and went to the kitchen, standing in the dark and lit only by the moon. As though he had been waiting to hear her move, she heard footfalls on the stairs, confident they were his. He appeared in the doorway and she turned to look at him, knowing she was ready to go to bed with him if that was what he wanted. Rachel almost ran to him, stopping only inches away. She waited for him to make a move, to kiss her. Rachel could hear their breathing, even the movements of their chests seemed audible in the late night silence. Rachel thought she saw him move his head a fraction closer to hers and she readied herself for the kiss.

It never came.

Gary straightened himself up and shook his head as though waking from a dream. 'This isn't right,' he said.

Rachel ran past him and quickly up the stairs, welling with disappointment and tears.

Problems in America, her father told her when they were suddenly gone one afternoon two days later. Rachel knew it was problems closer to home and she hated her parents for it, as though they had driven them out. For three months, Rachel expected Gary to call or write. He did not, and Rachel longed for him so much it made her frustrated. One afternoon, she sat on her bed and banged the mattress with angry fists until long sobs spilled messily from her. Things could not get worse she told herself over and over.

Then Daddy moved out. The emotional current of the Franklin household shifted and Rachel was carried along with it. By the time the separation and divorce were settled, Gary had become no more than an old photograph clipped from a newspaper. Even before then, Rachel had combined the energies of desire, lust and sex and projected them onto a polite boy called Colin, losing her virginity to him one weekend while his parents were away. For just the briefest part of a second, before Colin entered her, a thought went through her mind – it should have been yours, Gary. At least I'm not going to spend my life holding onto it for you, Gary, another voice quickly echoed in her head.

'You were really that keen on him, then?' her mother asked.

'Ten years ago, I was. It was the worst sort of schoolgirl crush you could imagine. I've used the emotional recollection from that period so often. I thought maybe you knew and that was why they went home. I really thought that for a while. Then you and Daddy. What happened?' Rachel asked.

'It wasn't your fault, dear,' her mother replied.

'But what happened? We've never talked about it. I've always been afraid to even ask.'

Rachel's mother held her hand up, indicating that it would not be discussed. 'The past happened, Rachel. Like it always does, and, when it does, it's done. My mother's favourite phrase, What's done is done.'

'I don't think Gary was interested in me anyway,' Rachel said, realising she was sniffling. 'I was so bloody awkward with him and every time he said anything to me, I went red. I shot my bolt too early with him.' Rachel paused, wondering if she should continue. She sniffed and smiled before speaking, trying to make light of her next sentence. 'The night after we went to Kew Gardens, I was with him in here, in the middle of the night. I think he was going to kiss me, but then he didn't.'

'My mother might have been right about what's done being done, but it doesn't stop you thinking about it. I've always tried to avoid regrets, Rachel, especially where you're concerned. God knows, I've had enough with your father, but this was one situation I've regretted for a long time and maybe now is the time to make it right.'

'What do you mean?' Rachel asked.

'I might not have given you that postcard ever, but when Lizzie told me you might go to New York, it got me to thinking. Then that bloody newspaper with Nikki Price. I don't ever want to think I might have been the reason for you missing out on a chance, then or now.'

Rachel hugged her mother and they wept the kind of tears that passed easily between a mother and daughter. She held her mother tightly and wondered if she really had missed out on a chance and if it would be folly to try for a second one.

Chapter Nine

It was Rachel's turn to wait in a hotel for Damien. Their relationship was mostly conducted in places neither of them would normally have frequented and the initial burst of excitement brought about by such novelty was beginning to wear off. All the sneaking around made the situation so unequivocal. Tonight, for instance, she knew they would have dinner, possibly in the tiny restaurant, but most likely off room service and then they would have sex. If they were an ordinary couple, they would have done the same, but at least dressed it up in a bit of romance.

It wasn't the only thing on her mind. New York was just two days away, the audition three. And after that? Gary? Rachel had thought her mind was more than occupied with the prospect of meeting Carl Milken and auditioning for *A Winter's Tale*. Her mother had changed that, throwing Gary into the swirl of thoughts in a way that was awkward. There had been occasions when Rachel had been considering one part, only to be offered another, which would cause some distress, but was always resolved satisfactorily through a choice. With Gary, it was not so simple. He played on her mind, got in the way of the mental preparation she was attempting for the audition. She would sooner have broken an arm or a leg, she thought, than have to deal with the idea of Gary at that moment. At least a broken limb was tangible and she could take her mind off it with thoughts of the play, but Gary was right there in the middle of her mind like someone talking to her while she was trying to concentrate on a book.

The hotel was in Banbury, a sort of midpoint between London and the studios of Damien's soap and Rachel had registered under the name Antonia Ford, resurrecting her character from *Crossed Wires* even though it seemed an unnecessary precaution for somewhere as quiet as Banbury. The hotel was too big to be a pub and too small to be a dignified country house, but it was comfortable, if a bit too plaid for her liking. Rachel had alternated fidgeting sits on the bed with journeys to the window to look for Damien's jeep. From the bed, she heard tyres on gravel and went to the window, pleased to see him draw up.

Rachel stood with the door ajar and heard him approach. He did not see her and his face was set in a frown and he was mumbling to himself. When he looked up and their eyes met, he tried to fix his face into a smile and Rachel would ordinarily have been happy with it had she not seen his face only seconds before.

'What's wrong, Damien?' she asked him.

'Nothing,' he said, brushing his lips against her cheek as he walked into the room and threw a hefty overnight bag onto the floor, his coat quickly following it with the force of an annoyed throw.

He went to the fridge and rummaged around, emerging with a bottle of beer in his hand.

'So, tell me about it,' Rachel said, sitting cross-legged on the bed.

'The producer gave me a telling off about our picture being in the paper, like it was my fault. Christ, it's like being back at fucking school.' His back was to her as he spoke, fumbling to get the top off the beer.

Rachel watched him drink and then patted the bed. 'Come and sit down,' she said.

He dropped himself onto the end of the bed, his back still to her. Rachel unfolded her legs and put them round him, moving herself close to him and hugging his back, looking at his reflection in the mirror.

'Did you talk to your friend?' he asked.

'Nikki's not taking my calls. She's probably embarrassed.'

'Don't stick up for her, Rachel.'

'I'm not. These shoulders feel so tense. What did the producer say?' she asked, kneading at his collarbone.

'Just this smarmy little speech about values and the image of the show. He did the same thing with Will last month when he talked to the *News of the World*. It makes me wild, the producer talking to the boys like he's our headmaster and fucking anything in the cast with a dress. Sometimes, I feel like chucking it in.'

'Just ignore it. They wouldn't treat you like that if they didn't have you under contract. And anyway, you'll be in the series long after the producer's been fired, if you still want to be in it.'

Rachel squeezed and manipulated the tight muscles of his neck with more force and Damien gave a sigh, one that was tense and still irritated. She continued until his muscles were loose and she could feel the warmth of his flesh through the material of his light blue Fred Perry. Her legs were thrown over his and dangled from the end of the bed. His anger excited her and she wanted to calm it and also for him to redirect it into another sort of energy. The strangeness of the hotel room, its perfectly scrubbed *Country Life* feel, made her want to sully it, to do something naughty.

Putting her arms under his and wrapping them around his middle, just under his chest, she kissed the back of his neck and felt the steady rise and fall of his chest.

Rachel leaned closer to his ear and whispered in it.

Damien turned his head to look at her. 'What brought that on?' he asked.

'Just do it, please,' she said.

He made a face that said he was not convinced.

'Please,' she said again, rubbing her hand over his chest.

Rachel climbed off the bed and stood in front of him. He grinned to himself and reached out for her, pulling her over his knee. Her midriff was on his knees like a pivot and her hands and feet touched the floor from where she was stretched out over him. It was an unusual position for her, but it served to display her behind for him. She felt him cautiously lift the short skirt and lay it in the small of her back. The cheeks of her rear were elongated into a stretch by her posture and the material of her white underwear was similarly taut across the flesh, almost as tight as skin itself.

Damien's hand lay itself on her behind like the footprint of where it would land when he put force behind it. Under the spread of his hand, Rachel's bottom seemed smaller to her and she clenched it tighter, her buttocks pulling the knickers into her. Damien was making a circular motion with his hand as though weighing up the target area. The more he caressed her, the more she wanted him to lift his hand and bring it down harshly on the delicate cloth of her panties and for it to reverberate through her. The crotch of her knickers was moist.

The hand was gone and then it was back. It landed firmly and squarely in the middle of her behind, lifting her cheeks for a moment. Rachel was sure her whole body had moved forward. The sudden weight of it made her gasp in surprise and pleasure. After the weight, a light tingling sensation followed which itself quickly turned to heat. Before Rachel could appreciate the feeling, his hand came down again and it felt as if it was in exactly the same position as the first time. It was a heavy thud in the midst of the radiating heat and it increased the depth of the feeling as well as its temperature.

By the fifth or sixth time, each spank concentrated in the same area of her backside, Rachel was moaning and squirming. The blood was rushing to her head as she hung over his knee, her head tingling almost as much as her behind. Damien pulled her knickers over her rear and Rachel was conscious of the air on her skin as he peeled them away. He pulled them to the tops of her thighs and delved between her legs, his fingers tickling the damp underside of her sex.

Damien's spanks sounded different on the bare warm flesh of her rear. The sound of skin on skin was sharp and in her mind Rachel imagined she could hear the whistle of his hand through the air. It was starting to smart and she was a little afraid she had asked for more than she could take, the naughty girl act running into Damien's bad boy. She tried to see the picture in her mind, her over his knee and he, still angry, spanking her behind. His free hand left her back and he was pushing it under her. Rachel shifted herself and allowed his hand to find her sex. She held her weight up for a moment until his hand was positioned and then she rested herself down on it, pressing it between her groin and his lap. In the compression of their bodies, his fingers wiggled and created a throb on her clitoris.

The movement was restricted, difficult even, but Rachel concentrated on it, taking pleasure from the way his fingers worried at her sex. His other hand now rested on her behind, occasionally stroking over it. The pressure from her clitoris was overwhelming, each previous spank seeming to flow through her and directly to the centre of desire. The heat on her behind and the hot swishy feeling in her sex were coupled with the rushing sensation in her head. The feeling was almost orgasmic in itself and Rachel wondered what it was going to be like when she came.

Rachel grunted and Damien worked his fingers harder, his palm sweaty and the knuckle of his thumb hard against her pubic mound. She twitched and felt the orgasm release inside her and she knew she had reached the point where nothing would prevent her from coming. It was a slow free-fall into it and her noises increased and became louder in time with her agitated movements. She tensed her body as though trying to fight it. Rachel held her breath, letting it catch in her throat as she tried to hold onto the few blissful seconds before orgasm.

Damien spanked her hard, his hand making a loud crack. The first one was enough and she yelled like a newborn baby. It had released the tension from her and it now spilled out as movement and sound, washing all through her. All the while she was coming, Damien's right hand was raining down on her bottom while his left hand quivered on her sex. The spanks increased the painfulness of her climax, a falling in the midst of her ecstasy in a way both methodical and cruel.

She kept her position as the orgasm subsided and her behind hummed. Damien worked her knickers off and lifted her off his lap, laying her face down on the bed and planting kisses on her behind.

'Have you got any cream I can put on you?' he asked.

'Look in my makeup bag in the bathroom,' she said.

Coming back, he knelt on the bed and Rachel heard him open something. The cream felt so cold on her it could have come directly from a fridge. Damien was careful in his application of the salve, smoothing it all over her buttocks, not pressing too hard on the sensitive flesh. Gradually, the coldness of the cream and the warmth of her rear melded at some midpoint and she glowed pleasurably.

Damien's fingers slipped into the crease of her behind and she felt the tip of his finger probe the wrinkled opening concealed between her cheeks. He put a large dollop of the cream into the fold and smeared it around the outer fringes of her anus. She heard his breathing, quiet but regular as though concentrating greatly on the task. Several times, he applied the lubricating cream to the area around the opening pushing it directly onto the centre of her tiny orifice where she felt it spread. He massaged the exterior ring of muscle with gentle fingers, loosening the whole area. He inserted his thumbs close to the hole and played her cheeks wide, letting them slip slowly and greasily through his grasp until she was closed once again.

Rachel continued to lay face down on the bed, still replete from the orgasm and spanking she had just received. She opened her legs a few inches wider and bit her lip in silence when the tip of his finger insinuated itself through the first band of muscle and slid deliberately along the small passage her clenched sphincters made. Rachel relaxed as much as she could to the ingression and Damien was making vague circular motions with the finger as he introduced it into her, loosening her in readiness. His finger was in to the last knuckle and it felt grainy in the tight hot passage, a strange presence in an infrequently explored and exotic place.

The withdrawal of the finger was a sudden and shocking sensation as it dragged itself out of her grip and she felt empty. He had done little more than meticulously probe her and yet she found herself wanting more. She raised her behind and moved it from side to side, leaning up on her elbows and feeling the stretch in her back. It was different to have the attention shifted away from her sex, her clitoris or her breasts or some of the many sensitive areas on her body and focused instead on the tiny squinting aperture.

After he had removed his clothes, leaving Rachel in hers, he was back on the bed and his finger worked more concertedly on her, soon to be joined by a second. It amplified the excitement far beyond the purely physical and before long, she was flailing on the bed, grabbing at the covers and pulling a pillow to her, burying her face in it and shouting into it.

'Put your legs together,' he said to her and she complied immediately.

Damien's cock hung down and lay on the cheeks of her behind. He was over her in the sort of stretched position he might have adopted were he about to do press-ups. His hands were either side of her shoulders and his feet next to her ankles. He was suspending his body so that only his erect member was touching her. He trailed it over her cheeks and she could feel its heat and she was sure there was fluid escaping him and lighting on her flesh.

He sat down, resting his behind on the back of her thighs. Rachel waited while he greased himself up. The end of his cock was burning as he pressed it against the centre of her backside, letting it nestle in the join of her buttocks and against the opening to her anus. There was pressure from the weight of his body and the resistance of her own. Damien remained in position, naked and astride her still clothed body.

It was hard to tell the precise moment at which he entered her. His phallus had been pressing insistently at her anus and then it felt as though it had become a part of her. There was a feeling of strain, but nothing unpleasant. Damien entered her almost by stealth and before she really knew it, the length of his shaft was in her. It was easy to discern the difference to his fingers, in both size and circumference. Because he sat astride her, the angle of entry was acute. When he was fully in and his groin was against her rear, Rachel felt at one with him.

Where he had been leisurely with his fingers, with his cock he began to thrust at a steady pace almost right away. He retracted half of himself and then lunged down quickly, the angle adjusting itself and making Rachel conscious of the rub of his hard cock against her quivering muscle. She adjusted to the rhythm and its enthusiasm, her sphincters relaxing to the point where she was able to squeeze him with them if she chose. Each time she did, he gave a gasp and pushed harder into her.

Damien was pounding at her, seemingly desperate to come. The force of his thrusts pushed her into the mattress and it creaked. The sound of the creak got closer and closer together as he went on at a furious pace. Rachel felt him straighten his legs out and was amazed that he was able to build up even more speed and depth from the position. In and out of her behind, his cock was a relentless onslaught, back in her almost as soon as it was out of her. It created a deep ache in her as though pushing against something that it could not topple over. It stimulated her but not enough to make her come. There would be time for that later, she reasoned, realising it was Damien who was most in need of release at that particular moment.

Rachel made encouraging movements and noises but he grunted and pushed her shoulders, indicating she should keep still. Rachel lay almost motionless as his movements signalled that the end was near for him. It was as though control no longer rested with either of them as he thrashed about helplessly on her prone and yielding body. Her behind still reverberated from what he had done to it earlier and now at its core, her anus was an overloaded mass of nerves that tingled wildly.

It was like no orgasm she could remember him having with her. He gripped her tightly and buried his head into her shoulder, nipping at her through the blouse. He gave several hard and decisive shoves with his lower body and let out a cry. Rachel was not sure if she felt him ejaculate but there was a warm and flooding sensation in her rear. She remained still as he jerked several more times and breathed hard against her ear, his weight bearing down on her as though the orgasm had sapped all his strength and he could no longer support himself.

Rachel undressed in the bathroom and went back to lay next to Damien who was still on top of the covers, naked and exhausted. She huddled up to his back and stroked his belly.

'I'm going to miss that while I'm away. What a send-off,' she said.

'You won't have to miss it. I'm coming with you.'

He spoke so casually and contentedly that Rachel almost took it in her stride. She let him go and sat up. 'I'm sorry?' she asked.

'I'm going to come and keep you company when you go for your audition,' he said, turning and laying so he could face her.

'Says who?' she asked.

'Oliver,' he said.

'Oliver? You don't even know Oliver,' she said.

'He called me and suggested I could go with you. He told me he was sorting out your travel arrangements and really thought I should go too. That you needed some moral support.'

'Oliver doesn't have your number,' she said, as though it made a difference.

'Well he got it from somewhere, obviously. Rachel, I've spoken to them about it at Oakwood and they're happy with it. We could do with getting away, somewhere we could be together and actually go out places. No fucking camera lenses pointing at us.'

Rachel looked at him.

'Damien, there is no way you're coming to New York with me.'

Chapter Ten

The yellow taxi had left the tunnel and been in Manhattan for almost forty minutes, stopping and starting in the late afternoon traffic. Rachel's neck ached both from the flight and from continually craning her head out the car's window as she tried to take in some more scenery, storing it like she were a camera. She flopped back into the leather seat, impossibly spongy and divided in two halves by a long stretch of gaffa tape. The photograph of the driver stared sombrely at her from his identification badge and the grubby laminate plastic made it difficult to read his name.

'Look,' said Damien suddenly, pointing out of his side of the car.

Rachel leaned across him and saw a theatre, its lights glowing in the dusk. As the taxi made a move of a mere few hundred yards, she saw more awnings, lights and posters. She smiled when she caught sight of the large Sony screen. They were, she knew without ever having been there before, in Times Square. Catching a glimpse of another theatre production she had seen in London made her realise they were the only things she recognised in a place that was otherwise alien to her. The only things apart from Damien.

What would it be like to be sitting here on my own right now? she thought. It would have felt lonely, she knew. Having Damien with her was comforting and he was fun to travel with, chatting everyone up along the way, but it had also made Rachel begin to worry about the real purpose of her journey. Originally, she planned to skip quietly across the Atlantic, go to the audition and possibly make a discreet, curiosity-satisfying visit to see Gary and then return to England. She had planned, in that event, to take a rather cowardly approach and call Oliver from New York to explain why she would not be back when her ticket said she would. Worse still, she might even have let her mother break the news. Instead, one of her boyfriends had insisted on arranging the trip and the other one was accompanying her on it.

They rode on in silence for another ten minutes and the taxi made a few abrupt turnings before coming to a halt outside the Larchmont Hotel, the one Oliver had recommended. A man in a green uniform piped with gold was opening her door and she stood and stretched her legs while Damien paid the driver.

'I feel like just going somewhere right now,' she said as their bags were being taken from the boot.

Damien gave her behind a gentle squeeze. 'There'll be plenty of time for tourism and romance,' he said quietly.

'And what about now?' she asked.

He smiled at her.

They sat naked and facing each other across the expanse of bed. Tiredness had given their passion a stop and start lethargy that had begun with them giggling and stripping off as soon as the bellhop left and had resulted in them currently sitting face to face, looking but not moving.

Damien's orangey auburn hair was in its normal tousled state and Rachel thought she could see the weariness in him, not just in his eyes but all through his nude, wiry body. She thought he was just gazing into space, the way she was herself, but she realised he was looking at her.

'What?' she asked.

'I was just imagining what Nikki Price would do if she could see us now,' he said.

'Get her notepad out and find the nearest phone,' she said.

'Were the two of you that good friends?'

'Not really. Nikki was a bit aloof and intense. We all got like that sometimes, but we knew when to stand back and take the piss out of it. I'm surprised someone as intense as Nikki can flourish in a tabloid gossip column. I'm sure she sees herself as a crusading journalist.'

'It'll blow over. They'll be onto somebody else by the time we get back. Still, when they're talking about you, they're leaving someone else alone. That's what my mum says.'

Rachel laughed.

'No, really,' he continued. 'I was getting a bit chubby at stage school and it looked like I was going to spend my teenage years playing the fat boy on Grange Hill and some of the kids teased me about my weight.'

'I find it hard to believe you were ever chubby. Puppy fat, maybe,' she said, reaching for his flat stomach.

'My Nan reckoned I put on weight because I got me sperms,' he said, mimicking an accent.

'Well, you seem to have plenty of those,' she said.

It was easy to forget where they were, casually sitting on a hotel bed, naked and chatting. What's this like? she thought. It's like we're a . . . couple. That was one outcome she had not expected with Damien, but she felt it. It might have been easy to pretend he was nothing more than a chaperon, but it was not entirely true.

While the thoughts traversed her head quickly, Damien was sliding himself nearer to her until their knees were touching. He reached out and put his hand on the back of her neck. Her spine and whole back stretched as she leaned forwards to meet his kiss. It was a brief, dry kiss that was a strange mixture of affection and desire. It was the sort of kiss men used in place of the three little words. Stop analysing it, she thought, pulling him into a hotter, deeper and wetter kiss.

Rachel stroked his thighs, feeling the smattering of hair tickle her palm. Gradually she worked her way up until she reached the crease at the top of his legs, where she let her hand light across his scant thatch of pubic hair before dropping to rest on the mattress. The skin of his ball sac was wrinkled and warm, loose as it lay on the bed, and his balls spread away from him. His shaft was semi-erect, tumescent but with the foreskin still partially forward. Rachel looked down at him and watched her fingers as they lightly stroked the smooth, dark skin of his cock. She did not rush, letting the brush of her hand awaken him slowly and resisting the urge to squeeze him. It was exciting and entrancing to watch him become gradually erect from her touch.

Rachel continued to gaze down at him the whole time, concentrating on the swelling flesh in front of her. When the stiffness was more evident, she took the shaft in her fingers and felt its circumference, weighing it as she did. It was hot in her fingers and deliciously long, his balls already tighter to his body than they had been only moments earlier.

Damien made fists with his hands and put them out behind him so he could lean back. As he did, his shaft pushed towards her, sticking out at an angle. Damien's cock was long, not enormously wide, but the length pleasing and exaggerated by his lithe frame. Rachel eased the fold of skin back across the smooth purple of his glans, only the faintest drop of fluid visible in the tiny slit. The head of his cock swelled with blood as she bared it. She encouraged him by squeezing the base of his shaft tightly between her thumb and index finger. Damien sighed through his nose, sounding somewhere between content and impatient. Their sex was usually rushed and frantic and Rachel was relishing the slow teasing way she was dealing with him.

Rachel masturbated him with a steady hand, holding him almost upright while she worked his increasingly pliable foreskin across his glans. Although he seemed as erect as he would get, Rachel noticed a hardening, almost impercept- ible, the more she used her hand on him, as though the density of his cock were increasing. A thin, watery fluid had seeped from his urethra and his foreskin spread it across the head of his cock, making it shine. Rachel imagined the convulsions of his body, the noise he would make and the contorted agony he would feel as he ejaculated a far heavier fluid.

Her sex felt long and moist, the lips puffed and heavy. She had not touched herself and would not yet. If she was going to torment him, make him subject to her rhythm, to perform an act on him she was sure he was proficient enough in himself, then she would also hold herself back.

Damien appeared content to sit back and let her take control, as well as doing all the work. She moved the sheath of her hand over his cock at a moderate pace, not fast enough to bring him to a swift orgasm. Rachel could tell he was greedy for the sensation of coming, but equally keen to delay its arrival and savour the process of getting there. She kept her grip on him and looked at him. His face was turned down to where she held him and he appeared fascinated, as though something new was happening to him. Damien's brow was furrowed and his lips slightly pursed, concentration evident.

When she stopped and eased him backwards, he looked up at her. As she pushed him back with a hand placed in the middle of his chest, she used the other to put his legs out on either side of her. He was sitting almost at the foot of the bed and as he went back, so his whole upper torso was off the bed, his head touching the carpet. The arch of his body was a delight to look at, the skin of his stomach stretching away in a smooth white sheet, his belly button stretched and his cock standing proud from his pubic hair.

'All the blood'll run to my head,' he said.

'I know,' she replied, taking hold of him before he could complain any further.

Rachel masturbated him with more force than she had previously, watching his balls jiggle and the whole of his pouch move up and down in time with her hand. She remained in her sitting position between his legs and took in the sight of him stretched out in such an unusual bow which made his body seem even more taut and in need of orgasm. His breathing was laboured and she assumed it was a mixture of excitement and the position of his body as the breath escaped him with a loud panting.

Carefully and quietly, she let the fingers of her left hand explore her own sex. Her labia was engorged, the crease between it slick with her juices. Rachel held her breath and made no sound as she delved into the hot, moist place, dipping in and then dragging her middle finger along until she touched the bud of her swollen clitoris. The whole of her sex was dewy and it anointed her secret fingers as she pleasured herself at the same time as she pleasured Damien.

It took a while for her to coordinate her efforts so she could masturbate herself and him at the same time. Damien was wriggling, trying to make himself more comfortable and Rachel kept her rhythm constant with him, fitting the manipulation of her clitoris into the pattern. She used the tips of two fingers to press at herself, her sex squirming and her clitoris whelming with the pent-up desire, needing release as much as Damien did.

Damien made some sighing noises and a few gentle groans that made Rachel wonder if he was nearer to his climax than she was. Would it be possible to time it just so and enable herself to use his noisy thrash to hide her climax from him. It felt voyeuristic to masturbate him in the way she did, as though he were a stranger she secretly watched, touching herself all the time. The thoughts opened the way to her orgasm, placing her closer to it in a matter of only seconds, her vagina rippling and quivering from touch.

Both her hands were lost in a flurry of movement. Damien's cock was a bulging and throbbing mass in her small hand, ready to burst over with his hot semen. Rachel kept as quiet as she could, shielding herself under his rising volume, wanting her orgasm to belong to her alone. She focused herself, slowing her hand on him while she speeded up on herself, shuffling her backside on the bed and feeling a tremble in her thighs.

Rachel came with a quiet power that surged all through her, emanating surely from her sex but quickly losing itself in all the erogenous areas of her body, sparking through her like electricity. Against the force which tried to move her, she sat rigid, letting the pleasure throb through her in tightly controlled pulses. It was almost like trying to conceal tears. She hunched her shoulders slightly, tensed her behind and seethed in silent anger, letting her sex take on the motion her whole body craved. It was more than she could take and she felt herself about to cry out.

Damien beat her to it. All through the blissful moments of her orgasm, Rachel had held onto him, continuing to stroke and tug at him almost automatically. While the last vestiges of her climax still reverberated, she was shaken rudely from it by Damien's sudden shout. He yelled loudly and Rachel watched his body tense as though pushed by some powerful internal force. Each breath was closer and closer to his previous, until he only seemed to be breathing out, catching air with the occasional grunt and snorting it back out again. A familiar twitch started, his legs restless and his rear flexing. As she prepared to feast over his orgasm, Rachel's hand was back on herself, attempting to draw out her recent release into something more potent.

Semen flew up in the air impressively as Rachel kept his cock upright. It was like watching it in slow motion as the thick globule flew gracefully through the air and landed decisively on his stomach, Rachel imagining she could hear a splat. The next two squirts were equally as forceful and followed by a thick spray of pearl-coloured sperm that spattered on his tight belly.

In a manner so unexpected it almost frightened her, Rachel came again. It was so soon after her first climax that it was both pleasurable and excruciating at once. Muscles and nerves which had only a minute earlier contracted and tingled with the rawness of sexual energy were now doing so again. This time, she was loud and obvious, crying out in a way that sounded helpless, using her fingers heavily as though trying to satisfy a deep yearning.

Ten minutes later, Damien spoke. 'What do you want to do now?' he asked.

'Let's go and eat and then tomorrow I want to do some shopping and all the tourist stuff,' she said.

'Don't you have to contact anyone here about the audition?' he asked.

'I don't want them fussing around me beforehand. It puts me off to get close to them before I've auditioned. It makes the process more uncomfortable and besides, I want to spend some time with you,' she said.

Rachel watched him as he rose from the bed and wandered into the bathroom to shower. When she heard the water running, she went to her carry-on bag and retrieved the postard from Gary. She looked at it for a moment before replacing it in a zipped pocket as though trying to put Gary out of her mind.

Chapter Eleven

On the morning of the audition, Rachel sent Damien off and spent time on her own. When she awoke, the first thing she had done was to check and see what condition her voice was in. It was excellent, the emergency throat spray unlikely to be needed. With Damien gone, she went through an array of exercises, vocal, physical and emotional. The material she had so scrupulously avoided since arriving in New York looked fresh once more, Oliver's advice coming back to her and helping her get a handle on what she wanted to do.

It was definitely time to work.

The holiday, short as it had been, was over. The afternoon before, she and Damien had paid a ghoulish visit to the Dakota building and then to Strawberry Fields in Central Park. Standing and reading the plaque, Damien could easily have been John, Paul, George or Ringo, his mop of hair shifting in the breeze. Apart from the shows, they had toured the Lincoln Centre with a chatty group of Italians, been up all the required tall buildings and circled Manhattan in a boat. Their time had been short, whetting her appetite for things she would like to do, but which would have to wait – galleries, museums and more shows. The couple of days had been fast and fun enough to distract her but now it was time to get down to the reason for her being in New York in the first place.

Rachel was superstitious about dressing too close to what she perceived the look of her character to be, although the problem was mostly overcome for her since she would play two parts in *A Winter's Tale*. If I get it, she thought, unhappy at catching herself thinking too many jumps ahead. The apprehension and anxiety was only just beginning, she knew. There were worries before the audition and during it and then, perhaps worse, came the waiting to hear, a restless time of imagined successes and failures, always secretly convinced the part had been landed. On it would go; first day of rehearsals, first read-through, blocking, speed runs, tech and dress rehearsals, previews, opening night, reviews, mid-run apprehension and apathy, closing night nerves and, then, it would all start again. I must love it all in some way, she thought, selecting her dark, loose trousers and a comfortable knitted top, glad she did not have more clothes to choose from.

Hailing a taxi was done for her by a valet who even gave the driver directions to the off-Broadway theatre, the exchange brusque but garrulous, an attitude Rachel was becoming familiar with in New York. The venue for the audition was currently home to one of Blake Jordan's smaller productions, a comedy of gay manners set in California. Rachel had sat through the matinee to get a feel for the theatre, barely noticing the antics of the over-handsome men. She thought the audition might have taken place in a studio or some other more intimate location, but then Carl Milken was a heavyweight traditionalist and Rachel suspected he wanted the formality and detachment a theatre would give, allowing him and Blake to lurk in the stalls while some hapless assistant director read with her. It didn't bother Rachel. It was a two-way thing and she would be happy to hide in the spotlight.

Blake had called to confirm the two-thirty appointment, telling her they were seeing actors in the morning for the roles of the husband and boyfriend. But I'm the one who'll have to act with them when I get the part, she had wanted to say. Wouldn't it make more sense to have me read with them, so we can all assess the chemistry? You're a long way from approving your own Broadway co-star, Rachel, she told herself.

Any new part, however big or small, and regardless of the amount of control she had, always raised lots of questions which could be addressed to no one in particular. As a result, auditions created a relentlessly interrogating internal monologue for Rachel, starting in the morning and continuing through the day until she was almost dizzy. The nearest thing she could compare it to was the early stages of drunkenness, a kind of serene melancholy.

Rachel was impressed that her extremely scant geographical knowledge of New York allowed her to recognise the area around the theatre as the taxi drew up. She paid the driver and skipped brightly to the stage door where an old man who could have been the stage door manager in any London theatre took her name and then mumbled it into a telephone receiver.

Blake Jordan looked more at home than he had at the closing night party for *Crossed Wires* as he strolled down the corridor.

'Hello,' he said, holding her elbow and kissing her on either cheek, lips barely touching her. 'How are you enjoying New York?' he asked.

Rachel expected such patter and as he led her through the theatre and towards the stage, she bantered with him, pleased just to be speaking, to have her voice working. One of her drama school teachers advised spending time chatting with friends on the morning of an audition in order to arrive ready to talk; the advice had always stuck in Rachel's head on such mornings as she guiltily enjoyed her solitude. She liked to save her chat for the moment and she was doing well, her nerves in check. Rachel was almost keen to meet Carl Milken. Most people want to have a nice time, she told herself. They have no interest in making this difficult for me because that would make it awkward for them too.

'Rachel, this is our assistant director Lucy Pattison,' Blake said.

Rachel nodded and shook hands with a svelte woman in her twenties with a shock of blond hair which stuck up at an obtuse angle and precisely drawn lines of good make-up.

'Hi,' they both said at once and Rachel instinctively liked her.

They were standing on the stage, in the middle of what Rachel knew was meant to be a tastefully and expensively well-furnished apartment in West Hollywood. Most of the furniture had been pushed back and she was glad to see a table and chair at the front of the stage; brightly illuminated, it was strangely welcoming, an island she could swim towards.

'Where'd Carl go?' Blake was asking Lucy.

'Bathroom, I guess,' Lucy replied.

'I'll let you get settled, Rachel,' Blake said, walking off stage right.

'Were you seeing actors this morning?' Rachel asked Lucy.

'Yeah. We had a few egos through here earlier. I told Blake and Carl they should have a casting director, but they insist on doing it themselves. You've come a long way for this,' Lucy said.

'I hope it's going to be worth it,' Rachel said confidently, removing her coat and throwing it onto an electric blue sofa with red scatter cushions.

'I'll give you some time,' Lucy said, beginning to withdraw discreetly.

Rachel stood alone on the stage, enjoying the feel of being on a set, despite the jangling of her nerves. It was quiet, much more so than during a show, when coughs and shuffles would sometimes spread through the audience in a contagious wave. She tried to adjust herself to the serenity, to let it seep through her. Rachel hoped to infuse herself with the calm as she went through final mental preparation.

All she had to do was meet Carl Milken and then do her stuff.

The shuffling was loud in the auditorium and through the glare of the lights, she could see two figures sneaking into seats several rows back in the stalls, moving nervously like latecomers. Rachel did not want to lean forward or squint, wishing to appear nonchalant. A third figure joined them but did not sit. Instead it bent forward and conversed before straightening up and heading towards her. It was Lucy, walking briskly and then clambering up onto the stage.

'They'd like you to read the speech on page twelve of the first act,' Lucy said.

'They?' she asked under her breath so only Lucy would hear.

'Blake and Carl,' she replied, making a sympathetic face.

Rachel had not expected a ticker-tape welcome but she had expected to be introduced to Carl Milken, instead of just standing on the stage, script in hand as though she had been shoved out of the wings to try out for a part in the chorus, a long line of hopefuls behind her like a super-market queue. Milken had a reputation for being difficult, but Rachel found the behaviour just rude. Don't let it rattle you, she thought, opening the script at page twelve and looking at the familiar words there. Lucy went off to the side of the stage, out of eyeline, and Rachel took a long breath.

Before any performance, there was a moment of pure emptiness, a second in which she was not anyone and knew nothing. In such instants, any words learned or characters developed were not there. The only thing which filled the space, bridged it and connected her to the performance was naked and exhilarating fear.

'For over three years now . . . '

In the long, eternal two and a half minutes that followed, Rachel became a woman who had never existed outside the head of Carl Milken or the words he put on paper. She lost herself in the woman, lettng the character fold its arms around her and protect her. It no longer mattered that she was angry at the unseen and staring eyes of Blake Jordan and Carl Milken; they could have been anyone at that point as Rachel performed only for herself and for her character, not to impress two men or to get a part.

The silence that followed was hard to read and Rachel waited.

'Okay. Try it again but start to let it unravel a few lines earlier, so she's really pissed at her husband,' rasped an unfamiliar American voice.

It annoyed her having to take directions from the un-known stranger that was Carl Milken, someone who did not have the grace even to introduce himself, but she held her tongue. Rachel did what she and every other actor she knew always did when given direction at an audition – she spent half a minute making faces to show the advice had sunk in and then proceeded to do it how she felt it should be played.

'Better,' came the crackling voice at the end and Rachel smiled to herself. 'Let's have a look at the daughter, page thirty-nine of the second act.'

Rachel silently thanked Ollie and wished he were there with her. She felt they had done just the right amount of preparation back in London a week earlier; it enabled her, coupled with the irritation at the process, to leave her nerves to one side.

Half way through the daughter's speech, as she sat on the edge of the table with one foot on the chair, Rachel was distracted by a noise in the wings. To her left, she heard Lucy's voice and another female voice she did not recognise, its volume slowly raising along with its pitch.

A tall woman in a long grey dress, hair pushed into a head scarf, marched past Rachel with long strides, her nose in the air and chin pointing out as though she were a silent movie star approaching Valentino. Except she *was* a movie star, Rachel realised, when she saw the profile. Gloria Vaughan, successful theatre and film actress, did not even acknowledge Rachel as she glided by, breaking the flow of the speech completely. Gloria Vaughan carried on until she was at the front of the stage, peering out into the dark with her back to Rachel.

'Blake? Carl, honey?' she was calling.

Because her back was to her and she stood on the edge of the stage, Rachel could not get in front of her to ask her what she thought she was doing. It was the first time Rachel had ever been downstaged.

Rachel turned instinctively to Lucy, her hold on the character gone. Lucy made a face and shrugged. The two figures approached the stage from the gloom of the seats.

Gloria Vaughan bent and reached out her hands. Like she were a queen, the two men carefully lowered her from the stage.

'Am I early? They tried to stop me at the door. Can you believe that?' Gloria Vaughan said.

Rachel got her first look at Milken. He was balding and all the skin on his head seemed tight around his skull, making him look skeletal. Small spectacles were perched halfway down the long bridge of his nose and his mouth was thin, revealing sharp teeth as he mumbled to Gloria Vaughan. It would have been difficult to guess his age and he certainly didn't look nearly sixty.

'What I thought I'd do,' Rachel heard Gloria saying.

'Excuse me. Hello,' Rachel said, making no attempt to disguise the annoyance or sarcasm in her voice.

Gloria Vaughan glanced over her shoulder at Rachel for less than a second, just enough to show disinterest, and then carried on speaking.

In the business, Rachel had a good reputation. Bright, funny, easy to work with, she was considered a trooper. Many in the profession were delicate constellations, their egos held together by only the thinnest threads of self-confidence and requiring the sort of fortification only the unqualified praise of others could bring. Either that, or they simply exploded, bringing the fragile artifice down around their ankles. The times when Rachel had blown up were memorable, to her and others, mostly because it was such an infrequent occurrence. In fact, Rachel could literally count those times on one hand because there had only been five of them ever connected with the greatest love of her life, acting. Part of her was sad that she was about to make it onto the other hand but there was absolutely nothing she could do to stop it as the anger coursed through her.

Inside Rachel, something gave.

Rachel turned, gathered her bag from by the table leg, and went to the sofa, putting on her coat. Her face was burning and she was shaking with anger. Get out of here before you say something you regret, was her only thought, a self-preservation instinct clicking in. Lucy approached her and Rachel held her hand up and shook her head as if to say, No.

'Rachel. Rachel.' It was Blake Jordan.

Just keep walking, she thought. Go home and have that rest. You don't need this.

'Rachel!' Blake said again.

He was louder and more authoritative, surprisingly so for such an unassuming man and, despite herself, Rachel turned and looked down at him standing in front of the stage.

'Where are you going?' he asked her.

'Are you serious? I've spent half an hour up here while the two of you sat in the shadows playing with yourselves like this is some, some fucking peepshow. I could have done this over the telephone.' She looked at Gloria Vaughan who was smirking. 'Then you let this haggard old cow march in with a tea towel on her head, acting like she's Garbo. Have you written in a grandmother character I don't know about?'

'You could be a little more respectful,' Carl Milken muttered.

Rachel trained her gaze directly on him. 'Respectful? After the way you've treated me? I got arrested on a demonstration once and was treated better than this. You write a couple of women characters and what? You want a medal for it?'

'Well, I can't recall being so insulted,' Gloria Vaughan chimed in her best fake English schoolmarm accent.

'Really?' Rachel asked. 'That's a pity, because if you had, you might be a lot less fucking rude. And you can save the Maggie Smith accent because it doesn't scare me – I've got one of my own at home.'

There was a hideous moment of silence, ghastly and empty.

'Rachel,' Blake Jordan said eventually, his voice low and calming.

'Don't,' Rachel said, raising her hand and feeling the stirring of angry tears.

'I think', Carl Milken began gravely.

'Go fuck yourself,' Rachel said directly to him, turning and walking out of the theatre too quickly to be stopped or to be seen crying.

Chapter Twelve

'How'd it go?' was the first thing Damien asked her when she entered the room. Part of her had been hoping he wouldn't be there, giving her more time to compose herself, while another part of her wanted to cling to him and bawl for an hour.

'It went fine. They'll get back to me,' she found herself saying with a cheery tone and a bright look on her face.

'What were they like?'

'Fine,' she replied too quickly and a little too sharply. She softened. 'They were nice. My brain's a bit addled right now and I get superstitious talking about auditions.'

'Do you think you got the part?' he asked, her superstitions not apparently concerning him.

An image of Gloria Vaughan marching onto the stage with her head in the air flashed into Rachel's mind and made her angry once again.

'Damien, it went well. Can we talk about it later?' she said.

'Okay,' he said, downcast.

'What did you get up to today?' she asked.

Damien visibly perked up. 'I got us invited to a party.' He smiled and sat forward on the bed.

'A party?' she asked, feeling her heart sink at the prospect.

'I was out looking round the shops and I went to FAO Schwartz because I promised my little brother I'd bring him something back from there. Then, I walked along and had coffee in the Trump Plaza – they've got this big pinky-gold water wall – and I got talking to an English couple.' He paused for a moment. 'They recognised me.'

'What are they doing in New York?' Rachel asked.

'They both work for the same fashion company, importing and exporting. I think they laid it on a bit thick, how jet set they were, to try and impress me, but anyway, they invited us to a party.'

'Did you say you were here with me?' she asked.

'What, the legendary Rachel Franklin?' he asked cheekily. 'I just said I was here with my girlfriend. They gave me the address of their friends' house. It's on Central Park West, not that far from the Dakota.'

'So this party is not even theirs, these people you met?'

'Russell and Dianne said it wouldn't be a problem. I thought you wouldn't mind. We don't have to go if you don't want to. We could go out to dinner, just the two of us. Or stay in,' he said.

The thought of Damien questioning her about the audition over dinner was not attractive. 'I wanted to see another show,' she said.

'We've already seen three. We've got one more night tomorrow, we can go to a show then.'

No we haven't got one more night, she thought.

'What time would we have to be at this party?' she asked.

'Not until eight o'clock at the earliest. We've got ages,' he said.

'Let's go,' she said, heading for the shower.

It was almost nine when they arrived, not wanting to be the first guests at the house of complete strangers. It was a big, solid building with wide ledges and large, square windows betraying little internal light to the night. The door to the apartment building was heavy and gilded, leading into a marble hall more like a prosperous city bank than a private residence. A polite doorman phoned up and relayed the complicated friend of a friend message Damien had given him. The doorman smiled, put down the phone and gave them token directions.

'Hello, I'm Patricia,' said the short woman with dark red hair who had opened the apartment door. 'You must be Damien. And this is?'

'Rachel,' Damien said.

'Rachel and Damien. Come in, do,' Patricia said in a knowing way, her accent as up-market New York as the dark pant suit she wore.

The door led to a raised area only a few feet square which looked over a sunken living room, an impressive expanse filled with vividly coloured antique furniture and about thirty people socialising in a warm and convivial manner.

Rachel was daunted by the prospect. Unfamiliar people in an unfamiliar place. 'Where's your couple?' Rachel asked Damien out the side of her mouth, keeping her voice down. The crowd was spread evenly in the mid-twenties to late-thirties age range, all dressed with obvious care, their colours, like the art on the wall, carefully coordinated. Music tinkled in the background, buoyed up by the wash of chatter and the odd laugh or clink of a glass.

Patricia had disappeared and a man too goodlooking to be a real butler was taking their coats.

'What do we do?' she asked Damien, standing on the raised entrance feeling obvious.

'We mingle?' he said, more like it was a query.

'Where are your friends?' she asked tensely as they moved through the light crowd, staying close to each other as though they were in danger of getting lost.

'I can't see them anywhere,' he replied.

For ten minutes, they circulated without making eye contact, like two children wandering through an adult party, clad in pyjamas and sleepy-eyed. They found a pillar to lean against, near a window and out of sight of most people, sipping wine from glasses lifted off a passing tray.

'Well, this is nice,' Rachel said, part-sarcasm at Damien and part in sympathy with him.

'You'll have to do your party piece in a minute, Eliza Doolittle,' he said.

She smiled at him, unable to be annoyed with him for very long.

A dinner gong was hit several times, eventually silencing the crowd.

'You didn't say there was dinner,' Rachel said.

'I didn't think there was,' he replied.

The small red-haired woman, Patricia, was holding the gong. 'Ladies and gentlemen, if you'll follow me into the dining room, we're all ready for you.'

They let themselves be carried along by the crowd, losing themselves in the gentle surge towards the double door at the far end of the room.

The dining room was empty, except for the stone-topped table set at one end as though for a buffet. The lighting in the room was subdued and the art different, blacker. It took Rachel a few moments to adjust to the low light; when she did, she was surprised.

Around the edge of the dining table, which measured some twenty feet long and half as wide, were short, fat candles spaced a foot apart. The wax looked yellow as each candle was illuminated by its own light. The bright glow they threw up reminded Rachel of footlights, mostly because of the way they shone on the two strangely clad figures standing atop the table.

A man in a black mask was kneeling on the table, his rear resting on the backs of his feet and his wrists bound together at the small of his back. He wore a leather harness whose thick, studded belts divided his torso into a number of muscular sections, chest and stomach criss-crossed by it. The mask concealed his whole head in shining latex, two outlandish pipes leading out the side to allow air into his nose and mouth. Rachel wondered if there were eyeholes.

She had read once about a mask that had only tiny pinholes out of which the wearer could see.

The woman was dressed more conventionally, lacy black bra and sheer panties plus high heeled shoes. Tucked through the side of her knickers was a riding crop. She faced the man, one foot forward and her hands on her hips. The woman was pretty, her hair long and blonde and her makeup carefully applied, accenting her eyes and cute nose. Utterly poised, she was almost motionless as she held her position, only the occasional blink indicating she was not a mannequin.

'You brought us to a sex party?' Rachel asked, making her voice as incredulous as she could in a whisper.

'Well,' he whispered back, 'seeing as that's Dianne on the table, I'm betting that's Russell in the mask. They didn't tell me they were on the menu,' he said.

The gong banged again, but it sounded more sinister in the dining room, the light faint and all the bodies pressed closer to each other than they had been in the more expansive living room. Rachel expected music to pipe up from somewhere, lurid peepshow tunes with a grinding beat or, more likely, modern classical music.

High heels clicking on the surface of the table as though it were made of glass was the only sound in the room. Otherwise, there was silence, Rachel certain she was only imagining the sounds of rising and falling chests and the beats of anticipation. Some of the audience stood close to each other, hugging intimately. She moved herself a step in front of Damien and rested her back against him as she stared at the two figures on the table.

The woman, Rachel could only think of her as that despite knowing her name, had stopped in front of the man and was regarding him coolly. When she walked around him and then stopped behind him, Rachel watched the slight movements of the man, the candle lights flickering. Rachel looked down at the man's cock as it dangled and touched the surface of the table. Afraid to make a sound, even a swallow or a blink, Rachel leaned against Damien and felt the hardness in his trousers.

The toe of one high heel rested between the man's shoulder blades and pushed him lightly. The man lolled forwards and placed his forehead on the table, his behind stretched into a tight, vulnerable round. The woman stood at the side of him furthest from the audience, so they could all get a view of her and her victim. She's done this before, Rachel thought. She's blocked all the moves out as though she's on a stage.

In the tense, expectant silence, the whistle of the crop through the air was amplified, sounding two or three times louder than it really should have. After the swish came the crack of contact. Noisy breath and a startled grunt escaped the air pipes, heavy and masculine, almost like the sound of a horse. Rachel shivered when she heard him and there were several mutters of approval from the audience. Her face felt hot, excited and embarrassed by the spectacle, the way it was being played out in silence, only the most necessary noises embellishing the moment. The crotch of Rachel's panties were damp and sticking to her and Damien's hard cock pressed against her buttocks.

Five more times, Rachel counting each, the crop fell. By the sixth time, a high whimper escaped the mask. The woman was totally methodical and dispassionate, neither lurid nor disinterested, simply precise. It was the precision which captivated Rachel and made her wonder what it would be like to participate in such a performance. The next three strokes had a cruel force behind them and, seeing the woman's arm muscles flex, Rachel could almost feel the weight of the blows.

The woman stood behind the kneeling figure, looked at it for a moment and then slowly slid the round leather handle of the crop down the front of her underwear, closing her eyes as she caressed her sex. When she withdrew it, Rachel peered and was certain she could see the handle glistening with the woman's juices. Before Rachel could look for too long, the woman had squatted down and was gently introducing the handle of the whip into the man's behind. Rachel saw his thighs trembling and his fists clenching, the leather thong binding his wrists clearly showing the strain. Again, groans came from the pipes of the mask, resistant at first, then submissive and, ultimately, passionate.

Rachel looked to one side and did a double take. A woman was on her knees in front of a man, taking his cock deep into her mouth while the man held her by the head. Two women were locked in a deep kiss, their mouths wide open and exploring each other. As she looked around at the anonymous audience, Rachel realised many off them were in varying stages of undress, engaging in sexual activity of different degrees.

'Do you want to leave?' she murmured to Damien.

He reached his hand up the front of Rachel's short dress and slipped his hand down the front of her knickers, letting his middle finger rest casually in the centre of her labia. With his hand pressed firmly into her pubis, he used it to pull her back hard against him where she felt the solid protrusion of his cock.

On the table, the woman stood in front of the man and used her hands to lift him by the shoulders to a kneeling position. The crop hung from him like a tail and his cock draped equally impressively. It was long and hard, angry red even in the soft light of the candles. The woman paused and seemed to be thinking for the first time in the ritual. This was improvisation, Rachel sensed, as the woman quickly bent and picked up a candle. Damien's finger probed her and nudged her clitoris as the woman dripped wax from the candle onto the cock of the unsuspecting man whose back arched involuntarily, pushing his cock out and making the crop trail the table's surface.

The woman placed the candle on the table and slid it

towards the man until it was directly under his scrotum. The candle was only an inch or two high but Rachel wondered how hot it would feel to the man. The candle in place, throwing light up so his erect cock casting a shadow across the taut skin of his stomach, the woman began to masturbate him. She gripped and manipulated him with the same quick confidence she had shown in all her other actions; back to the script, Rachel thought. The cock was thick, filling the woman's hand, swelling under the pulse of his blood coupled with a need for release.

Rachel heard a gasp from somewhere behind her and even though there was something unmistakable about the noise, it took her a few seconds to realise it was the sound of a woman coming. It was guttural and unabashed, cutting through the quiet of the dining room. Damien's finger was moving back and forth, pressing only a short way into the opening of her sex, her vagina wet and full with desire. She felt her inhibitions slip away and she reached behind her head to hold Damien round the neck while she writhed against his body, meeting movement with movement. Damien was crooking his arm forwards to allow himself deeper access and Rachel bit her lip and gazed around her, watching other people and being watched amidst the sea of spontaneous and heated eroticism.

With a cry that was made hollow and sharp by the pipes of the mask, the man came and it was as though he were the only person in the room. For a second, all movement and sound seemed to stop. Rachel watched as the man ejaculated several thick lines of semen into the flickering glow of the candle. Rachel imagined his seed spilling into the flame, hissing as it was consumed by the fire. The man's orgasm forced him to writhe against his bindings and his masked head snatched from side to side. The woman continued to use her hand on him until he had stopped coming and then she carried on still further. Rachel looked at the man struggle helplessly against it, seeming as though he were overloaded with sensations.

Rachel was almost hanging off Damien as she came, pushing her behind into his groin and letting her head drop forward. It did not concern her who might be looking at her as she flailed and whimpered, riding the tense climax while Damien kept his finger on her pulsating clitoris. She wanted to be seen and heard. The climax was a long exhalation of sheer bliss that came and went suddenly.

All around them, people were undressing, clothes thrown in unruly heaps or used as hastily improvised pillows. Body connected to body, couples, threesomes and other groupings, differing mixes of men and women. Damien lifted Rachel's dress over her head and then unclasped her bra. He worked her underwear off while he was still behind her. Rachel turned to face him and took him quickly out of his clothes. Still the strangers in the middle of people who seemed to know each other, they began kissing, dropping to a space on the floor. Rachel enjoyed the sensation of having him in such a public way, relishing the wiry muscles of his body and the enthusiasm of his kisses.

The gong banged just as Rachel was beginning to tantalise Damien with soft brushes of her lips. It was hit just the once and some people ignored it. Rachel looked up and watched as a large, upright box was wheeled into the room. It reminded her of a magician's box, the sort where a glamorous assistant stood inside and swords were plunged in. It was pushed smoothly through a side door by two goodlooking men with worked-out physiques. The box fascinated her from the moment she saw it. This square and wardrobe-like compartment held secrets, she could tell. It was a gradual process, but the two men wheeled it to somewhere just about in the centre of the room, people making way for it and stopping whatever they were doing as they stared up at it. It was like a procession, a royal throne being borne slowly through the crowd.

Patricia appeared next to the cabinet which was a good two feet taller than she. Naked, her skin was slightly pale and the triangle of her pubic hair dark against it.

'This is the first time out with the new toy,' she said, pleased with herself. 'Any takers?'

It was the same way it always happened when she had been at school. Whenever the difficult question was about to be offered to the class, Rachel's eyes would collide with the teacher's. Rachel had been trying to avert her glance and in the process had practically locked eyes with Patricia. She had no intention of getting involved until she knew what was in the box. Patricia probably wouldn't even remember her name, Rachel thought.

'Rachel?' Patricia asked, her tone quite stern.

Damien was looking at her. The people in the room did not know who she was, but they were following Patricia's eyeline to where Rachel was sitting. That's the point, she thought. No one here knows who I am. I can just lose myself for a little while and not play any part, least of all myself. No one knows me, she thought once more, as she stood and walked towards the cabinet, Patricia smiling warmly at her.

Patricia opened the door with a graceful and grand movement. Rachel was inquisitive, wanting to know what lay inside and she sensed the curiosity of everyone as they looked on. It was a well-balanced, reverential group, all of them apparently serious in their pursuit of pleasure. The atmosphere pervaded the whole room, quiet and church-like, not even any music. Feeling serious, apprehensive and excited, Rachel took a step closer to the box and looked inside.

At first, there was not much to see as her eyes grew accustomed to the darkness of the space. Even when they did, there was not much that caught her eye. On the floor were two footholds, a bit like the ones on skis, set three feet apart. Dangling from the roof at each front corner was a loop which Rachel assumed was for inserting a hand through. The interior of the box was painted black and the door looked as though it would close and seal out all light. Why would anyone want to stand with their legs spread apart and hands up above their head in a dark box? she wondered. It would be easier to travel on the tube in rush hour.

Then Rachel looked closer.

Hanging from the side and back walls, almost flush with it, were long black rubber gloves. They were fixed to the walls at various heights, probably twenty in all. Patricia had been watching her closely, as though trying to gauge her reaction. As though demonstrating, Patricia went to the side of the cabinet and put her hand through it and into one of the gloves. Rachel stood and watched, fascinated, as Patricia knelt outside the cabinet with her arm in it, flanked by the rubber gauntlet. Patricia disappeared behind the box and it was eerie to watch a disembodied rubber arm moving around, a thick black cock moulded into the glove. Behind her, Rachel heard approving mutters. Between her legs, she was damp.

Rachel felt a bit like Houdini when she placed her feet into the footholds and Patricia was reaching, with some difficulty, to help her hands through the loops. Rachel caught Damien's eye over Patricia's shoulder and he smiled encouragingly at her as the door began to swing closed. 'Don't worry, it's air-conditioned,' Patricia whispered conspiratorially just as the door closed. Of course it is, Rachel thought – this is sex uptown New York style.

It reminded her of the flotation tank she occasionally frequented in London, but without the comfort of all the saline solution bolstering her, she felt disembodied with only air touching her. It was the kind of dark to which eyes could not adjust, but it did not make her anxious. Had she been tied in and the door locked, she might have been worried, but instead it made her excited. Rachel couldn't hear any movement outside and she wondered what was happening, if Patricia was issuing instructions, or if no one was interested in putting a hand into a glove.

For a long time, nothing happened and Rachel worked on her breathing, keeping it regular and her chest steady. Holding her arms above her head had tightened most of her upper body muscles and the position of her legs spread her sex invitingly, so much so, she was tempted to slip a hand from the loop and caress herself.

There was a squeaking sound in the dark and Rachel heard a hand and arm filling a glove. It could have been off to her right or possibly behind her; the acoustics of the box made it hard to tell. It was odd because the sound was exactly the same as when she put on rubber gloves at home. It was joined by other similar sounds as more and more arms were entering the compartment, although none had yet touched her.

A tentative hand brushed her thigh and it startled her. The rubber was warm, a similar temperature to her body. Rachel could not tell if it was the hand of a man or a woman, its cladding disguising it. The hand continued to stroke her thigh on the outer edge, trailing up her hip and exploring the shape of the proud bone. As more hands joined the first and roamed over her, it occurred to Rachel they were as blind as she was, unable to see and having to feel their way around her. Sometimes the hands were clumsy and brusque, gripping and prodding at her with an eagerness but also a total lack of finesse. Her breasts, arms, legs and behind were all explored, her flesh warming under the touch. None of the hands had yet centred in on her hot and swollen sex and Rachel shifted herself, restlessly twisting her torso to make herself available.

It was as if the silent, unseen hands knew what she wanted and were conspiring in not giving it to her as they covered every part of her other than where she wanted. For several agonising minutes she was squeezed, tickled and titillated, the sensations playing through her body and tingling on the surface of her skin like electricity. Finally, the touch she wanted came. An inquisitive finger rubbed her pubic hair, searching for the breach that lay beneath its surface, finding it and dipping in. Rachel sighed, the sound flat and close in the enclosed space. The finger toyed at the opening of her sex, prying through her labia and resting on the wet orifice. It entered her slowly, the rubber deliciously abrasive against the soft flesh of her vagina.

While she was being entered, she forgot momentarily about the other hands, but was brought to a rude awareness when one which had been caressing her buttocks now worried at the wrinkled crevice between them. It pressed on the button of puckered flesh, threatening it, but not entering. Abruptly, the finger was gone, replaced almost immediately by the solid mass of a dildo. Rachel remembered the size of the plastic cock when she had seen Patricia wielding it by way of demonstration. A moment of panic set in – she would never be able to take it in her behind, not so suddenly and so dry. It lingered on her anus for only a few seconds before tracing down her perineum and then onto the underside of her sex. The rubber cock arrogantly pushed the finger out of her sex and then the top of the shaft was running along her outer lips, becoming lubricated by the fluids which seeped from her.

The unseen cock continued to rub her sex, going from the discernible head to the end where it connected to the glove. The position of her legs meant she practically straddled the dildo, feeling exposed and hungry for penetration. Two rubber fingers tweaked hard on one of her erect nipples, the intensity of the passion it released making her eyes moist. Rachel swallowed a heavy groan when the phallus pushed into her, passing unceremoniously through her labia and directly into her vagina. There was a brief moment where she thought, even in her lubricated and elongated sex, she would not be able to receive it. For a second, her muscles contracted, but she quickly yielded to the intrusion, accommodating it within the walls of her trembling vagina.

Rachel stood in a completely dark box, legs wide apart and arms stretched up while from behind an unknown, invisible hand worked a long thick dildo in and out of her sex. With no visual stimulation, it was left up to Rachel to conceive images in her mind, the dark a backdrop onto which she could project them. For a time, typical fantasies and memories sparked in her brain, popping like a flashgun. The longer it went on, however, she found the experience itself was enough, literally blinding her. A sly hand found where the dildo entered her and was toying with her clitoris in a knowing way, pushing her more quickly to the orgasm she was desperate to wring from her body.

She tightened her grip on the wrist loops and began to move herself backwards and forwards, meeting the thrusts. The hand on her sex went with her, following her clitoris with the precision of a shadow and keeping the pressure on. Several hands stroked her breasts and another her behind, sometimes knocking against the thrusting hand. With all the images burned out, her mind floating in the blackness, Rachel gave several heavy lunges back onto the dildo and heaved a sigh that was a combined mix of passion and relief as her vaginal muscles trembled and she came.

The orgasm lit the darkness with its blinding light, rendering all of her senses pure white, so bright and intense she could smell it, hear it, taste it even. She writhed and shrieked, letting her body hang from her wrists, her knees weak and thighs quivering as the orgasm reverberated through her, flowing out to every place she was touched and back again into the dark centre of herself.

One by one, starting with the rubber shaft, the hands withdrew and eventually she was left alone once again, the twitches of her orgasm subsiding and her breath returning to normal. When the door clicked open, even the dim light of the room was bright and it took her eyes time to adjust as a naked Damien took her hand and led her to the large, soft mat which had been laid out on the floor. Several people stared at her, but there was no applause for her unseen performance.

When they left the house, it was early in the morning, the dawn light refreshing. For many hours they had floated on the wash of unknown bodies, not needing to be themselves or with each other and finding it both affecting and confirming. It provided Rachel a glimpse of who she could be and helped her affirm who she was and as they walked along Central Park West, ready to hail a cab back to the hotel, everything seemed simple to her.

Damien put his arm around her when they were in the back of the taxi. 'Jesus, where do you go after that?' he asked her.

Rachel looked at him, the answer clear in her own mind even though she was unable to tell it to him.

Chapter Thirteen

Rachel brought the rental car to an abrupt halt at a gas station on the outskirts of Hartford, Connecticut. The rational veneer she had been attempting to stick over her actions was about to burst, possibly in one resounding, all encompassing moment. Until now, she thought, everything had been so calm. Slipping out of the hotel, going to Avis for a rental car, renting a decent sized one, catching morning traffic, finding the interstate, finding the cruise control on the car. Each act had been conducted with the eerie serenity of a contract killer. She did feel herself relax in one sense and that was to leave the bustle and the recent bad memories of New York behind her. Every mile further from Manhattan had soothed her.

Until now.

Rachel sat and stared, her eyes resting on no fixed point. It was as though the automatic pilot had been switched off and she was suddenly responsible for controlling her own actions. What am I doing here? How did I get here? At the end of the road, possibly, was Gary, but what did that mean in any case? Back at the start of the road was New York, Blake Jordan, Carl Milken and Gloria Vaughan. Both ends had painful memories, some fresher than others. Rachel felt nauseous from the lack of sleep yet restless and eager to decide exactly which way she was travelling. The frustration surged through her as though stuck in traffic and late for an important engagement. She felt utterly powerless and yet she was the only one who could do anything about it.

'Fuck!' she said aloud and banged the plastic steering wheel hard enough to hurt her hands.

Someone was watching her.

Rachel looked up and saw a nervous-looking boy standing about fifteen feet from the car, holding an off-white rag. She thought she saw him take a nervous swallow before putting his foot forward and heading in her direction. His shoulders were quite broad, but he was lanky nonetheless, as though someone had sketched the outline of a man but forgot to fill in the details. Rachel thought about just sitting in the car with the doors locked and the windows up, ignoring him. Don't be stupid, Rachel, she said to herself. She checked her face in the rearview mirror – it looked like she had been crying. Perhaps she had been and not noticed. Rachel fumbled for the electric window button and listened to the confident whir of the motor.

The boy leaned down awkwardly, resting a hand on the window.

'Are you okay?' he asked.

'Fine' Rachel said, sniffing. Her head was throbbing and her eyes were heavy.

'If you need gas, you're gonna have to pull the car over there,' he said.

Rachel looked at the fuel gauge, not really taking it or the boy's words in. How the hell did she end up in the middle of nowhere, miles from home, thousands of miles? 'Um, no. I, ah, don't need any petrol, gas,' she said.

The boy didn't seem to know what to say next. Rachel wanted to rev the car and screech off. The boy carried on leaning down, looking concerned. He couldn't have been more than about seventeen, his mouth a long, almost lipless, split and his eyes pale blue. A few sprouts of thin black hair protruded from under his baseball cap.

'I need, um. I mean, is there a hotel near here? Somewhere I can rest?'

He squatted to bring his head on a level with hers and

exhaled a long, icy breath. He screwed his face into a squint as he thought. 'About two miles on up the road, there's a motel. That's the nearest 'till you get in Hartford proper.'

'Thank you,' Rachel said.

'No problem,' he replied.

Rachel closed her window and waited while he used the rag he had been holding to buff the windscreen. She watched him absently, uncertain if he was looking at her or not. Without looking or smiling, Rachel was back on the interstate.

Half an hour later, she was sitting on the bed in the thirty dollar room of the Frost Motel. She had pulled the curtains to try and block the afternoon light, but they were too thin to offer much of a shield. The room smelled of cleaning fluid and was decorated in matching plaids that looked grubby. The television was old and attached to the wall mount by a thick silver chain, while its small, dubious-looking, remote control with only four buttons was on the laminated pine bedside table. In the bathroom was a tiny coffee pot and kettle, no complimentary toiletries and a shower that was little more than a piece of bent pipe fixed in one position. Rachel tried the chair in front of the mirror and the lower one in the corner, but neither were comfortable, their structure quickly prominent through thin cushions.

From her position on the bed, she stared at the oversized plastic phone. It was not so early in England. She could phone Oliver or her mother. She could call Damien in the hotel in New York. Or Gary at his coffee shop. And what could she say to any of them? That the audition had been a disaster and that she had let Gloria Vaughan rattle and, ultimately, upstage her? Rachel caught herself holding her breath in and exhaling it with each bad thought. Bad breath and posture the voice of her speech coach intoned perfectly in her head.

It was quiet in the dim room, the road far enough away to be nothing more than the occasional rumble. Rachel gazed at the scruffy mustard phone as though it were a hypnotist's watch, her eyes feeling heavier as her whole body relaxed and gave into the inevitable. She lay back on the bed and, in moments, was asleep.

Rachel could not tell how long the knocking at the door had been going on when it eventually roused her. The rapping sounded heavy and anxious, as though the person knocking knew she was asleep. Light still came through the curtains. Rachel checked her watch and found it was ten minutes past four.

Looking through the spyhole in the door, she saw the boy from the garage, his gawky frame done no favours through the distortion of the peephole. Rachel opened the door and he stood there, shuffling from foot to foot, the baseball cap in his hands. His hair was shorter than she would have expected, almost like a marine. He licked each side of his mouth but did not speak, not seeming able to muster a breath strong enough to enable him to do so. It occurred to her that she should say something, but her mind was sluggish from the nap, still deprived of proper rest.

'Hi,' he said, suddenly, twirling the cap. 'I wanted to make sure you were okay.'

Rachel gave him what must have been a puzzled look because he continued to speak, part-explanation and part-nerves.

'I got off work and was passing. I saw your car parked.' He motioned over his shoulder. 'You seemed upset, earlier. I just wanted to . . . ' he paused. 'Anyway,' he said, lifting his face into an exaggerated smile and holding both his hands out in front of him, 'you're okay. I'm going to leave. I just wanted to . . . make sure. You were okay.'

'Thanks,' Rachel said, waking more fully.

'Anyway,' the boy said, moving off the spot.

'No, wait. Thanks for checking. I was just really tired earlier, needed some sleep. God, I'm starving,' she said, appending it suddenly to the end of the sentence. She realised she had not eaten that day.

The boy stood at the door, blinking and fiddling with his cap.

'Is there somewhere I can get a pizza?' she asked.

'Great place less than a mile away,' he replied.

'Will they deliver?' she asked.

'I guess. I don't have their number but they may be listed. I could go fetch you some,' he said, brightly.

'I couldn't let you do that,' she replied.

'No, really. Please. Let me. It's no problem.'

'Are you sure?'

He nodded.

'Wait for a second,' she said.

Rachel found her purse and scrabbled through it.

'Will twenty be enough? I don't have anything smaller,' she said.

'Sure. What would you like?'

Rachel thought. 'I don't know. Pepperoni would be wonderful,' she said, feeling the urge to gorge taking hold of her.

'Back in twenty minutes or a dollar off,' he said, smiling goffily at his own joke.

It was only after he had left that Rachel realised she had just given twenty dollars to a complete stranger whose name she did not know. Nice one, Rachel, she thought, heading for a quick shower.

Almost twenty minutes later, there was a knock on the door and he was back with a huge square box balancing on the palm of his hand. 'I got some soda as well. I would have brought you some beer but they always card me there.' He handed the box to Rachel, which had some change on top, and he set the bottle of Coke down on the stoop. 'Okay,' he said, turning to leave.

'Hey, hey, hey,' Rachel said. 'Stop walking away. Come on in. There's no way I can eat all this on my own.'

'I don't want to . . . You know, be in your way. I'm not, like, hitting on you or anything.'

Rachel looked at him in his faded jeans, torn on one knee, his dark brown animal skin coat with the discreet fur collar. No, she thought, you're not trying to hit on me. It interested her even more than if he were.

'Come on in,' she said, smiling at him.

They sat on the bed, either side of the open box, eating pizza and drinking Coke from toothbrush mugs at five in the afternoon. He sat cross-legged, holding the slice of pizza in both hands. There was a faint smell of petrol about him and he looked happy as he chomped away.

'Do you work full time at the garage, Christopher?' she asked, hoping to find out more than just his name.

'No, just part-time. I'm a senior in high school. What do you do?' he asked.

Rachel was not sure what answer to give. 'I'm an actress,' she said, finally.

'Really? No way.' He had stopped eating. 'Have I seen you in anything? Movies?'

'I doubt it. I did a couple of films in England but they never got released here. I was in a television series in England that was a bit like *Murphy Brown*, although not as big.'

He raised his eyes, obviously impressed. 'Are you doing anything right now?'

'I finished a play in London a couple of weeks ago. I was planning to have a rest but I was just in New York to audition for a Broadway play,' she said, wishing it had all been as simple as she was making it sound.

'An actress. No shit,' he said to himself.

It made her feel a fake to be able to impress someone so easily, especially when she had made such a mess of the audition.

'How do you remember all of those lines? When we were in fifth grade, we did this Gettysburg address thing as a big group and I couldn't even do it with the book.'

'It gets easier, the more you do it. Will you be going to university?' she asked, hoping to steer the conversation away from herself.

He shrugged. 'I dunno yet. Should I be, like, getting your autograph or something?'

'Well, you never know,' she said.

'An actress,' he said softly, before taking a bite from the slice of pizza and chewing it thoughtfully.

It was nice to be sitting on the bed of a strange motel, eating pizza from the box with a strange boy. Still caught between the poles, not quite sure where she wanted to be, it was comforting to spend some time in a kind of limbo. It was like some kind of bizarre slumber party, the two of them overindulging in bad food and sugary cola.

'So how come you're out here if you were just in New York?' he asked.

'I'm going to Portsmouth in New Hampshire to surprise someone I haven't seen in ten years,' she replied. It didn't sound so bad said aloud, she thought.

'Ten years. And he doesn't know you're coming?'

'What makes you so sure it's a he?' she asked.

'Sorry. You, it just sounds like, you know, the way you said it. A friend,' he said, making his voice sound dramatic.

Rachel just smiled.

'Man, I'd like to see his face when you walk in,' he said, gleefully. 'Is he some old boyfriend?'

'No. I would have liked it if he had been. He came to stay at my parents' house, but nothing came of it.'

'Is that why you looked so pissed earlier? In your car. I almost laughed when I saw you shout "fuck" and hit the wheel. I get like that sometimes,' he said, his voice trailing off.

'I was just tired. Up all night,' she replied.

'So, is there like a boyfriend you have in England?' he asked, eagerly.

Rachel would normally have found such prying questions annoying and impertinent, but he was so earnest in the way he asked, it was hard to be irritated. She was charmed by the halting nervousness of his speech, as though he were interrupting himself.

'I have two boyfriends, sort of,' she replied. Rachel could see he was about to ask another question, so she cut him off with one of her own. 'What about you? Do you have a girlfriend?' she asked.

He took a big bite of the last pizza slice, letting it fill his mouth like a gag as he vigorously shook his head from side to side.

'I can't imagine why you don't,' she went on.

Christopher made a face as he chewed.

'I'm not, like, hitting on you, or anything,' she said, mimicking his phrasing in an exaggerated way.

Christopher swallowed the pizza loudly and awkwardly but did not speak. His baseball hat was on the bed next to him and he touched its brim, running a finger lightly along the stitching. He turned his head away from her and stared at the blank television screen.

In the silence, Rachel felt bad, as though she had spoken out of turn. The room was quiet enough for her to hear the Coke fizzing in her glass. She was about to say something to him when his voice stopped her.

'Can I kiss you?' he asked.

'I thought you weren't hitting on me?' she asked, her tone neutral.

'You could pretend it was just acting. Do it like you would in a film.'

'Have you ever kissed a girl?' she asked.

His eyes studied the cover and Rachel could detect the shine of a blush on his cheeks. She leaned over and cupped his face. He blinked at her and his lashes were long. Rachel looked at him and his nose twitched slightly, possibly from nerves. She leaned forward, conscious of the speed of his pulse where her hand was on his neck, and planted a long and deep kiss on him. At first he was passive but soon enough his mouth came to life. They held the kiss for a moment longer and then broke away. He exhaled loudly.

'I really shouldn't have done that,' Rachel said.

'I'm glad you did though,' he said, quietly.

Rachel looked down and realised she had been resting her hand on his leg and had not removed it. She tried to stop herself, but she let her eyes trail to the crotch of his jeans, knowing already what she would see. When their eyes met, he gave a smile and small shrug of boyish embarrassment. Rachel remembered what it had been like to be his age, the gawkiness and the nervousness. What would she have wanted to happen, had she been in his position with Gary all those years ago.

Firmly, Rachel pushed Christopher's shoulders until he was stretched out on his back, sidelong on the bed. He was staring up at the ceiling, a desperate look on his face. Rachel unbuckled his belt and unbuttoned his jeans, pulling them and his underwear only a short way down. Rachel wanted to feel how tight the skin would be over the muscular young behind and she glided her palms over his hips before scooping them under him and squeezing his buttocks. Playfully, she pulled them apart and saw the look of consternation on his face as she did.

'Pull up your shirt,' she said to him, taking her hands off him, and instantly he did, revealing white, soft skin.

His pubic hair was golden and his cock straining under its own pressure. Before she could talk herself out of it, Rachel held his youthful cock in her hand and began to masturbate it, rubbing the circumcised phallus with her fingers. She heard him gasp and let the tension in his body go from nervous to pent up excitement. Glancing up she saw the bemused and grateful look on his face, a grimace of concentration as he worked himself mentally towards his orgasm.

It did not take long.

'I'm coming,' she heard him mutter.

Rachel watched his cock in her hand, looking at the small slit in the phallus, wanting to see the semen squirt through it. Christopher's hips moved up and down, his behind coming off the bed and then pressing down into it. Rachel carried on, squeezing and stroking his cock as it pulsed in her hand and felt impossibly hard. With her free hand, she tickled the tiny rounds of his balls. Christopher yelped and whined, the climax shivering through his body. Erratic breathing was smothered by a cry and then his body convulsed as he ejaculated a spurt of milky semen onto his stomach. The potent fluid was irresistible as it lay on the perfect skin.

Leaning forward, Rachel covered him with her mouth and received the rest of his orgasm into it, letting the semen gather and relishing the powerful taste it gave off. When he had no more to give, Rachel let up with the movements of her tongue and took a long breath which she swallowed along with his warm come.

Over an hour and a half later, Rachel knelt on all fours and spat out a throaty climax as Christopher gripped onto her hips and spilled himself for the third time, his fingers digging into her flesh and his cries reaching a pitch of sheer desperation.

Finally, Rachel lay sleeping, secure under heavy covers. Curled against her, and with his arm thrown protectively across her, was Christopher, his lean young body momentarily spent.

Chapter Fourteen

The room seemed bright, even to Rachel's just-opened eyes. Across the other side of the bed, Christopher clutched the covers to him and slept peacefully. Rachel watched him for a moment before getting out of bed and going to the window.

Through the crack in the curtains, she saw the landscape had been frosted white by an overnight fall of snow. Everything was pure, the uniformity of the colouring reducing everything to an illusory same size. The roof of the rental car was piled an inch high, the trees and road beyond it looking like a snow dome. It was eerily quiet, as though no life had ever crossed the pristine landscape, and she wondered what the time was. Creeping to the bedside table, she checked her watch and saw it was only just six.

Christopher moved, his nose twitching and mouth opening a fraction as though about to speak. A troubled expression crossed his young face, followed by a grumble and then he was restful once more.

In the shower, Rachel tried to measure the time since the audition, glad it had been lost in the wake of the all-night party with Damien and the night just gone with Christopher. It was no longer possible to tell if the audition had been yesterday, the day before, or even a week ago and the passage of time was helping her forget just how badly it had gone. Rachel dried and dressed quickly, a single thought and word on her mind.

Gary.

When she reentered the room, Christopher was dressed and the covers thrown haphazardly over the bed.

'It snowed just like they said it would,' he said, rubbing his hands on his hips.

'I know,' she said, smiling. 'Will I still be able to make it to Portsmouth?'

'I can check on the radio but it doesn't look so bad. You should be okay. I can always put on snow chains if you need them,' he said.

'Do you want to get breakfast?' she asked.

'I should be getting back. You might want to get on the road now. There'll be less traffic and they should have ploughed them by now,' he said.

Half an hour later, the bill paid and a brief hug exchanged, Rachel cautiously pulled the car away from the motel, glancing up at the mirror and catching a last look at Christopher who was waving at her. With all the energy and resolve she could muster, Rachel tried to leave all of her troubling thoughts behind her, as though she had stopped off at Hartford and inadvertently lost them there. She wondered how long such a contrived brave face would last.

Several hours of careful driving took her towards Portsmouth. When she began to see signs for it, Rachel felt herself getting excited and nervous, counting off the miles. By eleven-thirty, she was driving past the sign welcoming her to Portsmouth. It was not as grand as the one which had welcomed her into the state of New Hampshire, but it gave her the jitters. Rachel had found the location of Gary's coffee shop in one of the several guide books she had purchased in London. It was off Market Street in the Old Harbour District and the books had not overstated their picturesque descriptions of Portsmouth.

Even without the snow, it could not have been more different to New York. Buildings were lower, more space between them and somehow more relaxed. On the drive from the outskirts of town, houses had been organic, white and cream clapboards rather than the harsh mineral of Manhattan skyscrapers. At the front of all the houses, Rachel was certain, there would be well-tended lawns beneath the snow.

Rachel drove with little sense of direction and was enjoying the scenery as it cruised past the window of her car. She did not realise how small Portsmouth was until she found herself approaching a bridge that was signed as leading to Kittery and the state of Maine. Rachel pulled the car into a slip road that led towards some docks and turned it around, deciding to find parking. She was wearing most of the clothes she had brought from England, layering them on top of each other to fend off the cold. It had been chilly in London and New York, but nothing like the iciness she had felt since setting off from the motel, the blower in the car a monotonous noise as it pumped out dry and artificial heat.

There was no longer a sensible chance of turning back, she thought. Rachel tried to imagine what ten years would have done to Gary Tate. People never looked quite the way make-up artists imagined them when they had to age a character, the trials of life worn in lines deeper than any that could have been painted on. Even meeting Gary for the first time, having secretly and longingly studied his newspaper picture for so long, Rachel did not believe it was him. Perhaps it was the same for people who recognised her. She parked the car and stepped out into the wintry brilliance of the New England noon.

It took her ten minutes and several polite questions to strangers before she located Cup of Joe, Gary's coffee house. It fitted into the row of other shops with the discreet uniformity of good teeth. Rachel's heart beat a shade more rapidly and on her first sight of the shop, she felt a flush. It had a glass double front with a tall entrance between the two windows, the handle a large wooden bar sloping across it at an angle. The glass held onto condensation and, behind its smokiness, she could see people seated at tables and a figure moving about. She wondered if it was Gary and swallowed. For a while longer, with her face cold, she stood across the street and watched the shapes and their movements.

Rachel crossed the street and entered the shop in a single move, almost like walking on stage and knowing there would be nowhere else to go once she was over the threshold. The warmth of the shop lifted under her like walking off a plane that had just landed in its tropical destination. The smell of coffee made up the total atmosphere of the place, warming her nostrils and soothing her nerves. The floorboards were bare and the furniture simple. The main hub of activity was the counter and the machinery behind it which gleamed in stainless steel while cups of differing sizes and shapes were stacked neatly. An old man with short grey hair that looked in need of a trim smiled brightly at her.

'What can I get you?' he asked. His accent was thick and like the ones she had heard in New York.

'I could use a cup of coffee,' she said, her eyes on the broad back of a tall man in a red checked shirt and blue jeans, his hair long enough to hide the nape of his neck.

Rachel had used her best English stage accent and it drew a glance over the shoulder from the tall man. Rachel knew it was him even before he recognised her. His attention had been turned back to the sink for a few moments before Rachel saw him stop what he was doing, his arms still and his head raising up. She could imagine the expression on his face.

'Rachel?' he said and then turned.

The college jock was gone. He wasn't as stocky as she remembered and it gave his movement a more light and youthful wiliness. Gary smiled at her and the folds of skin that ran from either side of his nose down to the corners of his mouth deepened. As dark and narrow as they had ever been, his eyes seemed to flit from side to side. Seeing him, it was difficult for Rachel to distinguish between what she remembered and what was in front of her there and then.

His mouth, one of the first things she had noticed even in his photograph, was the same unmistakeable shape, the top lip full and squarish. His hair was almost unrecognisable, still brushed back over his high forehead but extending down almost to his shoulder blades and tied back in a ponytail. The image of the college boy she had carried in her mind for so long had definitely gone. In its place was someone wiry and wiser, a relaxed exterior stretched over and even more serene inner core. She stared for as long as she could before speaking to him.

'Hi,' she said, opening her whole face into a broad smile and wondering what else she could say and wishing she, of all people, had rehearsed something in the car. Perhaps she had not believed she would go through with it, she thought.

The old man was watching them, head shifting from side to side as if he were at a tennis match. He seemed to have picked up on the unspoken flow of emotion between the two of them. 'Why don't you take a break, boss?' he asked.

Gary flicked his head as though checking he weren't dreaming.

'Sure. Hey, Joe, this is Rachel Franklin, a friend from England. Rachel, this is Joe. A friend from here.'

Joe nodded and reached across the counter to shake her hand. Someone entered the shop and stood behind Rachel.

'You two grab a table and I'll bring you a coffee. What'll you have?' Joe asked her.

The board was a bewildering array of coffee choices, even for Rachel who thought she had kept up quite well with the growing London obsession with caffeine. 'Cappuccino?' she said weakly.

'Why not try a latte?' he replied. 'Tall, double and skinny and you'll be set.'

'Okay,' Rachel said, not sure what she was ordering.

'And mocha for you,' Joe said to Gary who was lifting the hinged counter to join Rachel.

When they were seated, the table so tiny their knees were

almost touching, Gary still stared at her with a bemused smile, quietly using her name over and over again as though getting used to it.

'Rachel. Jesus. What are you doing here?'

'My mother gave me the postcard you sent,' she said.

'That was just after we opened back in January. I wondered for a while if you'd call but I figured you wouldn't. I didn't expect you to walk in off the street,' he said.

They were silent and Rachel struggled to find something in her mind that would connect the past to the present, some way of linking herself to him once again even though they had hardly known each other back then.

'This place is lovely. I thought you were going into business like your mother or going to become a football player,' she said.

He laughed. 'I worked a string of jobs after college and finished up working as a realtor in Portsmouth. That's how I found this place. Joe walked into the office looking to sell up and I found him an instant buyer – me. I didn't even imagine it myself. My folks certainly didn't.'

'How are your mum and dad?'

'Good. Still living over in Merimack. What about your parents?'

'They separated nearly ten years ago. Got divorced four years later,' she replied automatically.

'I'm sorry,' he said.

Joe came and set down cups in front of them. 'I called Katie and she's going to come in in about half an hour, so you can take off if you want to,' he said, moving away from the table before anyone could reply.

Gary smiled. 'Joe used to run this place. It was a deli and it was doing okay but he wanted to sell and get out. That's what he said, but you could tell it wasn't in his heart to leave. I'd just got back from a trip to Seattle and I was so wired about the whole coffee thing happening there. As soon as Joe said he was putting it up for sale, I knew. I made it a condition of me buying it that Joe agreed to stay. He's amazing. Still runs the place, almost. I don't think he thought he'd be in the middle of all this bonhomie.'

Rachel looked around and realised she was one of the more smartly dressed people in the shop. Lots of loose and hairy wool clothing, spectacles and male facial hair was in evidence. A cork notice board had at least twenty pieces of paper of varying sizes, amateur design and clashing colours pinned to it with over-used drawing pins. Acoustic music drifted along on the aroma of fresh ground coffee.

'Well, I've been given permission to leave, so we can spend some time together if you have it. You didn't say what brought you here in any case,' he said inquisitively.

'To Portsmouth?' she asked.

'The States,' he replied.

Rachel sipped at the smooth milk and strong shot of coffee through the spongy white foam. 'I had some business in New York and my mother gave me your postcard, a bit late really. I could have called ahead but I wanted to see the look on your face. It was worth it.'

'My mum told me she saw you on TV but at first she wasn't sure it was you. She'd turned on half way through, so she waited until the credits and then decided to call me and be all excited. You really went and did the acting thing then?'

'I really did,' she replied.

'And you're happy doing it? You look good,' he said.

A small twinge of yesterday, the day before and of New York went through her but she was able to smother it with the dreamlike state of the present.

'I love what I do,' she said.

'It took me a long while to find this, but now I wouldn't change it,' he said.

They paused, the silence some kind of indication of mutual but separate contentment. It made Rachel uncomfortable, as though she had brought some sort of agenda that would intrude on his life in an unwelcome way. She drank the coffee down quicker than she should have and felt the scald of the milk on her tongue. I shouldn't have come here, she thought, despondent at how difficult it would be to extract herself quickly from the current situation.

'Are you going to show me around Portsmouth?' she asked.

'I'd love to. It's a great town. Have you been to New England before?' he asked.

She shook her head.

'How long do you plan on being in town?' he asked.

'I'm not sure,' she replied, unable to meet his eyes.

Chapter Fifteen

It was dark when Rachel followed the tail lights of Gary's truck onto the gravel beside a wide detached house. The building was comprised of overlapping blue boards and a few steps leading up to a porch. Some gardening tools leaned against the screen of a side door and two cans were stacked one on top of the other, their yellow skins dirtied by oil which shone in the headlights. There were no lights on in the house and it made Rachel feel sad for him, to have to come home to it each night.

A long afternoon had been spent sauntering around the streets of Portsmouth. A late lunch had led to an early dinner via several hours of browsing around shops and what seemed like endless cups of coffee in different shops. Gary seemed to know a lot of local people and each time he stopped to chat, it had made Rachel feel spare and in the way. Throughout the day, he had not asked her where she was staying or, apart from in his shop earlier, mentioned the topic of how long she would be staying. She, in return, had asked him no questions about where he lived or who with. Through their silences, they had spent their time creeping around topics and creating a space they could occupy without too many questions.

Now, they crunched through the snow, Gary taking her large bag, and made for the front door. A hollowed out pumpkin filled with snow and looking soft round the edges sat on the porch rail. Their breath was visible, smoky and almost as white as the snow. It felt later than it really was as they stood in the cold silence and Gary put his key into what looked like the flimsiest and most token of locks and the thin door swung open on the cool dark house.

'Well, this is home,' Gary said.

The door led directly into a large square kitchen, big windows letting moonbeams fall across surfaces. It was hard to make very much out, but Rachel picked up on a sense of home, that someone belonged there, an ambience that was missing from the exterior. Gary closed the door and put the bag down, not switching on the light. With more firmness and apparent force than he had shown throughout the day, he took both her hands in his. Rachel looked at him through the silvery dark, his eyes glinting, and she let herself move a fraction closer to him in a way that almost threw her off balance. This is what should have happened the first time, ten years ago, she thought.

When their bodies made contact, they were already kissing. Rachel knew they had been waiting all day for it to happen. It had been present in every casual touch or brush, leg against leg or hand on shoulder, all small hints of desire. In the shadowy kitchen, barely inside the door and bags still at her feet, Rachel pulled Gary tighter to her and felt the warmth of his body and the hardness of his lips on hers. Rachel had been waiting a lot longer than just a day. Even through the many layers of clothes they both wore, Rachel could feel the connection their bodies made, basking in it as surely as if they had been naked.

Part of her wanted to break the kiss and breathe frantic questions about the wisdom of their actions but at a level of feeling that ran deep, she was sure she was right in what she was doing. It wasn't the time for questions, she thought as she kissed Gary hard and then flecked her tongue gently across his strong top lip, feeling the ridge of his teeth. He responded eagerly, no doubts evident on his part. The kitchen was quiet and the sounds they made in it amplified until they seemed abnormally loud.

Rachel warmed up, her clothes feeling like a constriction around her. She held Gary tight, caught in the flow of the present and the past, still thinking of what might have been ten years ago and what could be there and then. She wondered if he felt the same or if it was simpler for him. It was a delicious sense of satisfaction, of things falling into place. Each second that passed purged her of anxiety and fear until she was left only with the physical sensations of him and the desperate desire for more.

Gary clutched her hand and led her up a short flight of stairs that seemed to rise from the very centre of the house. Steep, almost like a ladder, they led directly to a tiny landing with doors leading off either side, a bathroom in front of her revealed by a half-open door. Gary took her into the room on the left and flicked on a lamp which filled it with a soft golden glow and made it seem instantly warmer. There was not much more in the room other than the bed, low and wide with a densely worked quilt thrown across it. The lamp was made from an old bottle, the shade slightly askew.

The kiss which had been interrupted by the journey upstairs was resumed with more ferocity. Rachel shook her coat off and let it fall to her feet. She reached into his jacket and pushed it away from him. They stood and kissed for a while longer before they tumbled together and landed on the bed. It was soft and Rachel rolled onto her back, feeling herself sink into the mattress, pressed down by Gary's weight.

For a time, they continued to hug, squeeze and kiss while still clothed, as though shy with each other. There was something about their fumbling which took them back to where they had been ten years before, on the verge of something they were both a little afraid to explore. Where years before their trepidation had arisen from ignorance of what lay ahead, now it seemed to come from sure knowledge. The silence between them was fragile and intense, making Rachel afraid to break it.

Tentatively, she moved her hand a layer closer to him by slipping it under the hem of his thin jumper. Beneath was the soft cotton pelt of a shirt encasing the muscles of his chest and stomach. Gary supported his weight over her, resting on his knees and elbows. Rachel squeezed at his side and then grabbed a handful of the shirt and wrenched it from the waistband of his trousers, wanting to touch his skin. It was as soft as the cotton and exuded a gentle heat that spread to her hand as she searched for and found his pert nipple.

From where he towered over her, his face illuminated in pale gold, he brought his body down until it compressed her gently to the mattress. Rachel worked her arm over his back and pulled him into her, kissing him once again. He planted small kisses and nips around her neck and nibbled on her earlobe, his breath hot. His hands groped at her clothing, pulling and tugging until it was messy and disorganised. When he undid the button on the top of her jeans, she let out a gasp, raw and uninhibited, and he glanced up at her for a second before continuing.

Rachel lay back and let him carefully undo each silver button on the fly of her jeans. The denim was tight around her rear and crotch and it was a relief to feel them open and loosen around her waist. He scuttled down the bed and removed her shoes to allow him to slip the jeans over her ankles. He left her fluffy white towelling socks on. His hands seemed big as they felt around under her, picking her up by the behind and pulling off her knickers. Rachel felt the scrape of the material over her thighs and knees and the feathery way they shimmered down her calves and ultimately off her feet.

Naked from the waist down, she felt vulnerable and protected at the same time. That morning, before setting off from the motel, Rachel had tucked a thin T-shirt into her knickers before putting another over the top, following it with her heavy green wool sweater. Their hems now lay across each other, barely hiding her sex from his gaze. Gary pushed all the material up as though it were a single garment, lifting it clear of her breasts. Rachel obediently raised her arms abover her and moved her head from side to side to let him finish his revelation of her. Naked, she lay on the bed and looked up at him, waiting for him to make the move.

During his undressing of her, Rachel had been in a curious state of denial about where it was leading, as though sex were not really the point of the frantic activity. When Gary abruptly dropped his head and buried his face into her wet sex, she froze for a second before succumbing to it. Greedily, she let her legs hang wide and rubbed the heels of her socks over his back, hearing the friction of fabric against fabric. Down in her sex, there was the more intense sensation of skin on skin as his mouth examined the most intimate areas of her. A man she knew only through memory and fantasy was suddenly probing the swollen and fiery abyss between her legs.

Gary's tongue was pressing into her, finding its way towards the opening of her vagina. Pausing, he did something Rachel would not normally have found exciting. He used his fingers to part the puffed lips of her labia, easing gradually until he held her open wide. She kept her eyes closed but could feel his breath on her. Rachel wondered what he could see, how it was for him to hold her apart in the way he did and peer into her sex. It was invasive and yet it sent a deep shiver through her as she realised she wanted to open herself fully to him and allow him to see all of her. It was a raw manner of achieving such an end but one she found irresistible.

The smooth inner curves of her labia were moist and her swollen clitoris was in the midst of it like a bud craving blossom. When his tongue flicked at it as though responding to some unheard call from her, Rachel tensed the muscles of her lower back and shifted her behind off the bed and towards the source of pleasure. Still with her lips spread, his mouth covered the whole area around her clitoris and his tongue worked away at it with a quiet insistence, a knowing sense of its own ability to bring her to orgasm. Rachel wanted to come while he was plastered against her and toiling away. She wanted him as close to her as he could be without actually being inside her when she had her first climax.

Gary slid his thumbs away and let the lips of her sex close, still keeping his mouth over her clitoris. Freed, his hands wandered over the tight skin of her stomach, thumbs massaging the temple-like bones of her hips. In the same way as when he had removed her knickers, his hands cupped her buttocks and she felt completely held by him, as though he might be able to sweep the whole of her body up in that manner and carry her off. Rachel dug her fingers into his long hair, running them through the gentle waves and onto the nape of his neck.

Rachel's orgasm broke free from her in short bursts. Her body clenched against it, trying to release it slowly and maximise the pleasure but she knew it was beyond her control. The stiffness she willed into her muscles dissipated and she shook violently, her back twisting about on the mattress and her hands in furious motion through his hair. The inner recesses of her vagina moved with a forceful rhythm and Gary rode the echoing movements of her body, going with her pleasure and pushing it on further. Rachel reached the summit and scrunched her face up, breath held in. For a moment of pure ecstasy, it was as though she had vanished into unadulterated whiteness before the air spluttered from her and she let the receding pleasure tickle her.

While she lay recovering, Gary was quietly undressing. Rachel was too exhausted to help, even though she wished she could have. Instead, she lay in the flush of her climax and watched him remove his shirt and vest by lifting them over his head without undoing the buttons. He did not undress in a rush, but neither did he waste time as he put alternate feet on the bed to untie the bright yellow laces of his heavy boots. Rachel stayed on her back and kept her legs askew, her sex still on display for him and her socks white like snow on her feet. He looked her in the eyes as he removed his jeans. Gary stood before her in only a tight fitting pair of grey briefs that extended halfway down his thighs. A tumescent outline snaked down the left leg, raising the soft nap of the cotton. He pushed them down over his hips and stepped clear, approaching the bed confidently and slowly.

Gary stood by the bed and his eyes perused her. He sat on the edge of the mattress and leaned one arm across her, staring into her eyes. Rachel reached out and stroked the outline of his chest, her fingers finding the stray hairs that peppered the skin. His hair fell forward over his face and he was smiling at her as he moved in to kiss her. Rachel rose up to meet him and got herself closer to him, wanting to feel the heat of his body. As they kissed, she let her hand drop onto his thigh and was surprised at how solid it was, the muscle prominent and near the surface, no trace of fat between it and his skin. The inside of his thigh was smooth and bald and, at its crescent, she found the loose skin of his hairy scrotum.

Kneeling up and stretching his body out above her, the muscles of Gary's arms flexed to support his weight. Rachel could not take her eyes from him, running her gaze along the length of his taut and enticing body. Gary had his hands spread wide into the mattress and his long cock hefted towards her. She reached out and held it, feeling the stiff hotness of the rod between her fingers. It pulsed with life and passion when she squeezed it, the head a large circumcised flower on the end of his rigid appendage. With both hands, she stroked and tickled him, using light fingers over it and he responding with urgent movements of his hips. The tumescence solidified into a full erection, a bead of fluid glinting on the tip.

Rachel's sex was well primed from his mouth, her vagina feeling sensuous and pliable. With her heels planted on the bed, she opened her knees and then spread her feet to make a space for him. He took the mute signal and knelt between her open legs, bending forwards and brushing her mouth with his lips. Gary's erect cock was pressed between the soft flesh of their groins, their pubic hair grinding out a pleasant friction. When he pulled up, Rachel looked down and saw the underside of his shaft covered in a film of her juices.

Gary stroked her pubic hair and dipped a finger between her labia. Rachel bit down on her lip as Gary's digit passed the threshold of her sex and burrowed into her vagina. He moved it in a circular motion which became slowly wider, as though preparing her for his girth. It slid further in and his thumb massaged her clitoris so deftly Rachel thought she might come again before he had even entered her with his cock. He withdrew and used his hand on himself, steering it with practised confidence, making himself as hard as he could for her.

Their eyes met for a moment as Gary rested the head of his cock against the lips of her sex. The pause allowed no time for full thought, only small fractions of desire and doubt, fear and excitement. It was good to have only partial feelings, to be ready to tumble down with them, wherever they led.

The head of his cock probed between her lips and in no time found the opening of her vagina. The delay was only brief and, with an authoritative push, he entered her. Rachel let out a low breath, a mixture of satisfaction and torment at being so overwhelmed by a man who had been not more than a boy the last time she had seen him. All her fantasies were remade into realities and then taken further, all through the most simple and direct of acts. He penetrated her forcefully, never slowing his path into her or allowing her a second of respite. It was the way she wanted it to be, so assailing and overcoming that it would become the only thing important to her for that short time.

Their groins made contact and he was fully inside her, stretching the walls of her vagina around him as he crammed her with himself. She could feel the depth to which he had plundered her and lifted her legs higher, arching them around his hips and making herself even deeper for him. He took advantage of it and pressed as far as he could go, making her gasp. They lay on the bed, he on top of her prostrate form, and she felt as close to him as she could. It was almost enough for her to lay there with him and feel the gentle pulses of his member inside her, the sure beat of a heart.

Gary was cautious in his movements, easing back only an inch or so, pulling himself from her. Rachel stroked the sides of his body and smoothed her hands over his rear, going with the inward thrust he made. It was slow and considered lovemaking, surprising to Rachel given their newness to each other. His self-control was total as he moved his sex in and out of hers with a definite and precise rhythm. Rachel was enraptured by the experience, wondering how long it would be before his resolve would crack, giving way to a more ruthless plundering.

Rachel's eyes had adjusted to the dimness of the room and she found the glow comforting and intimate. The cover on the bed was soft and warm, gradually ruffling under her from the slow build of exertion. Inside, Rachel felt the inescapable orgasm take hold and spread through her body with a tremor. She let his motion coax her, awakening the second phase of desire as he drove into her. Back and forth he went and Rachel sensed the urgency of it, the earlier gentleness replaced with something much more determined. His body was hard against hers, their bodies banging and the bed revealing all its creaks and strains.

In the cool room, they became hot from exertion. Rachel pulled his head into her shoulder and felt the burn of his breath and the faint rub of stubble. His back rippled and undulated under her fingers and his knees were buried deep into the soft mattress. Rachel kept her legs wrapped around him, loose enough to allow his lunges depth, her thighs against the smooth outsides of his hips. His cock was hard and an ominous presence in her body. Although she could only feel it, the sensation filtered through all of her senses, overloading her and making her feel pressed to the bed by him like a flower.

The lunging became urgent and less coordinated, Gary frantically rubbing himself against her insides, trying to achieve orgasm. The quest for it pushed Rachel to the edge and she teetered on it for pronounced seconds before letting herself tumble into orgasm.

Rachel used her whole body to grip him as she came. The muscles of her sex held him and then released him in alternating spasms of pleasure, the climax shimmering through her in the midst of the frantic activity. Her head felt light and her body tense as she drifted through herself like a ghost in her own body.

While she was still crying out and writhing beneath Gary, he let out a moan and his moves suddenly became more snatching and violent. Rachel gripped his tight behind and felt his body judder. There was a warmth down in her sex as he ejaculated into her. It spread and she imagined it firing from him and into her. Their two orgasms melded into a mutual cry of pleasure and a common set of movements and, she imagined, feelings. They rose and fell at almost the same time, each finding a peak and then descending with sheer elation.

Gary rolled off her and lay on his back, eyes fixed on the ceiling and his breathing heavy. Rachel moved herself closer to him and clung to his arm, stroking it with her thumb. His hair was spread about on the pillow, a gentle shine of sweat catching the light. Several minutes of silence passed, then Gary sat up and pulled back the covers. Rachel got into bed and he joined her, flicking off the lamp and leaving them in a darkness so complete it took her a long time to adjust to it.

She wanted to speak but could not find anything to say into the blackness. Soon, she found her breathing had synchronised with his and she followed him into a deep and untroubled sleep, his arm around her.

Chapter Sixteen

Rachel took a few light steps across the landing, heading towards the bathroom and wondering where Gary was. The smell of coffee wafted around her from the kitchen and she was about to go down to look for him when Gary appeared at the bottom of the stairs, carrying a tray and wearing only a pair of green checked boxer shorts.

'You made breakfast?' Rachel asked, still sleepy and fiddling with the hem of her T-shirt.

'Just coffee. All the breakfast you need,' he said, looking down at the tray in concentration as he ascended.

Back in the bedroom, Rachel looked at him laying there, the blanket concealing most of him, only his shoulders and arms visible as they lay on top of the covers, smooth and muscular. Gary's hands were large and slightly rough as though they had once been soft but had lately grown accustomed to hard work. All through the night, the hands had explored, stroked, manipulated or simply rested on various parts of her body. The gentle explosions of their lovemaking had followed, she supposed, from a fuse ten years along. It was hard to separate the fact of him from the fictions she had entertained herself with and it was surprising how quickly old feelings reintegrated themselves into her conscious mind.

Standing at the side of the bed, Rachel lifted the T-shirt over her head and watched his eyes scanning over her naked body as she climbed into bed next to him.

'What do you want to do today?' he asked, handing her a

mug of coffee, mist rising from the malty-brown liquid.

Rachel sipped it and felt it warm through her, stoking the glow of the previous night. 'Don't you have to go to work?' she asked.

'Not if I don't want to. Joe can manage without me and it's always easy to find people on short notice.'

'I'm in your hands then,' she said.

'I didn't want to ask last night, it seemed inappropriate, but how long are you staying?'

'I'm not sure. A day or two.'

She detected the slightest of pauses, a beat missed in the lazy morning chat.

'Well,' he said, 'we could go over to Kittery and check out the outlets, they're a favourite destination. If you want, I could take us up to Freeport in Maine. There's a prettier route than the freeway.'

Rachel took another swallow of coffee and leaned over to place the cup on the floor by the bed. She sat up straight, pulled the cover off him and then threw a leg over his prone body, straddling him. The soft cotton of his boxers caressed her bare behind and she enjoyed the feel of having her knees planted either side of him, spreading herself over him. Rachel sat down on his lap and felt the press of his cock through the fabric and against her skin as she made small gyrations over him.

The hardness in his shorts quickly became evident. Gary held her hips, letting his hands be carried by her motion. Rachel allowed the desire to wake her, stretching her back and straightening her arms to shake off the recent sleep. Her head buzzed from the caffeine rush and she was aroused by the act of writhing naked on Gary's lean body. Gary's erection had pushed upright and lay between her legs. Rachel felt a sudden flash of warmth against the underside of her sex as his shaft was uncovered by the slit in the fly of the shorts. She repeated the movement and felt his flesh once again, Gary sighing as their sensitive areas made contact. Several more times, Rachel made a grinding motion with her behind.

Rachel moved down until she was sitting on his knees and then she began to work the shorts off him. Gary raised his behind so she could slide them from under him and she had to hold his cock to free it from the folds of cloth surrounding it. She left the underwear around his thighs and took hold of him once again, feeling the heat and the stiffness, the skin sheathing a smouldering core. The glans were shiny and full, the lack of a foreskin making the line of his shaft smooth and sleek, Rachel running her finger along the veiny underside and watching his reactions.

Throwing the blanket fully off the bed and quickly tugging off his shorts, Rachel was seized with a pang of desire, a hunger she wanted to feed with Gary. Kneeling between his open legs, she voraciously took half the length of his stiff cock into her open mouth, plugging herself with it. The bulging shaft filled her mouth, leaving her tongue only limited room for action over it. Rachel found the area beneath his glans, where they joined on the underside of his phallus, and worked her tongue at the tiny rift between them. Gary seethed air and Rachel kept the pressure on, using the tip of her tongue to excite him.

Gary was reaching down at her and she wondered what he was doing. His hand moved imploringly on her side, almost pinching her. She realised what he wanted and he groaned approvingly when she turned herself and raised a leg over him, straddling him once again, but this time with her back to him. Rachel kept on mouthing Gary's cock and caught her breath when she felt his tongue begin to lick at her labia. Stretched out on top of him, sucking his cock and with her own sex rudely displayed right in front of his face, Rachel felt a surge of adrenalin in the morning hush.

Rachel held Gary's shaft halfway down and lifted it upright, flicking her tongue over the tip and tasting the acrid fluid that had oozed from the slit. She looked down at his balls, crammed together in their tight sac of skin and, beyond, the hairy graze of skin that led into his behind. One of his legs lay spread to one side, while the other had a raised knee, his foot planted in the mattress. When his cock was back in her mouth, Rachel squeezed his balls and jiggled them together. His pubic hair was a wiry mat, heavy and dark compared to the sprinkling of stray strands over his ball sac.

Down in her sex, Gary was working his tongue with the same practised ease he had shown the night before. Rachel's knees were either side of his head, pressing against his shoulder, and her breasts dangled towards him, nipples brushing the warm masculine flesh of his torso. His hands reached up and gripped her back, keeping her in position for him and feeling powerful where they touched her.

It was a tantalising mix of giving and receiving pleasure, their bodies connected together at their most susceptible points, a circuit of mutual gratification established. Each darting movement of Gary's tongue in her labia or on her clitoris made her suck his cock with greater passion and, each time she did so, his actions were in turn more animated.

Rachel's sex reverberated from the touch, the muscles of her groin shifting in a profound grinding motion, the walls of her vagina rippling. Juices flowed easily and she felt sopping, kneeling over his face and hearing him lap away at her. The muscles of her thighs tightened involuntarily, as did her behind. Gary clutched her tightly, controlling her movements and firmly pushing her onto him. Rachel squirmed on his face, his cock still in her mouth but her motions lacking coordination. He seemed to know she was close to orgasm, as though he could read it from the action of her sex.

Abandoning his cock, grabbing it as though to steady herself, Rachel twisted about as a climax took swift hold of her. She masturbated him, her hand sliding up and down over the smooth shaft and teasing the head. With her back to him, she was left only with her mental images as she came. It was enough, the potency of the moment and the fact it was with Gary, to inflame her.

Crying out and letting her upper body sag onto Gary, Rachel tightened and released her rear as she came, the bursts hot through her. The depths of her sex rolled and her clitoris was abuzz, tingling as the pressure of desire was released. The orgasm was brief and assailing, leaving Rachel spread over his body in a daze, her breath loud and fast and an astonished look on her face.

Without looking at him and with barely any time to recover, Rachel sat up and moved her body over his until she was riding him, only a few inches above his erect cock. Her back still to him, she held him at a right angle to his body and teased the quivering lips of her labia with the tip of his cock. The shaft bulged and strained under the pressure of the blood coursing through the veins, the head throbbing.

Rachel stared down at it, imagining in detail what it would feel like as it entered her, remembering the sex of the previous night. Kneeling over him the way she did meant the glans would run along the front wall of her vagina and the thought of being taken from a different angle was exciting. She got up off her knees and planted a foot either side of him, the mattress sagging under the redistribution of her weight. Now, she was squatting above him, her sex poised to receive him and he ready to become a part of her.

Steadying herself with one hand in front of her on the bed, Rachel reached between her legs with the other as she brought her body down to make contact with him. The very tip of his cock, blunt and round, touched the wet rim of her sex where her lips were puffed. Deeper inside, she still ached from the orgasm and was ready for another but still possessed of enough self control to tease Gary by caressing herself with him. He sighed and his muscles were tense, his whole body crying out for release, not just the swollen member she held so firmly in her hand.

The feel of his cock between the lips of her sex as it neared the opening of her vagina, seemed far larger than it had in her hand. There was a brief moment of consternation where she thought it might not be possible for him to enter her, as though it were far too large for her. Rachel hesitated, perched on him and his hands supporting her behind. Regulating her breathing and readying herself mentally to be invaded by him, Rachel eased herself down onto his long shaft.

It splayed her and the stretch was agonising for a moment or two, before turning into the most luscious expansion she could imagine. The opening of her vagina dilated and its walls eased wider to accommodate him. There was something brutal and harsh about the way she inflicted him on her, giving herself little respite once the initial moment of entry had occurred. Rachel moved her behind towards his groin in a way that was decisive and desperate, needing him in her.

Gary squeezed and parted her buttocks as Rachel continued to descend towards his body. His big hands made her feel delicate under their touch, the fingers hard and obvious over the soft, slightly sweaty flesh of her rear. Rachel shuddered when he stroked her lower back, reaching up as far as his hands would go, nearing her shoulder blades. With a long sweep, his hands travelled over her and were suddenly under her, touching Rachel's hand where it was holding his cock and then exploring the area where they were joined. He gripped her hand for a moment and then he was gone.

The spread lips of Rachel's labia came to the base of his shaft and rested on it, close to his balls, which she clutched tightly for a moment, getting a cry from him. Rachel leaned forwards, put her hands on his thighs, and carefully flexed the muscles of her vagina around the intrusion. The whole of Gary's body felt like one strong muscle as she sat atop it. His skin was a delicious shade of gold and the hairs over it were masculine and enticing. Inside her, his cock was large and powerful, able to bring her to the release she so badly wanted once more. Rachel wanted to do it as much for him as for herself, to provide him with freedom from the tension she could sense throughout the long stretch of his body.

Rachel put her hands on Gary's kneecaps and squeezed them, the heavy muscles of his thighs steely and harsh, defined as though from running or cycling. The whole of his body was athletic, designed for movement. Rachel recalled the different shapes and sizes she had imagined Gary's body to be, the things he would do to her and she to him. In her most intimate moments, before she was really knowledge-able enough to do so, Rachel would picture his cock in intimate detail, shocked that her imagination was so crude and heated. In the dark thoughts, she would caress and hold it, lick it and take it into her mouth, or masturbate it and let it spray its seed all over her body. The hardest part of the fabrication to cling to was the part where she imagined him inside her. Rachel would probe with a finger or two and, were she really daring, something closer to the shape she needed, but it was hard to tell if the sensation of penetration she envisaged would be the same in reality. In Gary's case, she never expected to find out.

Sitting on him and lost in memory, Rachel had not moved for almost a minute and it was only Gary's insistent squeez-ing of her behind and the movements of his hips that broke the concentration and fired her back into the reality which had occupied the central place in her fantasy.

Rachel squeezed his cock with the muscles of her vagina, the whole area of her pelvis moving in concert around the hard presence of flesh and blood. The walls of her vagina undulated in a throbbing motion, drawing him deeper into her and constricting the shaft. Gary sighed each time she clenched him and Rachel reached a hand down to tickle his balls, the wiry hair wispy on her fingers. Still holding him tight with internal muscles, Rachel moved up and down on him and savoured the rub of her flesh over him. When she had reared up almost to the tip of his cock, Rachel let her weight drop abruptly, thumping into him and gasping as his cock shot back into her with an agonising combination of speed and force.

The more she did it, so the harder she landed on him and soon her sex began to ache, her pubic bone warm from the banging against him. Rachel wondered if it was painful for him, the way she lifted herself and then pounded down. It would be his balls which bore the brunt of it, she thought. Whatever it felt like for him, he was not complaining. In fact, he was starting to bring himself up to meet her. Sometimes the rhythm worked and there was a profound sense of being penetrated in a manner so harsh and deep it was hard to imagine it could get any more intense.

But it did.

As well as the physical force, there was something building in her which was a mixture of physical and emotional. Their bodies were working together and in doing so produced something neither of them could have managed on their own. In Rachel, it manifested itself as a sense of urgency, a fear almost, that the sheer potency of the climax would be unattainable or, once attained, too much to handle. Their sex was a way of bridging the emotional and the physical, condensing themselves into basic physical acts that had so much more attached to them and the result of which was the release of emotion in jerking physical spasms.

In the room, still so early, Rachel shook and flailed about on Gary and waited for her orgasm to come. It was close, she could tell. It whispered in her, like a secret crying out to be told. Rachel knew she would not be able to hold it in for much longer and she readied herself.

It was Gary who came, surprising Rachel with the sheer volume of his cry and the strength with which he held onto her rear. His nails raked along the buttocks and Rachel seethed through clenched teeth. There were any number of ways in which she could have tantalised him, denying or prolonging his orgasm. The pattern of his noises suggested to Rachel that pleasure was coursing through him with a slow build, each shout slightly louder than the previous. Rachel moved firmly on him, listening to him and relishing the sound he made, the desperate and manly roar as his semen blasted forth. As she clutched at him with the walls of her sex, she thought about how his sperm would be shooting directly up into her, filling her with a hot pool of come.

Gary's cock was throbbing and Rachel's sex was sensitive to even the small dilation of her vagina caused by his shaft. Along the front wall of her vagina, the ridged underside of his phallus suddenly felt prouder than it had, scratching the itching need for a climax of her own and dousing her insides with fluid that had come from deep inside of himself. Rachel looked at Gary's legs, watching them quiver as his orgasm began to recede and she knew she did not have long before her now so pleasurable movements would become an excruciating pain to him. For the time being, he was still hard inside her and his hold on her was still strong. Gary's body jerked and he moaned, feet twitching on the bed.

It was how she had imagined it, the feel of him inside her. The touch of his hands on her. The feel of his body, on her, over her and, now, under her. The intensity of his orgasm, brought about by her movements alone. His semen now inside her, part of him was now part of her.

The thoughts were enough and she combined them with her movements and several quick presses on her clitoris to achieve a climax. It was the only way out of the feelings, to let them gush from her in one undifferentiated torrent. Rachel held onto him and let go of herself, pushing the orgasm through all the pores of her body and feeling it tingle in every nerve ending as it left her body. She shoved herself up and down on him with a roughness that took her by surprise. Rachel bore down on him and the deepest recesses of her sex rumbled, his presence in her as she came intensifying the experience.

Rachel almost fell from him, her body splayed out on the mattress, limbs thrown carelessly and her breathing hard. It was almost a full fifteen minutes before she was able to recover enough to lay by his side and stroke his chest as she hovered in a twilight brought on by exertion.

Gary was staring up at the ceiling, avoiding her eyeline. Rachel could feel something in the silence, words that wanted to be spoken. She did not intend to let the situation end up feeling difficult, as though they had woken up after an ill judged one night stand. Rachel leaned up and tried to look at him, but he turned his head to one side and dodged her gaze.

'What's the matter?' Rachel asked.

'Nothing,' he said, without looking at her.

'What are you thinking about?' Rachel asked.

'I'm not really thinking about anything,' he said.

'Gary, come on. Don't do this to me. The last thing I need right at this moment is for you to start some sort of mean and moody act on me.'

'Come downstairs with me. There's some stuff I need to tell you,' he said, finally looking at her.

Chapter Seventeen

Rachel sat in Gary's living room, holding a picture of a five-year-old boy.

'But you never married his mother?' Rachel asked.

'No.'

The boy had a tinge of Gary about him, a genetic hint, but not much more. His cheeks were slightly chubby and rose-coloured, as if from some recent exposure to the cold. Under the longish hair, which looked set in no particular shade of blonde, the boy's ears seemed large, but then Rachel remembered something about them staying the same size from quite a young age, although she could not remember precisely which. Perhaps that was eyes, or did they change colour?

'Zak,' Rachel said quietly, looking at the picture.

'Grace, that's his mother's name, still lives here in Portsmouth. She's back in school right now and also works in a book store.'

'When did the two of you split up?' Rachel asked.

Gary discreetly cleared his throat. 'Five months ago,' he said.

'Were all of you living here?'

'No. Gracie, Grace,' he corrected himself, as though embarrassed at using a pet name for her in Rachel's presence, 'has the other house. It's only a rental, like this place.'

Rachel looked around the sparse living room. It was basic and reminded her of something she might have lived in herself five years ago. Unhung picture frames leaned against a wall and a grey cardboard carton was filled with unpacked magazines. Rachel could not tell if he had arrived in a hurry or planned to leave in one. On a side table with a half-burned candle stuck into the neck of a wine bottle, an acoustic guitar rested, the multicoloured knit of its strap hanging across the steel strings. Apart from the sofa they sat on and which was pointed purposefully at the television, the only other piece of furniture in the room was an upright piano of dark walnut, its lid down and dust laying on it. The picture of Zak had been on top of the piano.

'How often do you see him?' Rachel asked.

'Twice a week usually. Sometimes he stays for weekends, but misses his mum and the cats after more than two days.'

'It must be difficult, both of you living in such a small town like this.'

'It'd be harder on me if she lived a long way away. Me and Grace are okay now. We're starting to work things through. Once in a while, we shoot pool together.'

Gary had simply shown her the photograph and told her it was Zak, his son, who was five years old. The statement had raised a barrage of questions for Rachel, making her feel inquisitive, but she was aware how invasive too many queries would seem. Carefully, as though trying to show respect or affection, Rachel set down the picture of Zak. The question that had immediately occurred to Rachel when Grace had first been mentioned was still at the forefront of her mind.

'Does, ah, Grace ever stay over?' Rachel asked.

'Not the whole night,' he said slowly. 'There was one time, back in September. Zak had a sitter and we were meeting to discuss something about his school. Anyway, we went out, had a few drinks, ended up back here.'

'And?' Rachel asked into the silence.

'And we knew our own heads were fucked up enough without making it worse, getting Zak involved. We realised we either had to be together or not be together. If we didn't have Zak, we could play games with each other, but not when he's in the middle. It was a mistake to do what we did, a misjudgment we put down to experience.'

Rachel wondered what she was getting into, if she were, indeed, getting into anything. 'But neither of you is really over the other, not so soon, surely?' she asked.

'Who knows?' Gary asked, shrugging.

A pot of coffee, two cups and a milk jug were on the floor, a broadsheet newspaper acting as a place mat. Rachel bent over and poured herself a cup, putting in more of the creamy milk than she should have. While she busied herself, she casually asked another question, the way a doctor might talk about the weekend while performing major surgery.

'What made you split up in the first place?'

'Just drift. Nothing dramatic. We were gradually going off in our own different directions, like floating out to sea and not realising how far away the shore is. When I bought the shop from Joe and gave up the realty job, it was pretty selfish. There was money from when my grandmother died and some of it is put away for Zak but the rest went into the shop. Everything I've got is tied up in it. The shop was for all three of us, or it would have been.'

He spoke as though answering questions he had been asked many times.

'It wasn't because of anyone else you broke up?' Rachel asked.

'Not when it finally happened. Grace came close to fooling around once, but that was a couple of years ago. I'm sorry, you don't want to hear all this crap,' Gary said, looking away.

'Have you seen anyone else since you split up?'

'No. The shop's been enough to keep me going. There's always another hour you can do there, something else to keep you busy.'

'So, when you sent the postcard to me, you were still with Grace?'

'Yeah. I was just sending a whole bunch of cards out. I

mailed a couple to people I know in Europe. I was so hyped about having the little postcards made, that everyone I knew got one, all saying more or less the same, "Drop in if you're ever passing by". You're the most travelled to have done it so far. There was no agenda in me writing you, I promise.'

Rachel knew he was telling the truth. Why wouldn't he be? She sipped at her coffee and tried to integrate the new information about him into her feelings. It shouldn't make any difference, she thought. She was only passing through and, in a day or so, would be on her way. Enjoy the now for what it is, she told herself, ignoring the strong undertow she already felt from the deep emotional waters she was wading into.

Gary took them to Kittery in his truck, the drive out mostly silent. Rachel wondered what he was thinking about as she let the earlier conversation settle in her head. The quiet was not hostile, the way it might have been had they fought. Instead, it was considered and delicate, the intensity of their passion tempered by the information he had shared with her.

They pulled head first into a space in the middle of a vast car park. The outlet village was a collection of low, mostly wooden huts that could have been out of an old western except the buildings were emblazoned with high class badges. Names like Ralph Lauren, Calvin Klein and Donna Karan had flitted past her eyes on the way in.

'People come from all over to shop in the outlets in New England,' he said as they walked along a wide, raised promenade.

It was still early as far as Rachel was concerned but there were plenty of people around. Gary put his arm around her waist and gave her a squeeze, but he didn't linger.

It was late afternoon when they arrived back at Gary's house. Rachel felt the kind of holiday tiredness that came from wandering around shops and having no place in particular to go. The day had sapped her energy in a pleasant way and the first sense that she was having a break had taken hold of her. The things they had discussed that morning, Zak and Grace, now seemed less important, the sharpness of it worn away by her spending time with him, accommodating him. The camaraderie engendered by the need to crunch through snow and occasionally hold each other up had made them physically at home very quickly.

'There's some live music happening at the shop tonight. I thought we could stop by there, if you want,' Gary said.

'I don't mind. Whatever,' she replied.

Rachel sat on the sofa where earlier in the day they had talked. Zak's picture surveyed them, back in its place on top of the piano. The lamp on the side table was switched on, pouring light down onto the guitar. Gary had carried a cassette player in from another room and music drifted out from where it was placed on top of the television set. At the opposite end of the sofa to Rachel, Gary sat, his head swaying in time with the music.

'Where did you get the paintings?' she asked.

He gave an embarrassed smile. 'Those are my attempts at art, playing with colour because I can't really draw. It was a phase I went through a few years ago.'

'You should hang them up. It's a shame to leave them there, propped against a wall,' she said.

'Maybe someone will discover them in my attic after I'm gone and I'll be posthumously exalted, sell for millions,' he said.

'Why don't you put them up in the coffee shop?' she asked.

Gary laughed. 'You've seen the type of people we have in there; they'd laugh them off the walls and I'd be ashamed, besides. Did you have a nice day?'

She went with the change of subject. 'Yes.'

'I'm sorry if I made it heavy earlier, all that stuff about Grace. I thought you should know,' he said.

'Don't worry about it, Gary.'

Rachel's feet were tucked under her on the sofa and she unfolded them so she could lean over towards him. She moved along and knelt next to him, stroking his hair. He continued to follow the music, his expression changing with each bar, the brow becoming heavy and serious. Rachel kissed his cheekbone and he turned to look at her, she meeting the gaze. Not for the first time that day, Rachel could not tell what was on his mind. Cupping his jaw, she brought her mouth to rest on his, the soft warmth of his lips mingling with hers.

Bereft of the layers of winter protection, Gary's torso was lean and discernible through the soft white cotton of the T-shirt that remained. The light blue of his jeans had faded to almost white in some places, areas where the fabric stretched to accommodate the movement of his body. The wide leather belt pulled his waist in and, below it, his crotch bulged where the legs of the jeans ran into each other.

Their kisses became more prolonged and deeper, less hesitant. Rachel pushed her tongue into his mouth and he drew on it. Rachel sensed a shift in Gary's body, more of an urgency evident as he moved from his sitting position and manoeuvred her down onto the sofa. Rachel yielded to the direction his body took hers in. He was heavy on top of her, his shoulders broad enough to make it seem as though he was smothering her. Rachel gripped onto him, her lips aching from the growing ferocity of their contact with Gary's.

Rachel was spread out flat on her back across the three cushions of the sofa, the combined weight of their bodies pressing into the springs. Any doubts or questions left her mind, as she knew that would be the moment close physical contact was resumed.

The clothes Rachel wore were no obstacle for Gary as he pulled her sweater over her head, quickly following it with the shirt she wore. Not stopping to look at her, he was down at her waist, unfastening the buttons of her jeans and pulling them down her legs. He seemed to pause for a second, looking at her in only her knickers, before he pulled them down also and she was naked.

Gary stood up and removed his own clothes, down to his underwear in only moments. Rached eyed the bulge in the crotch, the line of his erect cock clearly revealed by the dark fabric. Gary put his thumbs into the waistband and pulled down his shorts. She could make out the line where the broad elastic had made contact with his skin. From the midst of his pubic hair, his cock stood out, filled with blood and drooping bulkily.

Kneeling on the edge of the sofa, Gary ran his hands over her, touching her breasts and concentrating on one of her nipples. He leaned down and bit at the tip gently, rolling it between his lips and wetting it with his tongue. Rachel gasped, her pent up passion quickly released by a touch somewhere so sensitive. While he fed on her, the flat of his hand made circles on her stomach, her flesh elastic beneath the undulations he made. Gary broke away from her and, without speaking, turned her over onto her stomach.

Rachel lay, unable to see him and wondering what he would do next. He resumed his position on the edge of the sofa and the hand which had previously rubbed her stomach was now examining the pert cheeks of her behind. She lay her head to one side, looking at the seat back and enjoyed the light, tickling sensation the brush of his hand gave. A kiss was planted in the small of her back and it made her quiver, as though his mouth were buzzing on her and sending echoes along her spine. Gary's fingers began to trace along the groove where her buttocks met. For what seemed like a long time, his fingers teased along the crease, Rachel's breath almost a purr.

When he touched the underside of her sex, her voice went down a register, a low groan of contentment emitting as he gradually eased nearer to where she wanted him. Her sex was wet, its muscles free and lax, ready for him. Gary put his finger into the outer folds of her labia, the small hard digit enveloped by her moist flesh. It quickly burrowed its way to the opening of her vagina, barely stopping before it was penetrating her. Rachel lifted her head clear of the cushion and arched her back. Gary's thumb lay between her buttocks and one of his fingers, she could not tell which, was sliding into the humid channel of her sex.

Quick and methodical, Gary's only interest seemed to be preparing her for him. A second finger was not long behind the second and Rachel twisted her shoulders, head moving from side to side, as Gary manipulated her sex. The act was so focused, directed solely to quick and purposeful sex with her, that Rachel was overcome by the need as strongly as he seemed to be. The harder and more rapid his movements, the deeper she found her response. Pushed against the cushion, her clitoris was inflated and sensitive and Rachel was only able to tease it with small movements of her groin.

Gary mounted her in a swift movement, one knee either side of her hips, pushing her legs closed. Her sex felt confined, hard to get at because of the way her legs were shut. She felt the weight of his cock on her upraised bottom, the head of it rubbing over the soft globes of flesh.

Rachel had been confident she was ready for him, but the abrupt intrusion of his hard cock into her sex was severe, making her whimper at first and then, as he splayed her sex wider, she roared. Her body was closely compacted to the sofa, pressed down by his masculine weight and yet she felt rent asunder where he entered her. Rachel closed her eyes, raised herself up on her elbows and let her head hang loose, relaxing the muscles of her vagina at the same time.

The wiry brush of Gary's pubic hair scratched the cheeks of her behind and then his groin pressed firmly against her, embedding his cock as far into her as he could.

They lay still for a moment, Rachel face down and Gary straddling her, legs now stretched out and against the outer edges of her own and his cock buried deep in her.

'Touch yourself,' he murmured.

Rachel felt him ease his weight off so she could raise herself from the cushions and work her hand down into her crotch. Her fingers were pushed flat and Rachel moved them in a wave which culminated in the tips of her fingers pressed into the area around her clitoris. She put her free arm under her head and rested on it, massaging herself and waiting for Gary to begin thrusting.

It was not a long wait. Gary pulled himself out slowly and just when she thought he was about to pop out of her, he sank back in. The sensation was the same aching swell as his first entry into her, but now he was wasting no time with finesse. A few more deep lunges in and out of her and then he picked up speed. It was an unusual angle and her sex felt tighter than normal because of the position of her legs.

While Gary drove in and out of her, Rachel used her hand to massage her pubic bone and the area around her clitoris. Her orgasm was on the verge of bursting from her, the combined movements of Gary's body and her hand edging her continually closer. His cock felt wide in the tight passage of her sex, the walls of her vagina expanded by his presence. Where they were joined, the skin was moist with sweat, adding to Rachel's own lubrication. She wondered if she could reach her hand far enough under her to touch his shaft where it spread her labia.

Rachel exhaled and shouted into the cushion which absorbed most of the noise. Gary's stomach was banging into her lower back forcefully, his movements indicating the approach of his orgasm. Even from so few sexual encounters with him, Rachel already felt she knew him well enough to appreciate how sudden and out of character such a ruthless bout of lovemaking was for him. The previous night and morning, she had found him to be considerate and assertive.

Now, she was enjoying the onslaught of a firmer, more demanding approach to their sex.

Almost without noticing, and certainly without trying, Rachel came. She fidgeted under his weight, her body shuddering and the muscles of her back twitching. The walls of her sex stirred in a long spasm, clenching him and then letting him free. Rachel fumed with the orgasm, as though the energy it released was transformed into a kind of anger. On her clitoris, her hand fingered in the constricted space, keeping the flame of the climax burning through her.

Gary's body shook on top of her and he had all but stopped thrusting. From stillness, his orgasm shimmered through his body and Rachel felt it transmit through all of his muscles as they twitched against her prone body. As the first long pulse of semen juddered from him, Gary pushed himself decisively down, smothering her, his groin stuck into her behind. He heaved up and down on her several more times, riding her naked body with his and ejaculating into her, the feel of the semen hot and heavy.

In a stupidly mutual orgasm, they thrashed on noisily for a long time, pushing it beyond its comfortable limits as though trying to delay the moment when they would become themselves once again, their passion a desperate act.

'Rachel,' he said in a long breath that was hot on her ear.

The sound of the word made her panic, the intonation implying that something grave would follow it, something she was not ready to hear, not sure she would ever by ready for.

'Don't say anything, please, Gary,' she whispered.

Between them once again, oppressive with unsaid words, was silence.

Chapter Eighteen

Cup of Joe was busy when Rachel arrived with Gary, more
bustling than the first time she had seen it. The people, if it
were possible, seemed even more relaxed than before. A
corner had been cleared, no more or less illuminated than
any other part of the shop, but the focus of it nonetheless.
There was a free seat at the counter which Gary directed her
to. Joe was there, pouring steaming milk into a cup, and a
young woman who could have been a student was shaking
cinnamon onto froth. Gary slipped behind the counter and
spoke to Joe, his head close to the old man's and Rachel
unable to make out the words as Joe nodded thoughtfully.

'What kind of coffee would you like?' Gary asked, returning.

Rachel scanned the board and ordered a latte flavoured
with caramel.

A woman with a guitar case, long frizzy hair and a heavy,
intricately knitted jumper approached them.

'Carole. Hi,' Gary said. 'This is my friend Rachel, from
England.'

They exchanged hellos and handshakes and then Rachel
was alone on the stool, Gary over in the empty corner with
Carole, smiling and chatting as he helped her set up. Rachel
surveyed Gary's world, he in the middle of it. She pulled
herself up when she found she was imagining herself inserted into his milieu in some way. Tomorrow, she would be
gone and it would be over. In the honest part of her heart,
she knew she had already outstayed her time in Portsmouth.

Still, a sadness tugged at her as she thought of leaving the safe cossetted world, all the frozen snow, welcoming layers of defensive clothing and endless hot coffee.

'Did you want coffee?' a voice asked.

It was Joe, beaming at her. He looked out of place in the middle of it all she thought. His shirt sleeves were turned back twice, hanging just below his elbows and he wore a white apron, clean and crisp. She repeated the order for latte to him and he relayed it to the woman as he lingered, hands on the counter, looking at her as though he had something to say.

'How are you enjoying your stay?' was all he asked.

'Fine,' she said.

'He's had a rough ride, lately,' Joe said.

She glanced at Joe and saw he was looking past her and at Gary who was talking to three people seated at a table.

'He's a good guy,' Joe continued, his tone almost reverential. 'There's been a lot of unstable things in his life. He needs to find some calm.'

Rachel was about to respond when Gary's amplified voice came over the tiny speakers.

'We've seen her here before and I don't need to make any big introductions. Carole Carney.'

Over the applause and whistles, Rachel leaned close to Joe. 'I'm not here to cause him any trouble. Him or his family,' she said.

'I didn't mean it that way,' he said, touching her arm lightly. 'Maybe you're what he needs.'

'I forgot your coffee. Sorry,' Gary said, returning and putting his arm around her waist as he stood behind the stool on which she sat.

'It's on its way,' Joe said, withdrawing.

Gary kissed her neck and squeezed her. Rachel was flustered by the public display and felt herself shrink slightly from his clinch, although he didn't seem to notice.

The music began, folky and almost painfully from the

heart. Rachel would not normally have liked it but was glad of the distraction.

'You didn't mind having to come here?' he asked.

'No,' she said.

The combination of guitar and voice was not loud, fitting in with the ambience of the room. It was easy to listen to, sailing out over the crowd, who swayed their heads, drank coffee and, in some cases, discreetly carried on chatting.

'I had a really nice day,' he said.

'Me too.'

'When do you have to leave?' he asked in her ear.

'Soon, Gary,' she said.

'You could stay on a while longer.'

'Gary—'

'I'm sorry.'

The music wafted over the words once again.

They undressed for bed like a couple that had been together for years instead of just days. Rachel felt a tired ache running through her limbs, the small of her back and her legs stretched by the gradual exertion of all the walking she had done with Gary. Free of her clothes, she was looking forward to getting under the bedclothes with him, clinging to his body and warming herself with it.

Gary pulled his shirt over his head, lifting his hands high in the air as he did. While the shirt covered his face for a second or two, Rachel stole a glance, looking at the smooth, velum-like skin of his stomach stretching over the natural musculature. He was inviting, too inviting, and Rachel was finding herself falling into the apparent easiness of his suggestion that she stay on longer. Standing in the bedroom with him, watching him undress, all the earlier conversations and their attendant worries faded away. The thoughts shot through her mind in the small fraction of time it took for him to remove his top.

Naked, they climbed into the bed, pulling the heavy covers over them. Lazily, their bodies found each other in the expanse of sheets and they clung close together, their breathing regulated. Gary lay on his side and Rachel hers, facing each other with their limbs entwined into a single entity. Her head lay on his outstretched arm and one of her hands was resting on the bone of his hip. She leaned into him and felt the press of his partly tumescent sex against the soft down of her pubic hair. All of his body was lean, nothing in excess. He was, at different times, calm and passionate, underpinned by the serenity and confidence Rachel had detected when she first laid eyes on him again.

Rachel turned onto her other side and backed herself against him, their bodies slightly bent and fitting into each other. Gary's free hand stroked her breasts gently, feathering the nipple with deft fingers. When he squeezed the sensitive point of one between thumb and forefinger, gradually increasing the pressure, Rachel moaned, the tone of her voice raising in time with the physical tension. He released his hold and returned to a softer motion, a relief. Against her behind, his cock hardened, an insistent signal of the desire that lay at the core of his sensual caresses.

Gary bit her shoulder, nibbling along the bony ridge at first and then closing his mouth over her flesh, a faint sucking action discernible. His touch made a tingle reverberate, spreading from her upper back and down her spine, culminating in a wiggle of her hips. She shivered despite the pleasant warmth. The hand which had fondled her breasts was increasing its range, slowly but definitely. Using long sweeps, his fingertips ran a line along the outside of her thighs and on between them, always stopping just short of her sex.

The room was lit by the now familiar soft lamp. Rachel nestled herself into the welcoming curve of Gary's body. Soon, his hand was fondling her sex, tracing along the join of her lips and tickling her pubic hair. Rachel felt moist and her clitoris was aching for his attention. Gary rubbed the flat of his hand over her pubic bone, moving the whole area of her sex in a deep arc. His finger pushed into her labia, spreading the lips slightly and insinuating itself into her wetness. He put it deep in her with barely a pause, exploring her vagina in a way that was crude and brazen. She shifted the position of her legs to make it easier for him. Had she not been aroused, the presence of his finger would have been excruciating, but she was ready for him, physically and emotionally, willing to go in the direction he chose.

Rachel laid her hand on top of his, feeling the rise and fall of his knuckles as he laboured on her. She pushed down on his hand and in turn he pushed deeper into her, delving at her further reaches. Arching her back, she was stiff with the passion and full of anticipation and desire for release. As she curved her spine, her behind moved free of his groin and Rachel felt the heavy flop of his erect cock on her cheeks. Removing her hand from on top of his, she reached behind herself and found the sturdy, stalk-like shaft. Between her fingers, the flesh was hot and hard. It always surprised her that a part of his body, any man's body, could change in such a way, from soft to hard so simply and to such purpose. With some difficulty, she managed to trace the tip of his phallus across the taut flesh of her buttocks.

Letting go of him, Rachel concentrated her mind on her own pleasure. Gary was sliding his finger in and out of her with increasing speed. The angle of his hand ensured that he stimulated her with each stroke and Rachel tried her best to move with it, maximising the contact. In a way that was unassuming, their movements had taken on a kind of vigour. The main source of activity was his hand in her sex, but they rocked energetically back and forth as he masturbated her. They were quiet, as though doing something secret, something to be hidden from prying eyes. In her mind, Rachel could picture his face, yet all she could do at that moment in a tangible sense was feel him. It was enough, stirring her and pushing her closer to orgasm with each second that passed.

In what was a final push, their bodies jerked about, still contained within a small range but infused with the density of feeling, a pure concentration of their energies directed towards the goal of her liberation.

Rachel climaxed as Gary used his hand on her. She pushed herself into him, getting as much of her body near to him as she could manage. The muscles of her back and legs were tight, slowly easing the tension of her whole body through them. Rachel panted heavily several times and he gripped her securely, pressing his cock into the cheeks of her behind as she held herself aloft on the surge of the orgasm.

While she was still recovering, Rachel was surprised when she felt his hand slip away from her pulsating sex and begin to stroke the outside of her buttock. She remained laying on her side, exhausted from her climax as though it had required intense physical activity on her part even though she had barely moved, Gary making the pace. Rachel's eyes were lightly closed, the lamp light visible through her lids; she opened them when Gary's body eased back from hers and his hand dipped down between her buttocks.

Gary resumed his earlier kissing of her shoulder but this time it seemed as if he were trying to distract her from what his hand was doing as it explored the area where her sex ended and a patch of sensitive skin led to a less familiar area. His finger stroked her perineum as if scratching an itch. Rachel felt it through her as surely as if it were electricity and she shivered at the touch. When the tip of his finger found the grooved cleft between her buttocks, it paused, becoming coy. He probed the border of the fissure, not attempting to penetrate it and Rachel sighed in a way she hoped communicated her desire to him. It was unusual for her to be aroused by a touch of such a kind, but she was, and she wanted him to go further.

He did. Carefully, his finger massaged the dry ring of muscle, stretching her cheeks apart and pulling at the orifice while he did. Rachel felt wide open and exposed as Gary used his hand to spread the cheeks of her rear so wide, revealing the anus. Each time he pressed and pulled at her, she felt herself relax and the muscles loosen. If, when he had first touched her, the idea of what he might do seemed impossible, it now began to seem inviting as he gently fingered her, never venturing too far beyond the outer fringes of her quivering orifice.

The finger stopped abruptly and disappeared. His hand was on her shoulder, easing her over from her side and onto her front. Rachel rolled with the movement, pulling a pillow under her chin and resting her head on it. The covers were pulled off and she shivered from the sudden rush of air and the chill on her back. The mattress sagged as Gary knelt between her legs, Rachel opening them enough for him to fit himself in the gap. For the first time, Rachel heard him murmur and then a long breath of approval. She lay and waited for him to continue, wondering what he would do next.

On the soft skin of her buttocks, his hands felt large and slightly coarse, enough to create a pleasing friction. He cupped her behind and then massaged the globes, pulling them wide apart in a way that was crude and revealing, the air cold on the normally hidden area around her anus. As he carried on, she became conscious of his thumbs pushing in towards her, his hands moulding her flesh like clay. The two thumbs met at her anus and he used them to pull the tiny cleft wider. Rachel felt the resistance of her body and moaned at the straining feeling he was creating. She raised her head from the pillow and stiffened her back while he probed his thumbs a fraction and managed to enlarge her further.

The whole of her backside, the puckered fissure of her anus especially, were warm and slack and Rachel found it hard to tell exactly what he had done to her, but she felt ready for him. A wet finger pressed onto her anus and before she realised what he was doing, the first half of his finger was inside her. His finger was barely lubricated enough but she was able to accommodate it, the intrusion rough and creating a burning sensation. With his free hand, he eased her sphincters apart to enable his finger to get further into her and it felt more like he was fitting her around himself rather than he penetrating her. Gary wiggled his finger and the radius of his movements made her realise how tight she still was.

Rachel cried out when the finger withdrew, the wetness long since dried and the passage of the digit harsh. Gary was leaning over the side of the bed and then he was back where he had just been. She heard the sound of plastic, a cap being flipped up. Even though she knew what would follow, it was still a shock when the cold lubricant ran onto her anus. The feel of it was liquid and she wondered what it might be. Baby oil, she thought. He poured some more on and the groove of her buttocks ran slick with it.

In the midst of the oily fluid, Gary's finger returned and almost floated into her. The transition from him being outside and then inside of her was virtually impossible to discern. She bit her bottom lip as his finger went in all the way to the knuckle and examined the smooth interior of her anus. He explored deeply and thoroughly, touching her in places she would never have dreamt he might. It was so intense and personal and yet by sharing it with him, she felt at that moment as though he knew as well as she did herself. At first, his finger was implanted as far as it could go, the broad knuckle wedged into her as he made powerful circular movements. Then, he started to make thrusting motions in and out of her.

The act of his using her behind in the way he was had

become almost an end in itself to Rachel and when he stopped, she paused for a second and wondered what he was doing. She heard the sound of the bottle being squeezed but felt nothing on herself. He was slicking his cock up, ready to complete what he had so coyly began. Rachel imagined him kneeling behind her, his legs slightly apart and his strong hand rubbing oil over his cock until it glistened in the light.

With one of his hands resting near her shoulder and the other, she assumed, guiding himself, Rachel felt his phallus tracing over her as though aligning itself with her in readiness. He brought the head of his cock to her anus and, with barely a pause, pushed. The ring of muscle did not yield to his first attempts and Rachel wondered if he would be able to enter her. The circumference of his cock was greatly different to that of his finger, however well he had prepared her. He tried again, the both of them grunting, Gary sounding frustrated and slightly impatient. Rachel felt something give, as though the muscles of her sphincters had relaxed. He seemed to sense it too as he made a decisive shove and Rachel felt a stab of panic as she realised it really was about to happen.

The noise they both made when he entered her mingled into a shout of triumphant surprise. It was as if she could see him entering her with every sense in her body. There was a feeling of invasion, of crudity, of discomfort and, ultimately, of pleasure. Gary slid himself in to the hilt in much the same way he had done with his finger and Rachel felt his groin bump against her buttocks. He was supporting his weight on both hands and the area of his pubic hair was the only one which made any real contact with her own body. The position gave him the freedom to lever himself back and forth with ease.

At first, he moved in and out slowly and with no great depth, giving Rachel a chance to become accustomed to his presence. The restraint he showed gave the first moments of the act a tenderness along with a hint of the ferocity to come. Rachel gripped the pillow tightly as he made small lunges, her muscles relaxing a little more each time he did so.

Gary withdrew and Rachel closed as tightly as she had been a few minutes earlier, as though he might never have been there. She felt his hands on her hips, pulling her up to a kneeling position. Rachel complied, going up on her knees, spreading them wide and keeping her head down on the pillow, displaying her behind for him. He moved about, adjusting his position, and Rachel felt more exposed in the new posture, her anus brusquely on dispay for him. The posture stretched her buttocks taut and made her feel as though it had tightened her and that it would make his entrance more difficult.

He wasted no time, pushing into her quickly. Rachel backed onto him, grinding herself from side to side. The thrusting started immediately, ruthlessly quick and efficient. His cock felt harder to Rachel, but she could not be sure if it was because she had never done this with him before or if it was the novelty of the act that had increased his excitement and, therefore, his size. Slowly, Rachel became used to it, the relentless nature of his pounding into her. The sensation was initially focused on the tight clench of her anus but slowly spread through all of her body in a warm wave.

Gary's hand, so adroit, reached round her and toyed with her sex, making swift caresses all over before massaging her clitoris. It had not occurred to her that she might have an orgasm in the course of this but his sudden groping enlightened her as to how close she actually was to a climax. What would it feel like to come while he was in her behind? she wondered. It would not be long before she found out if he carried on in the way he was, she thought.

The rhythm of his hand and of his whole body synchronised to the point where he was plundering her methodically while working diligently at her sex. Rachel sighed and gave up the last vestige of control as he inflicted himself on her.

When it came, her orgasm was a mix of everything; what he was doing to her, what she thought about it and what she thought about him. It was devestating to have an orgasm that was so intimately tied to that moment whereas normally she would soar free from the situation as the pleasure momentarily blinded her to the world outside. Rachel forced the orgasm from herself in desperate sobs, her breath practically gagging and the neglected muscles of her sex undulating.

Gary's movements took on the tenor of near climax, his cock hard and fast in her backside. He slowed down and then he speeded up again, as though unsure what he wanted, faced with too many options for release. Eventually, it no longer seemed to matter as he flailed about behind her, calling her name over and over as he ejaculated into her behind. Rachel did not feel it as precisely as she would have had it been in her sex, but there was a tingling sensation of warmth that she knew would blossom into a long lasting glow. While he ejaculated, his strokes took on a final harshness that made Rachel wide-eyed, crying out almost as loud as him in the shocked feeling of strain he sent through her. When the lunges subsided, they collapsed into an unruly pile on the bed, Rachel's chest aching from the frenetic breathing.

'Rachel,' he said between breaths.

Again, it had the ponderous tone, something lurking behind it and wanting to make itself known. It had been there in the silence of the last few minutes as they lay next to each other, looking up at the ceiling. Rachel wanted to stop him saying anything else, but she could not.

'I think I'm falling in love with you,' he said.

She lay, not speaking, the enormous complications brought about by his simple expression of feeling already too much to contemplate.

Chapter Nineteen

She found him in the kitchen, leaning against the sink and looking out of the window.

'Snow's cleared,' he said without turning.

'You're up early,' she said.

'You're leaving today, aren't you?' His back was still to her.

'Yes.'

'Why?' he asked.

'Because I have to,' she replied.

'You don't have to do much of anything you don't want,' he said, barely any tone in his voice.

For the first time since her arrival in Portsmouth, she remembered who she was. Who she really was. The real Rachel Franklin she had tried to leave back at her stopover in Hartford. Names and thoughts banished for the previous days suddenly besieged her mind. Oliver and Damien. Blake Jordan, Carl Milken and Gloria Vaughan. Her mother, Liz Benton and Nikki Price. And, of course, at the centre of it all, Rachel Franklin. Is that person really me? she wondered. Did I do those things? The audition – a nightmare, surely.

'Gary, this was only meant to be a brief visit. Whatever might have happened, has happened; I always knew I'd be leaving. So did you,' she said.

'I thought you might stay, at least for a while.'

Rachel hovered by the table, not sure if she should approach him. She wished some of his reserve and calm would display itself. Even if he seemed placid on the surface, Rachel could sense the strength of the feelings buzzing away under the surface.

'Gary, it's so obvious, I shouldn't need to say it. Look at us,' she said, raising her arms at her side even though he couldn't see her. 'Look at me, Gary,' she said.

He turned and leaned against the sink, his arms folded.

'The business in New York, it was an audition for a part on Broadway. I made a real mess of it and it's been wonderful to hide away from it all out here, but I have to go back now and face it.'

'You never mentioned an audition.'

'I've been trying to forget it since I arrived. That's the problem with being here, it's too damn easy to forget everything. I remember the first holiday I went on without my parents, just me and two girlfriends, and we spent the last three days planning to live in Greece. We were so certain we would do it.'

'So, do it this time,' he said.

'Gary.' She paused, trying not to get angry. She wanted him, needed him, to make it easier for her. 'Gary, even if I stayed here another week, I'd still have to go back. It's better if I go today.'

'What you mean is, you're afraid if you did stay here a week more, you wouldn't want to leave.'

'I have a career, family, friends. I've known you for less than two weeks even if you count the time ten years ago.'

'It was you that came here, Rachel. No one forced you.'

'No one forced me,' she repeated, as though weighing up the words. This time, it was her voice which sounded flat in the stillness of the kitchen, the same room where it had started a few days ago and similar to the kitchen at her mother's house where they had faced each other in moonlight ten years earlier. 'I'm aiming to leave late this afternoon, so we could spend some time together today.'

'Zak's coming over this morning. I'd like for you to meet him,' Gary said.

Rachel drew in her breath. Images of meeting the small child and possibly his mother flashed before her eyes unpleasantly. The situation suddenly closed in on her and felt constricting. It was like discovering her least favourite aunt and uncle were coming to visit, the desire to run off and hide upstairs until they had left.

'You didn't mention this yesterday,' Rachel said.

'Is it a problem?' Gary asked.

'It seems a bit, I don't know, of a bad idea? What will he think if he sees you here with me?' she asked.

Gary just shrugged.

'I'm not going to play that game, Gary,' she said.

'What are you talking about?' he asked.

'Playing house, here with you and him. That's not fair. I remember how confusing it was when my parents split up and I was sixteen. No,' she said, the last word a mix of defensiveness and decisiveness.

'All I want you to do is meet my son.'

'No,' she said again, more to herself as she fidgeted on the spot, eager to be moving. Almost before she realised it, she was walking out the room.

'Where are you going?' he asked, following her.

She was halfway up the stairs when he called out loudly and firmly. 'Rachel!'

'What?' she asked, stopping and turning.

'Where are you going?'

'I'm going to pack. I'm leaving,' she said.

Gary massaged his temples with the tips of his fingers. 'Look, we need to talk this out,' he said.

'You might need to, but I'm going,' she said, starting back up the stairs.

'So you're running out again?' he asked.

'That's right,' she said flippantly. Inside, she felt herself switch off from the emotion of the moment as though she were floating somewhere above it. She went to a different, more peaceful part of her mind where she no longer had to deal with the situation.

'Do you know why we left early, when we were in England?' Gary said.

It stopped her dead and snapped her back to attention. Her foot was in the air, about to hit the step. For a moment, she paused.

'Do you?' he asked again.

'No,' she said, wanting desperately to know.

'That night, when we were in the kitchen together and you ran off?' Gary said.

He was making each sentence into a question as though trying to draw her to ask what happened next. She would not respond and yet she was rooted to the spot, her back still to him.

'I was going to come to your room. Really, I was. I felt it so bad and I stood in that kitchen for a long time wondering what to do,' he said, his eyes distant as he focused on the memory, his eyebrows arching in thought. 'When I looked up, your mother was standing in the doorway, just looking at me, like she knew what I wanted to do. Like she knew even better than I did.'

Silence.

'She was looking for me, Rachel, I swear it. She's never told you that, has she?' Gary asked.

'You're lying,' she said quietly.

'Why would I do that, Rachel? We were in that kitchen and the next thing, she's opening her robe.'

Rachel looked at him, finding it hard to keep her eyes on him. What he was saying did not make sense but it had a horrible ring of truth to it. She swallowed and tried to speak but was unable to find words.

'I still think she told your father about it, probably because she wanted to make him jealous. He exploded and before I knew it, we were all on a plane on our way back.'

She put her hand to her mouth which was hanging slightly open, as though she were looking at something awful. The muscles of her jaw felt weak and the whole of her face trembled with emotion. Gary was measured in his words, the earlier badgering rhetoric replaced by a sadness that chilled Rachel. She did not know what to do, a restlessness making her shake. Rachel ran, taking the last half of the staircase two steps at a time. She slammed the bedroom door shut and began gathering up her things frantically, shoving them into her bag.

Gary was still in the kitchen when she marched down with her bag. She had not even bothered to collect her things from the bathroom, she was so keen just to get away. His look was one of genuine surprise, as though he thought she might just have been in her room sulking.

'Where are you going?' he asked, standing.

'I told you before. I'm leaving.'

Gary ran beside her all the way to the car and she thought for a moment he was actually going to try and stop her physically. All he did was call out her name, over and over.

He was still calling it as she pulled away, the wheels of the car spinning noisily on the gravel until they bit into the ground and she made the first lurch towards home, her eyes filled with tears.

Chapter Twenty

'Come on, come on,' Rachel snapped as she butted at the bell on Ollie's entryphone, waiting for the speaker to crackle into life.

It was not possible, Rached had discovered, to rush back from somewhere like America to somewhere like London. It was possible to *be* in a rush, to want to arrive as quickly as possible, but the enormity of transatlantic travel and the various stages of the chain militated against it. It was like running into an oncoming wind. She kept to the speed limit most of the way to Boston, the snow thinning to almost nothing the further south she got. At Logan Airport, she paid an outrageous surcharge to leave there instead of delivering back to New York and she was about to dump or give away most of her luggage when she walked past left luggage. Her original return ticket no longer relevant, Rachel toyed with the idea of getting a shuttle to New York and then Concorde. The cost did help define just how much of a rush she was in, but the idea of it still nagged at her until she finally found a flight almost about to leave.

'Come on, Ollie, for Christ's sake,' she said again.

The Picadilly line from Heathrow had seemed the quickest way of completing the journey, Rachel had felt unable to face sitting in the back of a taxi, fidgeting her way along the elevated section of the M4. Instead, she had fidgeted on the train, counting off every stop and continually revising her estimated time of arrival in Covent Garden. It was just after ten-fifteen and something she had not counted on in the long distance dash was Ollie not being at the other end of it.

'Hello?' It was Oliver's voice, scratching through the slits of the metal speaker.

Rachel was just turning to leave. 'Ollie, it's Rachel. Let me in.'

'Rachel?' His voice was already alert.

'Let me in,' she repeated.

The door buzzed.

Oliver met her at the door of his flat as she clumped up the stairs with tense, straight legs.

'Where on earth have you been, darling?' he asked as she pushed past him.

'To hell and back,' she said.

'What's wrong? I was worried about you. All your mother would say was not to worry, which of course made me worry even more. I tried calling Blake but he wasn't taking calls and Damien was no use at all.'

She turned and looked at him, his stout hairy legs sticking out from the dark blue satin dressing gown. 'You are alone, aren't you?' she asked.

'Of course,' he replied.

The resolve, the tension, the anger and the fear of the previous few days gave way, along with her facial muscles. She threw herself at him, clinging to him and sobbing loudly. He rubbed her back but did not ask questions and she was grateful for it.

There had never been sex like it between them before and she did not expect there ever would be again. Still, he did not ask questions, as though not interested in her reasons for it or who she might be imagining him to be. Oliver was strong, silent and there for her at that moment and, in a way, she loved him for it.

Rachel removed Oliver's robe and directed him to the bed where he lay on his back, propping his head up on a doubled over pillow. He stared at her and Rachel returned the look with a gaze that felt mesmeric to her. The loose clothing, comfortable to fly in, came off easily and quickly and soon she was standing naked at the end of the bed. Most of the needs she brought to the moment seemed to be emanating from her subconscious and Rachel was not sure how much control she had over the situation.

Sitting astride him, resting her backside on his knees, she set to work manipulating him. He seemed tired, a little off guard so early in the morning, early at least for Oliver. His shaft was tumescent as though it had been erect recently and lolled back into its current semi-ready state. Like the rest of him, it was warm from recent sleep and Rachel was comforted by the heat. She tickled at the hairs covering the tops of his thighs and the sac of his balls, squeezing them tenderly and drawing a gasp from Oliver.

She moved herself closer, bringing her sex nearer to him and rubbing his shaft gently over her pubic hair, watching and feeling it become harder. When he was fully erect, glans straining at his foreskin, she used the tip of his cock to stimulate her clitoris. Rachel did not let him enter her but just played the head of his cock into the centre of her labia. There was a timeless feeling to the moment, brought on by the effects of the time difference she was suffering and the desire to escape her emotions, however briefly. It was hypnotic, automatic, the way she sat on him, knees spread wide and sex exposed, toying at herself with the swollen phallus.

With no sense of how long it had taken to get there, Rachel came. The shocking force of it was enough to stir her from her rigid composure, the sensation of the climax softening the set of her muscles and giving pleasure in a long release of energy. She kept his cock pressing on her, harder than she might have normally, as though searching for a deeper release, something locked away. The orgasm died with a quiver in her vagina, an empty clench that demanded more.

Rachel had barely recovered from the orgasm when she found herself turning her back on him and squatting over him, lowering her behind and feeding his long shaft into her eager sex. The suddenness of it caught her unprepared and she was tighter than she might ordinarily have liked. It did not deter her as she sunk onto him, using the weight of her own body to force him in. There came an instant when she felt the large blunt head pressing on the opening of her vagina as though unable to go any further. Rachel paused and felt the hardness on the unyielding muscle and was overwhelmed by the fact that he was outside of her but would soon be inside of her. He made no effort to shove himself into her and Rachel anticipated the prospect of penetration for a while longer, trying to keep the current feeling in her mind as she readied herself.

'Uh.'

It was a small word on her lips, tight and strained as it came from her throat. Rachel pushed down, using her full weight, and her eyes widened as he passed over the boundary of exterior and interior. It felt impossibly wide, hazardous almost, but it was what she wanted more than anything else she could think of right then, crying out as she sank with her full weight onto his tremendous cock. Along the silken tube of her sex, his cock advanced, dilating her crudely and probing far inside her. Her behind came to rest on his pubic hair and she put her hands on his knees, but not before reaching under herself and carefully jiggling his balls, pulling them from where they were pressed between the cleft of his closed legs.

Rachel rode him powerfully and soundlessly. It was animalistic but in the most placid way, the act of sex overwhelming. When she found the correct momentum and posture, Rachel was able to use a free hand to touch herself, feeling where he opened and entered her. Crouched over him, her back arched, his cock buried in her and a hand masturbating herself, Rachel ground away until she could do nothing other than climax. In the midst of the long strokes she made on him with the movements of her behind, Rachel came a second time. She was able to incorporate her orgasm into the whole act of making love to him, barely missing a beat as she sat atop his throbbing cock and let her vagina shimmer with elation. Her sex had slackened and lubricated itself to accommodate him and it now fluttered around his bony member as she contorted her body from side to side in heated paroxysms.

The orgasm, like the first, subsided swiftly and it seemed to her that climax was no longer the point of the sex. There had been times in the past when sex had brought on several hard fought and won orgasms but now they seemed to flow from her with ease, without a fight, and it gave the act a relentless feeling as though it could go on forever until she gave far more to it than she could ever take.

Oliver's hands squeezed, stroked and parted her buttocks, his first real sign of involvement. She knew he liked to do it in their current position, where she could have been anyone as far as he was concerned, man or woman. It suited her too, being able to use his body simply for sex and literally not have to face him. In her first real acknowledgement of him, she took her hand from herself and let it roam on his scrotum and then down the scratchy line of his perineum, using the edge of her fingernail to create a friction. He squeezed her behind encouragingly and she carried on tickling him, feeling his cock pump up inside her.

Images began to form in her mind, populating what had been up until then, a wilderness. The plainness of just having sex with Oliver became something more complex, involving Gary, Damien, Oliver and New York. Christopher. Her mind had gone from empty to full in a matter of seconds and now she brimmed with passion as though suddenly reconnecting it.

A moistened finger probed her anus gently, pressing only an inch or so into her. Rachel squeezed Oliver's balls in her hand, increasing the pressure until he yelled. She lifted herself up and down off of him with gathering speed, pushing both of them towards orgasm. Rachel leaned further forward, putting both hands on the bed and changing the angle at which he was entering her. She moved from side to side, wriggling on his cock so firmly implanted in her. They paused, taking a breather, respite before the final onslaught and she used it to flex herself around him and adjust her position until she felt confident about the prospect of another orgasm.

Rachel resumed her movements and Oliver too joined in, lifting his groin to meet her and his hands still stroking her buttocks and caressing the tiny knot between them. Each time he splayed her buttocks wide, his large hands holding them almost fully, she felt under his control and on display for him. Rachel thought about what he would be seeing, the dark centre of her rear pulled wide into a lazy pout and the sight of his cock disappearing into the folds of her dripping sex.

It happened even quicker than she expected. She had been thrusting wildly and noisily for not more than a minute or two when Oliver began to fidget and shove his groin more insistently, not just reciprocating her movements but demonstrating his own needs. The thought that he was almost ready to come inside her made Rachel shudder, the resolve to hold her next climax back crumbling. The idea of him heaving beneath her as his thick and hot semen ejaculated into her was overpowering.

Rachel was coming again, crying out and shaking her head from side to side, when she heard Oliver cry out and felt his hands clamp onto her behind with a vice-like grip. For a moment, she regretted not being able to watch the contortions of his face but the noises he made and the struggle he put up were enough for her to measure what was going on. In the midst of her own orgasm, the long aching contractions of her vagina, she felt the pulse of his sperm and its steadily spreading warmth. All the while she climaxed, her insides were being sprayed with his semen. It was a long and intense orgasm for them both, the mutuality of it far greater than the sum of its parts. Rachel held onto him, riding him far beyond the boundary of his desires and her own, until they both cried out, the physical nature of the act painful when no longer directed towards freeing themselves from pent up desire.

She lifted herself and removed his cock, covered in her juices and still quivering, much as her own sex was. Rachel flopped down on the bed, her head near his feet, cheek resting on his calf and one of her legs draped over his torso. She felt the semen move inside her, a light trickle of it on the innermost part of one thigh.

'Ollie, make me come one more time,' she whispered.

Rachel lay on her side, head towards the bottom of the bed, eyes closed and one leg raised in the air as Oliver sat up and put his hand between her legs. His hands explored her recently plundered sex. Rachel felt loose around him, wet with her own juices and filled with his seed. As Oliver masturbated her, his whole hand working itself at her, Rachel lay and felt the strangely hot and itching nature of it. The passage of her vagina was overheated and his fingers, it felt like more than one, slid easily up her. It was audible, his rough manipulation of her. It was as though he knew she wanted him to be quick and cruel.

She lifted herself onto an elbow and seethed, her face hot and sweat trickling down a reddened cheek. Rachel opened her mouth wide and made long heavy panting sounds. Her head dropped back to the bed and she ground her forehead into the mattress in time with the squirming of her groin onto his hand. It was his large, square fingers plying her where he had so recently been, that finally moved her. In a set of twitching movements, Rachel orgasmed, the feeling emanating from every recess of her sex. Her body shook, first violently and then with a tremble. Rachel cried small tears and held herself in check for a few moments longer, working against the climax before letting her muscles yield to it. Rachel flopped onto the mattress, out of breath and finally spent.

Ten minutes had passed before Oliver spoke.

'What was all that about?' he asked, as he laid a gentle hand on her hip.

Rachel sat up, turned herself around and lay her head on his chest, his arm falling onto her and pulling her close.

'I've fucked up, Oliver,' she said.

'Tell me what's happened.' He stroked her back and planted a kiss on her hair.

'Where do I start? The audition was a disaster. I was so ready, so focused, and then I let myself get thrown. It makes me angry because I am usually so calm when it comes to the crucial moment of something like that.'

'When Damien and I spoke, he said you had slipped off. I told you Blake wouldn't take my calls, still less return them. You must have made quite an impression,' he said.

'I found out when I got there that Gloria Vaughan was up for the same part, which is fair enough, but the bitch gatecrashed my audition. I couldn't believe it.'

'And?' he asked.

'And we got into a huge row. I was rude to everyone,' Rachel said.

'Everyone?'

'I told Carl Milken to go fuck himself.'

'Hmm,' was all Oliver said, as though weighing up how reasonable such a statement might have been. 'And then your disappearance.'

'Not really. I was going to tell you when I got back in any case. I went to visit a friend in New England, a boy I haven't seen for ten years. We spent the most wonderful couple of days together and I'd probably still be there now if

I hadn't got panicked by the speed of the situation.'

'This boy, he's the road not travelled, I take it? He's special?' Oliver asked, his hand soothing on her shoulder.

Rachel nodded her head against Oliver's chest and sniffed.

'Two weeks ago, I was at the end of a successful West End run, turning down offers of work to have a break and get myself centred again. Now look at me. I'm a mess, for Christ's sake. I'm trying to renew a schoolgirl crush and I told one of the twentieth century's greatest living playwrights to go fuck himself.'

'I wouldn't have minded seeing that,' Oliver said, drily. 'Is it possible to rescue the situation with Blake and Carl? Do you want me to try and intervene?'

'It's nearly Christmas, Ollie. I want to leave it, talk to Liz and Mum. And Damien.'

'You might as well know this,' Oliver said.

'What?' she asked.

'Details of your trip to New York leaked out. Your erstwhile friend and fellow student Nikki Price featured it in her column.'

Rachel had a sudden recollection of the sex party.

'What did it say?' she asked, anxiously.

'Just that you and Damien were spotted on a romantic pre-Christmas shopping trip. The usual guff, no pictures.'

'How the hell did she find out?' Rachel asked.

'Darling, the tabloids stake out departure lounges. Either that or you have a mole.'

They lay in silence.

'Do you love this boy in America?' Oliver asked.

'Ollie,' she said.

He squeezed her. 'You should be in love with someone. You shouldn't be with an old bastard like me, old enough to be your father. I rather hope you do love him.'

'Thank you,' she said, drifting into sleep comforted by his words.

Chapter Twenty-one

Rachel sat in Liz Benton's office, two days before Christmas, and nibbled at the corner of an ever-shortening nail as she listened to the noises of acknowledgement, agreement and neutrality Liz made during a mostly one-sided transatlantic conversation with Blake Jordan.

'Okay, bye,' Liz said, pausing for a moment with the receiver before setting it down gently, as though afraid to wake it.

'Well,' Rachel asked, her hand still to her mouth.

Liz sipped from the can and spoke almost as she swallowed. 'It's not looking good. Milken was absolutely furious with you. Blake is trying to be conciliatory and I think he knows they were in the wrong. Gloria Vaughan has a movie offer, one of many, but one that interests her and the whole production of which is awaiting her say-so. My friend at William Morris says Gloria enjoys the power that gives her, the idea that a simple yes from her can put something in motion, sets built, that sort of thing. That doesn't surprise me. Movie stars,' Liz finished.

'So, is she going to do the play?' Have they offered her the part?' Rachel asked.

'Blake's too polite to say. I think she would be their first choice. And, being frank, their second choice. I can understand them wanting to string you along in case, but basically, dear, you should think about that rest and put all of this behind you. I thought you didn't want the part in any case?'

'Yesterday, I didn't. The day before, I did, and, the day before that, who knows? You know what irritates me the most about all of this? For all the rudeness and how stupidly badly the whole audition fiasco went, I just can't keep away from the script. The characters won't stop smouldering away in me and I can't put them out,' Rachel said.

'So, you do want the part? Today, at least?'

'Is there any way at all you can turn this around for me, Liz?' she asked.

'Nothing will happen before Christmas. Go down and join your mother in Oxford and forget about it. We'll talk again in the new year.'

'I'm not going away this year. I've decided to stay at home,' Rachel said.

'What does Susan think about that?'

'Mummy doesn't mind. Every year she says I can do my own thing if I want and I've always secretly thought she'd balk when I finally did, but she's been fine with it all.'

'You're not going to spend Christmas alone, are you?' Liz asked, her voice concerned and inquisitive.

'No, of course not,' Rachel lied indignantly.

In fact, spending Christmas alone was precisely what Rachel planned on doing. The idea of some self-imposed solitude was appealing. There was something comforting and monastic about the prospect of being at her own whim over Christmas. Her mother had asked her to go away to the sanctuary of the house in Oxford as usual, Ollie had suggested Rachel could tag along with him, wherever he ended up and even Damien had hinted he might be willing to be dragged from the security of his precious family on her behalf. Each offer was appealing and appalling in its own way and Rachel had opted to be nowhere in particular over the next few days. Christmas was still two days away and it gave Rachel a buffer, a period of time she could use to avoid the thought of what Christmas alone was actually going to be like.

The only small hitch in the plan was she had not yet told her mother. As far as her mother knew, Rachel would be arriving in Oxford tomorrow. Whatever lie she made up, there was a danger Liz might call her mother, although Liz understood as well as Rachel the sacrosanct nature of the country retreat and the highly unfavourable way any phone calls were looked upon.

'Are you going to tell me where you disappeared to after the audition?' Liz asked.

'I had to see a friend. I'd been planning it in any case and when the audition went wrong, it was the best time to do it.'

'Only that your mother seemed so certain you were okay, I might have jumped on a plane and gone looking for you. When Susan told me you were not to be disturbed, that's fine, but I could live without having to field a phone call from an angry producer during which I have to pretend I know my client's whereabouts when, in actuality, I don't.'

'I'm sorry', Rachel said, nodding and feeling comprehensively told off.

'You don't strike me as the prima donna type, Rachel, unless you're planning to age into it.'

'Like my mother,' she said, the inevitability of it suddenly frightening.

'Don't think your mother, think Gloria Vaughan. Is that how you want to be? I was more worried about you than anything else. You're not the first person to have disappeared when things go badly. From a career point of view, I wouldn't worry about it. It was a very contained incident as far as I can see. If you'd done the same thing in London, with Peter Hall or someone like that, well . . .' Liz let the sentence hang in the air.

'Point taken. I have no plans to do it again, believe me. It wasn't all my fault. Not even half of it was my fault. Twenty percent, maybe, but that's my only liability. I don't want to labour this point, but all I'm saying is, if you can turn this around for me, I'd be ready to give it another go.'

Liz was writing something on a small piece of paper. She handed it to Rachel. 'Here's a number where you can get me over Christmas. Call me if you want to. If I hear anything in the next day or two, I'll call you. Now is not the time for us to look too keen.'

'Thanks.'

'Are you sure you'll be alright at Christmas?' Liz asked again.

'Of course,' Rachel replied, plastering a falsely confident smile over the words.

Chapter Twenty-two

Swathed in warm clothes which began from a tight-fitting thermal core and gradually layered into gently flowing lines, Rachel sat on the bench outside the Coach House Cafe in Marble Hill Park. It was ten minutes before eleven, ten minutes until the cafe would open, and ten minutes before Damien was due to meet her. The lack of cloud cover made the air sharp on Rachel's face, the high sun making no apparent difference. Rachel lifted her scarf to protect her neck from the icy draft and wiggled her toes in her boots, trying to keep the blood flowing through her extremities.

Damien's disguise was becoming almost as distinctive as his normal image and as he strode along the path in baseball hat and sunglasses, Rachel recognised him instantly, even from a distance. She couldn't see his eyes behind the dark sheen of the lenses but she imagined they would be regarding her with detachment. On the phone, when they had arranged to meet, Rachel found his responses frosty as she had expected, only the minimum yes or no answers passing between them to arrange the current rendezvous. Rachel did not blame him for being so distant under the circumstances. What would he be like by the time the afternoon was over? she wondered. He came and sat next to her almost as though they were strangers about to exchange secret information.

'Hi,' he said.

'Hi. How are you?' she asked.

'I'm fine. I'm cold. Can we get coffee?'

'It doesn't open until eleven, I think. Are you going to take those glasses off?' she asked.

He complied almost immediately, using both hands to lift the frames away from his head. When he had done so, he still did not look at her, his eyes set on some distant point in front of him. Rachel stared at him and watched his eyelashes as he blinked. Sitting on the bench with him had the awkward feeling of a second date to which there would not be a third. The park was empty save for a woman walking a short, squat dog along a far off path. In the background, Rachel heard the faint click of crockery as the cafe readied itself for a slow day. The cold had penetrated all of her clothing with a stealth that had left her numb rather than shivering. It was a profound feeling of cold, not one that chattered over the mere surface of her body. Rachel found herself wondering what it would be like to work in the comforting small cafe behind her, not to be so involved with everything all the time. Would it be the same way in Portsmouth, at Cup of Joe, with Gary, she wondered too quickly to be able to put a lid on the thought.

'Damien, I'm sorry about leaving you like that. Things got out of control and I needed to get away.'

'I only went in the first place to keep you company. Oliver convinced me you wouldn't really want to go on your own. If you didn't want me there, you should have said.'

Sitting on the bench, twiddling with the plastic tortoise-shell frames of his sunglasses, Damien looked and sounded so young to her that it made Rachel want to cry. She reached out and rested her hand on his, stopping his fiddling with the frames. For the first time, he made eye contact with her, but only in his petulant, Damien way. They were, in truth, not close enough to each other to inflict any real kind of emotional hurt. They related to each other almost like wilful teenagers, able to squabble and make up quickly in the space of sentences and Rachel enjoyed the freedom that gave them both.

'We could go back to mine and I could make hot chocolate,' she ventured.

Damien smiled.

Hand in hand, they walked along the towpath. The
worst of autumn was over for the trees, harsh twigs and
thin trunks revealed. The river was choppy in the breeze,
churned up by the occasional boat which sent long waves
lolloping towards each bank. Off to the right, the houses at
the top of Richmond hill were lined up as though at the
very edge of the horizon, nothing behind them but a sheer
drop.

'What's happening in Birmingham at the world of
Oakwood?' she asked.

'Closed set right now. You remember Charles Turner
who played the bank manager supposed to be involved in a
fraud and who did a runner?'

'Yes.'

'He's coming back into the show and the producers have
been trying to keep a lid on it.'

His grip on her hand was casual and unforced and the
walk pleasant. It was so close to Christmas and yet Rachel
felt nothing like festive. Her mind was in so many places at
once. However much she tried to find a peaceful, thought-
free part of her brain, it soon led back to familiar questions. *A Winter's Tale*. Gloria Vaughan, Carl Milken, Blake
Jordan, Gary. All of them so far away physically and yet so
proximate mentally.

Bed seemed the natural place to drink hot chocolate in the
middle of a chilly winter weekday. Rachel had left the
heating on before going to meet Damien and the house was
welcoming. When she entered the bedroom carrying two
steaming, oversized mugs, Damien was already in bed with
the covers pulled up around him. His sprout of hair stood out
vividly against the denim blue of her sheets and pillowcases.
Removing her robe, Rachel got into bed with him, aware that
as comfortable as the situation was, her bed was not the best

place to tell him what she had been doing in New England.

Their small sips were the only thing breaking the silence, the chocolate absurdly sweet and yet still bitter in the aftertaste. Damien drank more greedily than she did and after only a few gulps, his cup was half-empty. Snuggling up to Rachel, he lay his head on her shoulder and put an arm over her body. She smoothed the hair of his crown and felt the rise and fall of his chest against her side. At times, she found he could be brash and cheeky, their sex crude and athletic, and yet at other moments, like the one they currently shared, he could be shy and sensitive, a passionate lover for his age. Rachel wondered if he did it consciously, recalling times when he had put on a performance for her solely for the purpose of getting his own way.

'Are there things you wished you'd done?' Rachel asked, stroking the skin on his upper back.

'Got the part in Dr Who,' he said.

'Not like that. I mean with other people. There must be things you'd like to do that you never tell anyone about,' she said.

'This isn't one of those dare games, is it?' he asked.

'I'm serious. You must have fantasies about what you'd like to do.'

'I suppose,' he said, warily.

'Tell me one, then,' she said.

Rachel felt his breath on her when he sighed. 'Rachel,' he said.

'You're not shy are you? Not Damien Todd,' she said, teasing.

'We've done plenty of things, Rachel. I'm not sure there's much left. That party in New York was pretty wild. A lot of things went on while you were in that box,' he said.

'I know,' she replied.

'Not just for you. I meant me, too.' He paused. 'This couple, man and a woman, were coming onto me, really stronging it. They weren't much older than me.'

Rachel listened, excited. Damien's voice took on the London lilt it always did when he was revealing a secret, reverting to character as a shield. Each time he betrayed another cast member in the soap, his accent was the same as he leaned towards someone and spoke in a low tone.

'What happened?' Rachel asked.

'Nothing too heavy. He wanted to watch me and her, I think. Then he got a bit more involved, with both me and her.'

Rachel held her breath, feeling the tingle of her sex between her legs. 'What did he do?'

'Just touched the both of us. Ran his cock over my back and stuff. He was more interested in getting himself off. I was on top of her, kissing her and stuff, and he starts putting his cock between us, wanting us both to kiss it.'

Damien paused and Rachel realised he knew it was exciting her and that she wanted to tease it out of him. It made her feel naughty to ask such questions.

'And did you?' she asked.

'What?'

'Kiss it.'

'It was no big deal. It wasn't like a full blow-job or anything. The next thing I know, he was gone and then he came all over my back.'

'That wasn't your first time with a man though, was it? What about that boy you told me about at stage school?' Rachel asked.

'Yeah, but he sucked me then. This time, I was curious and it was a sort of now or never thing.'

'Did you enjoy it?' Rachel asked.

He shrugged his shoulder against her, as though it were no big thing either way.

'You're getting off the subject, anyway. I asked if there were things you wanted to do with me, not other people.'

'Is this one of those Christmas present things, where I get you to dress up as a maid and chase you round the room with a cane?'

'Maybe,' she said. 'If that's what you want. I'm just being nosy, that's all.'

'There was this girl I used to go out with when I was eighteen,' Damien said. 'She was gorgeous, a bit shy in some ways. I was going through a heavy magazine phase, stories more than pictures, not that I told her, but I got this real hang-up about wanting to come on her face, like you read in those stories. I was too scared to ask her in case she thought I was a pervert. It was a big deal for me at the time, but don't ask me why.' He stopped. 'And don't ask to do it now, please, it'd be chronically embarrassing.'

'Embarrassing because you want to?' she asked, hoping to tease him.

Damien did not reply. Rachel unlinked herself from him and leaned over to look him in the eyes. His face had a demure expression, the trace of feigned indifference Rachel always saw when Damien was trying not to betray his true feelings. For a moment or two, she let him dwell on it, glancing at him occasionally. When Rachel acted out whims and fantasies of her own, she was always surprised at how quickly desire could take hold of her, how easy it was to go in a certain direction once her mind had tipped that way.

Rachel nuzzled herself into Damien's chest, her own breath hot as it came back in her face. Finding a nipple, she kissed it and closed her mouth carefully around it, letting her tongue toy at the soft point of flesh as it slowly hardened. Moving further along, she planted kisses on the rubbery, taut skin covering his stomach, curving her back to get further down the bed, the covers still over the pair of them. As she found the edge of his pubic hair, she was in darkness, only able to feel him. His cock was already hard and Rachel held it in a firm grip.

Damien raised a leg and his groin moved nearer to her face. Briefly, Rachel took him into her mouth, not intending to linger for very long. Easing his foreskin back while his cock was in her mouth, she felt the skin unfurl through her lips and found the protuberance of his glans under the head, tunnelling her tongue into their cleft. There was a musky, manly smell which aroused her as it engulfed her. Rachel sucked lightly on his cock, using her lips as a fine sheath. From above the bedclothes, she heard his gasp as her tongue darted about over his phallus, the blood engorging him and making him spasm involuntarily in her mouth.

The movements in his legs were twitchy and restless and Rachel thought he might be about to come. She was deciding what to do when there was a rush of cold air and a flood of light as Damien threw back the covers. He removed himself from her mouth and rolled her from the hunched position on her side over onto her back. Rachel lay motionless, letting him determine what would happen next. Damien got to his feet on the mattress, its springiness appearing to make him uncertain, and placed a foot under each of her arms. Squatting down, be brought his cock level with her face, one hand on his shaft and the other stretched out to keep his balance. His small round balls hung away from him as he crouched over her. Rachel could see the fine hair from his ball sac glint in the light and she followed the trail along the smooth skin that led to his behind.

Damien was masturbating himself with a definite and precise rhythm. Rachel had never seen the act at such close quarters and it fascinated her to watch his stiff cock and the foreskin going back and forth over it to reveal the bright red phallus. His hand looked thin and delicate around the dark-skinned stalk it gripped. When the foreskin was back, she looked at the slit in the head of his cock, thinking of the way heavy pearls of semen would spurt from him. How often did he do this alone? she wondered. The position of his body above hers was difficult for him, crude and dominant and yet there was something about it which was tantalising, the idea of him using her in that way to achieve his orgasm. To achieve his climax and then spray its results over her face.

Laying on her back and watching him manipulate his cock, Rachel found herself longing for him to come. She wanted to feel the splatter of hot semen on her cheeks, her forehead and on her lips, letting it gather on them before slipping out her tongue to get the acrid taste into herself. There would be a good view of his climax from where she was and when it happened, she would feel very much a part of it.

Rachel tickled the base of Damien's balls with the tips of her fingers and she could almost feel the tingle in her own body.

'Finish me off,' Damien said to her, tension in his voice.

She took hold of his cock and worked the shaft between her fingers, letting most of the pressure fall on the ridge of his phallus and the glans beneath the head. His body felt as though it were resisting the orgasm, straining against it. Staring up at his torso made his body seem impossibly long and slim, a wave of pleasure visible all through it. Rachel kept the speed of her hand steady, not too slow or teasing, but more directed to bringing him swiftly to the edge and allowing him the relief of tumbling over it.

Damien let his head fall forward and then stretched it back, grimacing towards the ceiling as though looking for something. The muscles of his legs stood out from the strain of maintaining his position, an unusual and excruciating posture for an orgasm, Rachel suspected. Although she was in control of the movements, it was still Damien who dominated all else. Squatting over her, his cock pointing rudely at her face, he was the one who would shower her with his seed.

As she felt, sensed almost, the beginnings of his climax, Rachel no longer allowed her eyes to roam over his body and, instead, came to rest on what she held in her hand. Focusing on his cock and its bloated head and straining shaft, Rachel waited for him to come. When his body rocked and his muscles tightened, all movement becoming more intense, Rachel picked up speed, using her fingers on him with a relentless speed.

Damien gasped, sounding almost surprised, and Rachel braced herself.

When the first long spurt left him, Rachel was looking hard at the eye of his cock and was amazed at the speed with which it ejaculated. The heavy string of semen travelled a short distance in a perfectly straight line before falling onto Rachel, landing on her left cheek. Even as the wet heat radiated from the patch of come, another was issuing from him and this time landing on her forehead. The third ejaculation hit her where she wanted it to, had so carefully been directing his cock to ensure it did – on her lips. The semen formed a small pool, running into the join of her closed mouth. Rachel opened her mouth and licked her lips eagerly, his fluid hot and infused with his sex. Several more loads of sperm came from him like a fountain and Rachel moved her head from side to side, letting herself be showered by him.

Semen, hot and pungent, covered her face and Damien remained in position over her, breathing noisily and erratically. Rachel let him slip from her grip, turning her attention to herself. Her fingers still tingled from masturbating him and she used them to gather the semen from her forehead, poking her tongue out to collect what he had deposited on her lips. Rachel licked her fingers clean and used them to carefully retrieve his come from the various parts of her face. The taste was profound and sexual, a way of taking him into her that was both novel and exhilarating. She realised that Damien had been staring down at her, watching her as she toyed with the moist skin of her face.

Damien shifted his body and leaned over her. He gave her a long, deep kiss which excited her because she knew he would be able to taste himself in her mouth. When he spread her legs and shoved his head between them, Rachel cried out and held him tightly, lifting her back off the bed and writhing until she could do no more than call his name out in a triumphant climax.

Chapter Twenty-three

It was too early for Rachel to be able to tell if spending Christmas alone was going to be a mistake. Ollie was away in Prague and had readily accepted Rachel's story that she would spend the holiday with her mother. Damien thought she was at her mother's and her mother thought she was at Damien's, the gulf between the two of them a useful screen behind which Rachel could hide. There had been only one phone call so far that morning and it had been a wrong number, a child trying to phone an uncle to say thank you for a present. Rachel had found herself putting on a deliberate cheerfulness with the small voice at the other end of the line, an overly breezy tone that she thought was unnecessary. Eventually, the mother had come on the line and apologised profusely for disturbing Rachel, eager to let her get back to things. Let's talk for a while, Rachel thought about saying, I don't have any things to get back to. It was only after she had put the phone down that Rachel realised it was the first person she had spoken to that day, the first words she had uttered apart from the usual test of her voice on rising.

Rachel had never been alone on Christmas day and it was interesting to let each moment pass and use it as a measure to see how well she was doing. It seemed absurd to be on such tenterhooks the whole time, as though waiting to catch herself bawling at the slightest thing. Today was going to be a day like any other she had told herself. She would be happy with her own company, like she was during the many solitary days she passed throughout the year. Yes, I am enjoying myself, she said to herself.

Then why did it feel so strange? There was an atmosphere, a silence that seemed to hang over the whole of London, making her feel as though she had to creep around the house. If I'm no different to the way I am on any other day, she reasoned, there must be something mystical and specific about the day itself. Still in her robe, she sat on the sofa with her feet tucked under her, an oversized mug of chocolate on the side table and the heating on a degree or two higher than normal. A little later, she would have a bath, perhaps read or listen to music. Her *Pygmalion* was being repeated on television later that day, but she didn't have the heart for it.

Soon, there would be one or two small lies in the form of telephone calls to Damien and her mother. At least neither of them would ask to speak to the other. What were they doing now? she wondered. And Ollie, where was he? She smiled to herself when she thought of what he would most likely be doing, an image of him as a santa surrounded by scantily-clad elves filling he mind.

And where would Gary be?

Since arriving back from America, Rachel had more or less suppressed all thoughts of Gary, putting him back into the place she had kept him for the last ten years, where she should have left him in the first place. He had made no attempt to contact her, although after she had ran out the way she did, it did not surprise her. It was no different to the way he and his family disappeared ten years earlier, and now she knew why. How could she face her mother? The exchange of Christmas gifts between them had been more muted than Rachel was expecting, as though her mother knew what Rachel had learned, had sent Rachel there to find out.

In the quiet of the house, not even the sound of passing traffic to distract her, Rachel floated as though in isolation. At some point in the middle of the silent contemplation, her hands worked at the belt of her robe and she let it fall casually open, as though unnoticed by her. Her actions must have been connected to the emptiness of the house, the feeling of being a naughty teenager left alone while her parents were off for a dirty weekend.

With no more than a shrug, the cloth fell free of her shoulders and on down her back. The light rush of air it created made her shiver but the room was warm enough for her to go naked. Perhaps she would go naked all day. A completely nude Christmas. Possibilities began to suggest themselves. There were things she could do, pleasurable things that did not involve anyone else. Rachel felt brazen in her nakedness and it stirred fantasies in her. She was tempted to see if she could find a pizza shop open that would deliver so she could surprise the delivery boy by going naked to the door, giving him a Christmas present he wouldn't forget, whatever he was like. An image of young Christopher flashed in her mind, stretched out on the bed and crying out in desperate, inexperienced joy.

The thoughts made her wet down between her legs and the idea of a hot bath was enticing. In her mind, she tried to think of implements in the house she could use on herself, anything with even a slightly phallic shape suddenly springing to mind. However confusing relationships may have got, Rachel still burned with a desire requiring satisfaction, regardless of who it was harnessed to. She wondered if she would ever find someone towards whom the energy she had would flow and be returned in kind. When it happened, she trusted herself to recognise it. It was almost like that with Gary, she said to herself.

Ignoring the thoughts, Rachel submerged herself into the realm of the purely physical, concentrating only on her body and needing no one to reflect the potency of her desire. The bath running slowly, Rachel stood in the room and, surrounded by rising plumes of steam, carefully caressed herself, teasing her body awake. Not even sure if she was trying to make herself come, her manipulation was light and, she supposed, selfish in the true sense. The stroking motion became almost hypnotic and she lost herself in it, her eyes out of focus and staring off into an impossible distance.

Rachel knelt in the bath, the water a mite too hot but her skin adjusting to it. The water did not make it even half way up her thighs and she had plenty of room to get at her sex. Wetting her hand in the water and warming it up in the process, she enjoyed the feel of slightly hot fingers on the pliable lips of her labia. She bit her lip and pushed a finger into herself with a slight force, testing the way before she began in earnest. Inside, she was slick and ready for herself, her mind concentrating on no particular person or act, fantasy hardly required in the face of the basic physical release she needed.

The sound of the water as it fell from the tap in a thin line and on into the bath was soothing, making her feel a bit sleepy even though she had not long been out of bed. It was the sort of day she could easily drift through in a pleasant haze, as though anaesthetised by a small amount of alcohol and letting time buzz past her.

Only a little stimulation was required and Rachel gripped the edge of the bath with one hand while the other fiddled between her legs, tweaking her clitoris. The tight channel between her legs was practically itching for something more and Rachel trawled through her mind once again, certain there was some implement so deliciously perfect for her and yet she was unable to remember what it was, still less where it might be.

Even the thought of finding something, along with the gentle noise of the water and the rawness of the act on such a special day, were enough. Rachel's legs quivered and she made waves in the bath as she climaxed. The surface of the water rippled with the movements of her legs, a visible record of the surge of pleasure sweeping through her insides and on into the world through the energetic spasms of her muscles. Rachel's sex moved in short clutching actions and a shiver went down her back, all of her muscles tightening and then relaxing after a blissful moment in which she was not certain if she was moving or completely still.

Laying back in the hot water, Rachel refused to let her thoughts come back to anything specific. Even though she knew all of the things that played on her mind were still bobbing about below the surface, Rachel was content to douse them for a while.

The doorbell sounded louder than usual and made her jump, firing her quickly from the reverie. Any trace of the earlier sleepiness was quickly purged, all her senses functioning and questions firing off. Who was it? What did they want? It was a nuisance to get out of the bath but it could have been important. It was Christmas, after all, and no one should be calling on that day of all days.

As quickly as she could, Rachel hopped out of the bath, towelled herself with quick dabs and put the robe back on. She pulled the dressing gown tightly around herself and put the chain on the door before opening it. She peered round the side and through the gap.

'What are you doing her?' she asked Damien.

'I could ask you the same,' he said.

'I promised I'd give you a call later,' Rachel said.

'You didn't say where from, though. You're supposed to be at your mum's in Oxford,' he said.

Rachel removed the chain from the door and stood on the threshold as though defending territory.

'So?' she said, a trace of petulance in her voice.

'So? So, I was feeling bad and missing you and decided to give you a call at your mum's,' he said.

'Oh, Christ,' Rachel said, imagining the drama that would surely follow. She was surprised her mother hadn't rung already. 'What did you say to her?' she finished.

'Well, lucky for you I didn't get a chance to say much. I was about to ask for you when your mum went into this big one about how nice it was of me to invite you to spend Christmas with my family,' Damien said, smirking.

'And what did you say?' she asked anxiously.

His smirk broadened into a grin of self-satisfaction. 'Please. I recovered fine. I told her I was phoning to wish her a merry Christmas and that you didn't know I was calling. I wanted to thank her especially for letting you come. And I said you'd call her later.'

'I'm impressed,' she said.

'Can I come in now?' he asked.

'What are you doing here?' she asked.

'Are we back to that again? I wanted to see you.'

Rachel let him in, watching the way he eyed her. The naughty feelings returned and amplified with the presence of Damien. He was always ready to try something, she thought.

'I thought you had to be in the bosom of your East End family? Don't you all get drunk before midday, fight during dinner and sleep all afternoon? That's what you told me. It sounds unmissable,' she said.

Damien slouched on the sofa, his legs stretched out and his arms folded. 'I told you, I wanted to see you.'

'And it couldn't wait?' she said in a way that sounded strangely sympathetic.

'Not really,' he said.

'We didn't say merry Christmas yet, by the way,' she said. 'Do you want anything to drink? A brandy or something?'

'Rachel.'

The way he used the word stopped her and made her slightly apprehensive. His tone implied she might be about to hear something she didn't necessarily want to.

'What is it?' she asked.

'I, um.' He stopped and tutted, rubbing both hands through his hair. 'They've been filming this documentary about the show that's going to be released on video for the five year anniversary. I told you about it.' Again, he stopped. 'Nikki Price was on set because they want her to do some of the links and the voiceovers. Can you imagine why? We spend all this time being told to keep out of the papers by the producers and the next thing we know, we've got the tabloid gossip columnist from hell on set. I think they thought it would boost sales, the idea of this woman behind enemy lines.'

Rachel waited.

'I'm sorry,' he said and as he did, Rachel felt her heart descend through her chest and on into her stomach. She knew exactly what he was going to say. Not because she knew Damien, but because she knew Nikki even better.

'At first, she came on to me strongly and I thought it was because she was interested in you and me,' Damien said. 'After a while, when she kept on, it seemed like she was genuine.'

He stopped as though there was nothing more to say, that Rachel would be able to fill in the blanks. It wasn't too hard for her to provide the rest of it. Rachel smiled and let her head fall onto her palm. Slowly at first, she began to laugh, not a heavy or hearty sound, just a resigned acknowledgement of the stupidity of the situation. Rachel remembered the good times with Nikki, such as they had been, the way they had discussed men together and now, here was this boy, caught up in the middle of them and thinking he was in control.

The laugh subsided and she thought for a moment, looking at his expectant face.

'Damien, I know we didn't exactly swear chastity vows when we got together and I've never pried any more than you have, but didn't it occur to you that a situation with Nikki might have been slightly compromising?'

'She told me she wouldn't let it be like that.'

'But it was. Look at all that crap she wrote about me. I could have warned you,' Rachel said.

'That night, when your play finished and you came to the hotel, Nikki had already been to see me. She told me she'd seen you at the party. I could tell she enjoyed having the one up on you, but that wasn't what I wanted.'

'So you know what she can be like?' Rachel asked, rhetorically.

'Are you pissed off at me?' he said and she felt the full force of his boyish charm, its volume cranked up for her benefit.

'I just think you're bloody stupid,' she said, sighing.

'I thought you'd be well annoyed,' he said, still looking at the same patch of carpet he had observed through most of the conversation.

'When did she first turn up on set?' Rachel asked, knowing it was really a way to ask him how long it had been going on between him and Nikki.

'End of September,' he said.

Inside, it made her flinch slightly as she remembered how strongly she had felt about him during that period, horribly premature thoughts that she may have found the right one. Mostly, it felt like a close call, a near miss disaster. Her mother would wag her finger knowingly when it all came out.

'Is it serious, with you and her?' she asked.

'Yeah,' he said quietly.

'Damien, be careful,' she said.

'I'm sorry,' he said.

Rachel looked at him and for some reason, it was like a weight lifting from her. 'Just tell her to stop writing about us now or I'll have to reveal a few of her drama school secrets,' she said.

'Do you know what I'd like to do?' he asked.

'What?'

'To make dinner here and then go for a good long walk. What do you think?' Damien asked.

'I think that would be wonderful,' she replied.

Chapter Twenty-four

The small white bust of Mozart stared impassively back at Rachel who was cradling the cool, palm-sized piece of marble on top of her opened hand.

'Ollie, I don't know what to say,' she said, giggling.

'Darling, this was the *least* tacky, believe me. I thought I really ought to bring you back some kind of Christmas gift.'

In the lazy interim between Christmas and New Year, they were sitting in Ollie's Covent Garden flat, just before lunchtime, nibbling at some sweet walnut bread he had made, sipping wine and chatting amiably.

'I would have bought you something too, but I thought you weren't the present type, not after the way you railed on about your birthday,' Rachel said.

'Hate all the present bit, don't mind all the eating. I wouldn't have got you anything but you seemed so in the dumps before I left, not that Mozart will do much to cheer you up. He looks so bloody miserable.'

'I still feel bad, not getting you anything.'

'Darling, Prague was one long Christmas present,' he said.

'Meaning?'

Oliver sighed and made his eyes look glassy. 'I'm in a deep passion at the moment. I might not have come back at all except I wanted to see people over here, you especially. I worry. How was Christmas with your mother?'

'I didn't go,' she said.

Oliver sat more upright in the chair, leaning forward

across the dining table to look at her. 'What did you do?' he asked, his eyes boring into her as though he might be able to see the answer if he looked hard enough.

'I wanted to spend it on my own. After everything that's been going on over the last month, it seemed like the best thing to do. It got to the point where I felt I'd spoken to enough people and I wasn't getting the chance to listen to myself think. Do you understand what I mean?'

'Completely,' he said.

'I'd started this very solitary day and it was weird. I thought it was going to be like spending a day doing prep on my own, but it felt like I was the last person alive on the planet,' she said.

'A bit like the mother in *A Winter's Tale*,' Ollie said.

Rachel nodded. He was always so in tune with her. 'Anyway, half way through the morning, Damien turned up on the doorstep.'

'Trussed up with tinsel, I hope,' he said lewdly.

'Not quite. I assumed we would, well, do what we usually do when we meet, but he had come especially to talk to me.'

Rachel told Oliver the story of Nikki Price and Damien, surprised that she felt no real hurt or jealousy as she did. Oliver must have picked up on it in her tone.

'You seem remarkably calm about all this,' he said.

'I've known Nikki a lot longer than I've known Damien. In fact, I've also known Damien longer than Nikki has, so if anyone in the triangle should have the most perspective, it would be me.'

'Why would she do such a thing?' Oliver asked.

'Nikki? She could be jealous, possibly of me and possibly of Damien. I hope it works out for her, and for him, I really do.'

'I could tell he was a wily one, but Nikki Price?' Oliver pretended to shudder. 'I may be bisexual, but even I draw the line somewhere.'

'Damien can cope with her. He can be a right little sod when he wants to, a mummy's boy who can twist you right round his finger.'

Oliver exhaled sadly. 'In my day, we knew our bloody place and we were grateful that people wanted to even watch us do what we did. If you were an actor, you'd be stopping and thinking. This is so unnatural and the fact that someone will pay to watch me do this is amazing. Now, they think the opposite. We're lucky to get to see them. Well, power to them,' Oliver said.

'He's still young,' Rachel said.

'You're not old, dear,' he replied.

'I know, but he was starting to make me feel that way.'

'So, where does that leave you, my little spinster?'

'Back where I was a month ago, where I should have stayed before I got into all this. When *Crossed Wires* finished, I should have just taken the break like I planned. Sometimes, in a really facile way, getting excited about a part is like buying something you can't afford. All that remorse and worry.'

'I can't help feeling responsible. It was Blake that sounded me out and me who pushed the two of you together, and encouraged you to go to New York.'

She reached out and touched his hand. 'For God's sake, Ollie, I'm a big girl. I don't want you to take the blame for me just so I can feel better. It's down to me. I saw the part and got hungry for it.'

'Milken may have been a bastard, but it *was* a hell of a play, even the bit we saw. I'd play it if they'd let me drag up,' Ollie said.

'I know. That's the sting with it. Even just before Christmas I was harassing Liz Benton to try and rescue the situation for me.'

'And could she?'

'I don't know. I haven't even spoken to her since and I don't care. I'm over it. I want to be free for a while.'

211

'And do I stand in the way of this greater freedom?' he asked lightly.

'Of course not. We've never stood in each other's way. I want you to go and have your Prague passion. I can see you in your apartment in a silk dressing gown, typing away at your memoirs and being brought Earl Grey tea to aid you along. You should go for it, Ollie.'

'You might be right. If nothing else, I could corner the market in Mozart statuettes. If you do clear the decks for a while, what will you do with your time?' he asked.

'I still hadn't worked that out when *Wires* finished. Go off to Northen Italy and paint?' she laughed. 'Who knows? That was meant to be the fun part, the adventure.'

'And the man in America, Mr Right?'

'Ditto as the play. Over it. You get so wrapped in something, you forget how easy it is to just step back and say, No thanks. I was fine a month ago, I can be fine again.'

'Well,' Oliver said grandly, raising his glass, 'to freedom.'

'Freedom,' Rachel repeated.

Chapter Twenty-five

In the front room of the house in Kew, Rachel and her mother sat at opposite ends of the sofa, awkward and as though they were strangers meeting only for the second or third time. It was the first time since the swapping of Christmas gifts that Rachel had seen her mother and the conversation had yet to get going. Rachel remembered the silences as similar to the ones between her mother and father when some drama or other had robbed her parents of the will to communicate with each other.

Rachel realised she was never going to be able to talk to her mother about Gary and what he had told her. In retrospect, Rachel felt foolish that she had sat in her mother's kitchen, the room where it had almost happened ten years ago, and told her about her feelings for Gary. How must it have made her mother feel? Rachel felt no malice towards her mother. Why should she? Her father had philandered enough in his time and it seemed, if anything, a bit unfair that her mother's one transgression should practically end the marriage. That was so like her father, she thought. What was fine for him was not allowed for his wife. The involvement between Gary and her mother, whatever it may really have been, was, Rachel decided, not her business and she would be content to let it remain a long-term secret. Back then, her own feelings towards Gary were unrealistic in any case, she told herself.

'How did you enjoy Christmas with Damien? He seems quite polite, nothing like he does on the telly,' her mother said.

'I didn't know you watched it,' Rachel said.

'I've seen one or two episodes. Did you have a good time?'

'Yes. His family are hard work, though. Lots of them and they're all hyperactive like he is,' Rachel said, surprised at how vivid the imagined recollection was.

'Are you getting serious about him, now you've met his family?'

'Not at all. In fact, he's had his eye on someone else for a while and we've agreed to part ways, sort of. I think we'll still be friends, but nothing more.'

Her mother seemed to regard her with a kind of sad, but resigned shock, as though she had known a statement like the one Rachel had just made had been coming for a long time and now that it had, there was no gladness in being right. 'And you're not hurt by this, that he wants someone else?'

'Not really,' Rachel said.

'Is it anyone you know?'

'No. I hope it works out for him. Damien and I would never have lasted in the long run,' Rachel said.

'You were a bit too similar, the pair of you. Besides, it never does to have two on the go at once. Oliver Kelton must be very happy.'

'Honestly, Mother, the way you say his full name, Oliver Kelton, so formally, as though you're reading it out in court,' Rachel said.

'He's too old for you, Rachel.'

'You know what? That's exactly what he told me himself. Ollie is such a kind man. He wouldn't want to tie me down. I can't understand why you've never liked him,' Rachel said.

'I look at him,' her mother said, 'and I see that glint in his eye and it reminds me of your father and that's no good thing, Rachel.'

'So you think I've actually been going out with Daddy all this time? Thanks for telling me.'

'Rachel, don't be crude. You know what I mean. It's a roving eye he has.'

'Well, you'll be pleased, then. Ollie and I have given each other our freedom,' Rachel said, conscious she sounded a touch pompous. 'He's going to have a rest for a while, possibly write his memoirs. You might even be in them.'

Rachel could not tell if her mother was flattered or appalled at the idea. It was more likely to be pleasure as her mother could not resist attention of any kind.

'Rachel, what's going on? I may not have welcomed all of your boyfriends with open arms, but why the sudden need to be on your own?' her mother asked. 'Is it because of me running them down?'

Inside, Rachel managed a smile. Her mother could almost always find a route back to herself in any conversation. If she had done *A Winter's Tale*, her mother would have been such a resource.

'I just got bored keeping two of them on the go. Even with their cooperaion, it was a nightmare to schedule and I was the one who ended up with no time of my own. I thought I might as well go all the way and I couldn't really lose one and not the other. It wouldn't have been fair,' Rachel said.

'Wouldn't have been fair? You can be so cool and calculating at times, darling. I don't know where you get it from.'

'Of course not,' Rachel said.

'What a horrible year it's been. I'll be glad when it's finally over. If Damien and Oliver are off the scene, what are you planning to do?' her mother asked.

'What I should have done before. Nothing. I'm going to sit at home and read some books, watch television. I might go for a holiday somewhere.'

'The play in America is definitely off?'

'As far as I'm concerned it is.'

'Does it feel strange to say you're actually not going to be working?' her mother asked.

'A year or two ago, it would have. I think back then, I was afraid that if I stopped, I'd never get started again. Now, I just need to prove to myself I can take a break from it and live without it if I have to. It's almost like an addiction.'

'Well, if you need company, I'm always here. You only have to call or drop by.'

'Did you speak to Daddy at Christmas?' Rachel asked.

'He called me in Oxford on Boxing Day, wanting to speak to you. He actually sounded hurt that he wasn't told you would be elsewhere. I think he wanted to say sorry for missing your closing night.'

The phone rang in the kitchen and her mother rose casually to go and answer it.

Rachel sat and listened to how noiseless the room was, her mother's voice no more than a mutter in the background. Is this what it would be like for the next six months? One long Christmas break. At the moment, it was easy because most people were on holiday and in the mood to do relaxing things. What would it be like by February, when it was cold and everyone would be back at work, apart from her? How willing would people be to spend time with her, all chirpy and unencumbered. Perhaps she would be left with only her mother for company and they would merge into spinster sisters together. Rachel caught herself on a runaway train of thought and giggled.

'It's for you,' her mother said, returning to the room.

'Who is it?' she asked.

'Why don't you go and see?' her mother said.

Rachel hated it when her mother did that. Nervously, she walked to the kitchen and picked the receiver up off the counter.

'Hello,' Rachel said.

'Darling, you've got a recall. Blake Jordan wants you back in New York for another try,' said the voice of Liz Benton.

Chapter Twenty-six

In the mid-morning stillness of a rehearsal room off Broadway, Rachel sat in silence, her thoughts perfectly collected in her mind and her feelings under complete control. Coolly, she regarded Blake Jordan and Carl Milken as they fidgeted on their chairs in front of her. A few moments ago, Blake had asked, implored, Rachel to take the part in *A Winter's Tale*. She enjoyed the obtuse angle Blake's neck had achieved in the grip of his obvious tension and now she was making him wait, staring at him, then at Milken, then absently off into the distance. Rachel had decided she would not be the next person to speak.

'I know things went wrong last time you were here and I feel personally responsible for that,' Blake said. 'I should have managed the situation better. Not all stars have your grace and I must be losing my touch not to realise that.'

Rachel was not flattered by it, although part of her did feel sorry for Blake. She turned to look at Milken as if to say, Well, what about you? Milken gave Jordan a quick sideways glance and Rachel practically felt the mental kick given to him by Blake in order to get him to speak.

'Rachel. We, I, feel you would be ideal for this piece. Looking back, I'm not sure why we considered there would be competition for the parts,' Milken said, his lines not as well memorised or rehearsed as Blake's.

Rubbing her chin and trying to appear in deep thought, Rachel continued to give the best performance she had in a long time.

'It was good of you to come out here again, and at such short notice. I imagine you must still be interested or else you wouldn't have come?' Blake said in a friendly tone.

'The shopping is wonderful and you are paying for me to be here, so it's more like a holiday for me,' Rachel said, barely able to keep petulance out of her voice.

'The play is virtually finished and I'd like to get into rehearsal with it, once we've found the two actors for the husband and boyfriend. I think you'll like the way the story's developed even more than you did the original version,' Milken said.

'Well,' Rachel said. 'You live with a script and a part in you for a while and it always grows in directions that are unexpected.'

It was a neutral statement and Rachel could see it had irked Milken.

Blake Jordan sat back in his chair and Rachel could see he was wily enough to realise they weren't going to get an answer from her there and then.

'Take a day and enjoy the shopping, Rachel. Let's reconvene late tomorrow afternoon, say here at four, and we can talk some more. If you don't mind, I'd like to give Liz Benton a call,' Blake said.

'Feel free,' Rachel said.

'We'll see you here, tomorrow at four then,' Blake said.

'Looking forward to it,' Rachel replied.

Chapter Twenty-seven

'Hello,' Rachel said, the sound of the phone in the hotel room strange and oddly disconcerting.

'What are you doing here?' she asked.

She listened for a moment longer.

'You'd better come up then,' she said, replacing the receiver.

Gary stood a foot or so away from the threshold of the room, as though afraid to cross it or not certain he would be invited in. It must have been on his mind as he asked, 'Can I come in?'

Rachel looked at him for a second and then nodded curtly, the gesture almost resigned.

'How did you know I was back in New York?' Rachel said.

'Your mum called me, told me where you were staying.'

'That must have been nice for you. What did you do, discuss old times?' Rachel said, almost giggling at the absurdity of the moment.

'I didn't come here to fight, Rachel,' he said.

'Well, I didn't come here to see you, Gary, actually.'

'Okay,' he said, lifting his hands up in the air. 'I'll leave. Is that what you want me to do?'

'I don't know,' she said.

'Look, I'm sorry for what I said and I'm sorry for trying to steamroller you. All that stuff with Zak was way out of line.'

Rachel sighed and sat down on the corner of the bed. He

walked over to the window and looked out of it, his back to her.

'What happened between your mum and me, it was stupid, but it had nothing to do with you. Whatever feelings you might have had back then, it wasn't the right time. But when you walked into the coffee shop before Christmas, that was different. And that's what I'm interested in, not a bunch of stuff that's ancient history now.'

'Gary, I'm back here because they're keen, very keen, for me to be in this show. I don't know if I'm able to say no to them anymore, even if I wanted to. It's a very tricky time and I don't need it to be any more difficult.'

'If you want, I'll give up the shop, leave Joe to run it,' Gary said.

'And what about your son, Gary? What's going to happen to him? You can't just give him up too,' Rachel said, thinking of the photograph she had seen of the boy.

'Something has to give, Rachel.'

'Why? Why does it have to give? It was a mistake for me to come and find you and that's my fault, but now we need to just get on, let it go.'

'When I said I thought I was falling in love with you, it may have scared you, Rachel, but I meant it. Still mean it. I *am* in love with you.'

'Gary, don't. You're making this really awkward for me.'

He turned from the window and stared at her. Rachel avoided his gaze but she knew he wouldn't speak again until she looked at him. Reluctantly, she met his gaze.

'I'll walk out now and I promise I'll never bother you again.' He spoke slowly and precisely. 'If you tell me to go, and that's what you want, then I'll go through that door and it's, "Have a nice lifetime". Tell me you want me to go.'

Rachel covered her face with her hands and exhaled, the breath hot on her hands. 'Stay,' she said, the word claustrophobic as it reflected back at her from cupped palms.

The end of the bed lolled under the combined weight of their bodies sitting on it. Rachel let her hands drop from her face and rested them on her knees. Gary put an arm round her shoulder. The arm which was resting on her shoulder trailed down her back, resting in the small of it and leaving a tingle beneath it.

Rachel sat still, not wanting to move, afraid it would take her in a direction she did not really want to go. Gary's fingers rubbed at the skin beneath the fabric of the blouse Rachel wore, his caress light and easy, leaving it up to her. This was as much pressure as he was going to place her under, she realised. How long could she resist? What about all the resolutions she had made, the clarity of purpose she had felt in London, telling her mother and Oliver she would be taking a break for sure, going her separate way from Damien. Didn't all that mean something? How could she sit there and just throw herself right back into the same situation that had failed her not once, but twice so far?

Turning so she sat side on to Gary, Rachel held the back of his head and kissed him. Still, his response was measured, as though not wanting to be the one who could be blamed for anything. That did not worry Rachel, who felt secure and convinced about what she was doing, both at that moment and in terms of what it might imply beyond it.

Rachel pushed Gary back onto the bed and clambered over him, her breath heavy and fast. There was something animal and desperate in the way she mounted him, their garments rubbing against each other as she mimicked in her clothes what she wanted to do when they were naked. Already, she could feel the hard and urgent push of his desire as she straddled him. From nowhere, her temperature had risen, making her face flushed.

They kissed greedily, almost biting at each other as Gary began to warm up as well. Their bodies were stiff at first, unfamiliar and awkward after their short break from each other, but slowly finding each other again. If there should have been questions in her mind, troubling thoughts about what she was doing, Rachel could not find them at that instant.

Slowing the pace, she began to undress him, not wanting to rush him to nudity. Still sitting astride him, she pulled him until he was sitting up and pushed the jacket he wore down his back, the faded grey cotton shirt beneath framing the broad set of his shoulders. Rachel undid the first two buttons on his shirt to reveal the line of his chest and put her hand on the warm curve, surprised at how pert the nipple felt as it protruded from the smooth flesh. Running her hands down his sides, she pulled the shirt free of the waistband of his chinos, slipping her palms beneath and brushing them over his hips and around his biceps.

Gary was looking at her, a smile somewhere deep in his eyes. Rachel found herself staring back at him so hard, she was almost looking past him, gazing at a distant point. Slowly, she popped two more shirt buttons open and took in the sight of his skin, so inviting. After a brief kiss, she pushed him back down and lay on top of him, resting her weight on him and enjoying the pressure their bodies created. His hands had begun to roam over her behind, squeezing it, the first real gesture of his involvement.

Rachel lifted her blouse over her head, quickly opening the cuffs so she could discard the garment. Reaching behind herself, she opened the clasp of her bra and then leaned forward to allow herself to spring free. The tightness of the strap left a slight ache when it was removed, a not unpleasant feeling that was almost like a tiredness. Immediately, Gary's hands were lifting and toying with her breasts, touching the nipples and cupping the pendulous globes in his hands. His touch roused her, made her want to rip the rest of her clothes off and ride him quickly, pleasuring herself on his rigid body, but she resisted, knowing the reward would be greater for the wait.

The position of her legs over him made her skirt ride up around the outside of her thighs and Gary pushed it up further, exposing her underwear. Reaching out and around her with his arm, he slipped a hand into it, squeezing one of the cheeks of her rear. In a sly motion, his fingers slid into the crease of her buttocks and pushed under to the sensitive flesh that led ultimately to her sex. Already, Rachel felt wet there, his touch bringing it on even more. Against the soft cotton crotch of her knickers, her sex felt as if it were bulging, her clitoris almost distended. Gary tickled the patch of skin with light fingertips and Rachel slumped towards him, the will to remain upright gone.

Gary slipped from under her, rolling her onto her back as he did. She lay and looked up at him, the light from behind his head framing him, casting a shadow across one side of his face. They remained still, appraising each other in silence. Rachel wondered what was on his mind, not sure what was on her own.

He stood, leaving her half-naked on the bed, and she wondered what was going on, a second of panic taking hold when she thought he might be about to leave. Without rushing, he undid the last buttons of his shirt, the ones she had not. Gary removed his shirt and unbuckled the belt of his jeans, fiddling with the top stud and then pulling the fly apart to reveal his underwear. Down on one knee, she heard him unlacing his boots and the heavy sound they made as they hit the carpet. When he stood and came back into her field of vision, he wore only boxer shorts, not the baggy kind, but ones that hugged close to his narrow hips.

The sight of him made her anxious and urgent for him, her remaining clothes suddenly seeming like a constriction. She reached a hand out to him, encouraging him to come back to the bed. Still standing, he leaned over her and removed her underwear, reaching under her dress and tugging at it. Rachel took the skirt off herself, barely able to wait. Gripping his hand, making sure she had him, Rachel pulled him back down onto the bed with her and they clung to each other, rolling around and kissing. There was the desire for sex, pressing away under the surface, but they were also able to simply be close, to toss themselves about on the large bed.

Side by side, they lay facing each other. Rachel stroked his flanks, then down over his hips and on finally to the tight curve of his behind. Gary's stomach was hard and flat, the suggestion of rippling muscle not far from the smooth veneer of skin. Trailing her finger down the line of hair beneath his navel, she groped into the thatch of his pubic hair, warm and wiry to the touch. From it, the base of his cock emerged, the long shaft hard and hefty. She held it in her hand, feeling its heat and remembering the feeling of it inside her, wanting it once again.

Gary laid his arm over her and the weight of it was comforting and exciting. Rachel moved closer to him, closing the gap between their bodies and feeling the heat where their skin touched. As they kissed and held each other, she felt connected to him by their physical gestures, understanding that their thoughts were synchronised.

Rachel felt his hand running down the bumps of her spine, over her behind and into the join of her legs. She raised her knee to open herself to him and his fingers trailed along the lips of her sex which were slick from her juices. His fingers probed, as though testing her or preparing her for something deeper. Gary was gentle with her, caressing the sensitive skin and then prying it apart and entering it with the hard and bony tip of his finger. In the tight but lubricated channel of her sex, the intrusion was like an itch that scratched itself, so deliciously agonising as it stretched and plundered her. As she became accustomed to the presence of his finger, so he seemed to push it further and then it was joined by a second digit, making her sex feel rudely dilated and invaded by him.

Back and forth, Gary used his fingers severely. Rache

fought against it, trying to hold back the orgasm that was trying to burst from her. It was difficult to resist the temptation to come suddenly and loudly but there was a certain pleasure in resistance. Rachel kept her mouth closed firmly and held herself in check, feeling as though she were already at the point of orgasm and was now simply allowing him to increase the intensity of the impending moment. The feelings were echoed in her sex which had become looser, her clitoris a hard bud in its centre.

Using him to steady herself, Rachel grabbed Gary by the shoulder, her muscles in a tremor across the whole of her body. The sensation was like a shiver, a chill which made her shake and was about to be burned away by the power of her climax. Gary moved his two fingers more quickly, the speed invigorating her and enabling him to probe deeper into her. She could feel the way his fingers expanded the narrowest part of her sex and made it pliable to his touch, ready for what would follow.

Rachel climaxed, still holding him and digging her nails into his flesh, soon coming up against muscle. The walls of her sex vibrated with the release, the orgasm gushing through her. It was a quick and vigorous action, intense in its nature but short in duration. Rachel bucked her hips, moving her groin against his hand, regulating the speed and riding the emotional high.

For a while, they lay and only the sound of their breathing could be heard in the room. The shadows were getting longer and the corners of the room were hidden in late afternoon darkness. Rachel stroked him, running her hands over his body and feeling the desire in herself and the power he had to satisfy her.

Moving herself upright, Rachel knelt between his legs, pushing his knees apart as he lay on his back. Leaning down, she held his erect shaft and put her mouth over its head. In her mouth, it felt warm and the flavour was slightly acid, the bitter-sweet taste of his sex. Not wanting to tease him, she simply used her mouth to make him harder, sucking and licking at him until he was full, almost bursting out of the sheath of skin that contained him. While she mouthed him, Rachel heard him groan and sigh, the noises almost surprised, grateful even. It would not be enough for her just to satisfy him by using her mouth. Rachel wanted him inside her.

Squatting over him, astride his lap in much the same way the situation had started out, she brought her behind down to his cock, which he held upright. Quickly, she found the tip of his phallus with the opening of her sex. Often, it was a slow and delicate process, the way she toyed at her sex with a man, a procedure consisting of part titillation and part need to be fully prepared. Not this time, she thought.

Boldly and heavily, Rachel sat down on his cock, letting it thrust through the outer lips of her labia and enter the narrow passage of her vagina, the juices easing the path of his cock. On his face, she saw how much he had enjoyed the suddenness of her act and she imagined it must have felt exquisite to be so suddenly covered by the hot and moist cavern of her sex as it smothered his inflated member.

Resting her hands on the bed, she let herself lean forwards and looked down at him. Rachel's hair hung across the sides of her face and tickled at her. She felt the finest veneer of perspiration over her forehead and also on her breasts, which Gary had once again begun to toy with. After the abrupt way she had allowed him inside her, Rachel took a pause, her behind resting on his groin and the tight sac of his scrotum against the join of her buttocks. Inside, his cock felt large, pushing far into her and pressing against the walls of her vagina.

Rachel used sharp movements that emanated from the area of her groin and stomach, rough lunges that brought her down onto him with a hard and bony bump. Gary's eyes widened as though taken aback by the ferocity of what she did and he lay there, leaving her to take charge. Her eyes were wide and as she arched her back, brought herself up and then back down onto him, she stared directly into his eyes, watching the way he flinched each time she buried him back in her.

The bed felt soft under them, the mattress unable to cope with the brute force of her attack on him. Rachel sensed he would not be able to last long under the weight of her onslaught but she was not troubled as she too needed freedom from the tension that had built in her, an urgency that was getting harder to control by the second. Without noticing, she had begun to grunt. Animalistic and base, it was the perfect vocalisation of what she did physically. The more she pummelled herself onto him, so he too made noise.

Rachel speeded up, surprised she had such strength within her. Partly she wondered if she were doing it as a way of scaring him, as though warning him about what he was taking on. Certainly, the expression on his face was a mixture of excitement and shock. Gary alternated between opening his eyes and then closing them, Rachel fixing her eyes on his the whole time so that each time he opened them, she met him with a stare.

Gary groaned in surrender and Rachel could sense he was about to degenerate into orgasm. Cruelly, she slowed her thrusts down until she hardly moved. He made a pleading noise and she gripped him with the muscles of her vagina, feeling the shape of him inside her. Soon, she would grant him liberation, but for a few moments longer she wanted to hold him in her grip, in a frantic last demonstration of her power before she gave into him.

Rachel knew it was over and began to speed up once again, maintaining the sort of rhythm she knew would give him what he wanted. When she did give it to him, Rachel knew that she would follow him into the orgasm, possibly tumbling at the same time as him and that they would be lost in it together. It made her feel unaccountably happy and sad at the same time, as though knowing she had reached some kind of peak and found something there she had long desired.

There were a few seconds, just before she felt him spurt inside her, when Rachel could do nothing other than look at him, all her other senses on hold as she pored over him, her eyes watering from the strenuous focus, or it might have been the first inklings of tears.

Gary cried out helplessly and Rachel timed the movement of her body, using it like an instrument and making it coincide with the audible cues Gary gave. The anticipation of his orgasm had made her edgy and anxious for her own climax and Rachel felt it stirring. Desperately, she concentrated on it, trying to bring it to life while still pleasuring Gary in a deft balancing act.

The overworked muscles of her sex tensed and then released, the flow of the climax soothing and ecstatic at the same time. Rachel was conscious of the way she was riding his cock while it emptied itself into her and she received his hot seed into the contracting depths of her sex. There was so much movement, at every level, that the motion was overwhelming, kept in check by the pleasure she felt all through her.

Rachel held onto the side of his body, feeling the waves of motion that his orgasm had forced through him. Gary's climax was tight and snatching, all his energy seemingly concentrated through the pulsing shaft that was embedded in her. Rachel's orgasm had passed the peak and was in the giddying decline that would last well into the next hour, whereas Gary still seemed to be twitching and groaning. It was a long and painful climax and Rachel kept going until he finally put his hands up and shook his head, asking her to stop.

Lifting herself clear of him, she knelt back between his legs and licked at his cock amid his loud cries of protest. Still hard and covered in a slick of her own juices, Rachel looked at it quivering and lifted a heavy pearl of semen off the head with her tongue in an operation so delicate she could tell his sensitive member had barely registered it. The taste of it was familiar and potent, the musky mixture of their sex lingering in her mouth like a residue of the effort they had expended.

In less than a minute, she was back at him, not finished yet by a long way.

Chapter Twenty-eight

Rachel flicked through the revised script for *A Winter's Tale* that Blake and Carl had insisted she take away from the meeting the day before. It was good stuff, she thought. The kind of material on which careers could be built. Rachel looked at her watch and decided to give Liz Benton another try. It would be almost nine-thirty in the morning in London and, although that was a bit early for Liz, she might be there.

The phone rang six times and Rachel was about to replace the receiver when the ringing stopped abruptly and Liz's voice echoed a hello down the line.

'Liz, it's Rachel.'

'Rachel, where have you been? I tried calling you last night but there was no answer. I thought you'd gone walkabout again.'

The phone ringer had been unplugged for most of the night, Rachel not wanting to be disturbed.

'I was out. Sorry.'

'Blake called me yesterday and is expecting to hear from me in about half an hour, your time. He wants to make a deal, Rachel.'

'What kind of deal does he want to make, Liz?'

'Pretty much whatever you want, darling. They know they fucked up once and they don't want to do it again. If you take the part, they want to go into rehearsals in the middle of January and do a preliminary out of town in Boston for ten days before opening in March on Broadway.'

Suddenly, it all sounded so tangible and real. They were making it too simple.

'Is the money good?' Rachel asked, hoping to find a reason to be unhappy.

'Very. There is something else though,' Liz said.

'What?' Rachel asked.

'I was talking to Greg Warren at Monk Productions. They've been let down on a movie. You know who let them down as usual. If you step in, they're convinced they can get it right this time, ride the Jane Austen wave. It'd be a starring role in a costume piece and the money would be better than doing the play. Shooting's scheduled for after Easter. But either way, Rachel, the money's good, so it's really down to you. It's decision time, darling.'

'It sure is,' Rachel mumbled.

'Sorry?'

'Nothing. When do they need to know how we feel about a movie?'

'They need to know we're keen. They've been put back once and the schedule's tight. They've got enough tied up in preproduction costs to hurt them if they cancel. It's the play that needs the immediate decision, that drives everything else,' Liz said. 'I can hold them off for a day or two on the movie but I wanted you to know about it in case it affects any decision you might come to.'

'There's no way we could do both, reschedule the shoot?' Rachel asked.

Liz laughed. 'So, go from doing no work to do doing two jobs at once? From what Greg tells me, it's been a nightmare for them to get clearance to film the exteriors in London and they want April for the right light or something like that. I can't quite see you commuting back from New York to do it after you take off your makeup, dear.'

'I could always not do either of them,' Rachel said.

'That's always an option and I'd back you if you go that way.'

'What do you think, Liz?' Rachel asked.

There was a sigh. 'Blake and Carl want you, you can smell the hunger, so if you let them down, I still think they'll understand. If you did the movie, it would be a favour. I don't want to put you down, dear, but they'd find somebody else if you don't take it, just the same way Blake and Carl will. You have to decide if you want this to be your moment or not.'

'You know I'm seeing Blake and Carl in about an hour and a half?'

'Yes. I still think Blake wants me to call him. It will be good to show we've talked. Let me make him think he's got the inside track. I'll mention you've been offered something else, see what he says. Then I'll give you a call back, you can go meet them and we'll talk again afterwards. I feel I should be there with you.'

'I'm big and ugly enough to deal with these boys, Liz, trust me.'

At ten minutes past four, which she considered to be suitably late, Rachel breezed into the rehearsal room where Blake Jordan and Carl Milken sat with palpable unease. They looked as though they might have been in the room for over an hour, fidgeting and waiting nervously, as if it were a dental appointment.

Blake, charming as ever, was on his feet and smiling as soon as she was in his eyeline. Milken remained seated and tapped a pencil on the pad that rested on his knee. Rachel took it to be a gesture of writerly composure.

'Thanks for coming back,' Blake said.

'No problem. I was passing anyway,' Rachel said lightly and they all laughed with ease.

'I spoke to Liz Benton earlier. You're a girl in demand,' Blake said as they seated themselves in the same tiny circle they had the day before.

'Things come out of nowhere. I told myself when *Crossed*

Wires ended that I was having a break. If I'd been desperate to work, I imagine the phone wouldn't have rung once. People have a habit of wanting you when you're indifferent to them.'

Blake gave her a broad smile and then remoulded his features until they were slightly more serious. He leaned forwards in the chair and put one hand on his knee, looking like an old man about to launch into a story around a camp fire.

'What can we do to persuade you to be in our play, Rachel?' Blake asked.

Make Gloria Vaughan play my mother, she thought.

'It's very hard, Blake. I don't want to seem like I'm being difficult about this. I know we got off to a bad start, but to be honest, that's past. In terms of what's been offered financially, I have every faith in Liz, so that side of things is a non-issue for me.'

'It doesn't leave us much room. I can tell you like the piece, Rachel. If fits you, even more so since Carl met you and did some rewrites. Do you see the difficulty? You like the play and the money is fine and we think you're great for it. It's as though everything's been said but the word yes,' Blake said.

'Rachel, there's something in you that's right for this.'

Carl Milken's voice was almost a shock as he had sat so quietly throughout. Rachel had to move on her chair in order to look at him properly, realising at that moment that she had been freezing him out with her body language. In his eyes, she saw something burning and knew that, behind the look, there was a genuine passion for what he wanted to do. For the first time since meeting him, Rachel was struck by the feeling that she could work with Carl Milken, that there was something to the man.

'Hell,' Milken said, 'I haven't directed anything in years, still less wrote anything and the whole idea scares the shit out of me. I look at kids like you who make it seem so easy and it makes me jealous. We could learn a lot from each other if we do this. You can screw Blake into the ground on money and conditions if you want. For all I care, you can have my fee too. You know, and I know you know, that's not the real point of this.'

Rachel sat and did not speak. It was almost irritating that he was right. What about the movie? she thought. England. Time off.

'You're going to hate me for this,' Rachel said, 'but I'd like to think about this overnight and call you in the morning. I promise, one way or another, I'll give you a yes or a no.'

Chapter Twenty-nine

The door to Cup of Joe banged shut loud enough behind Rachel to make several people look up. Almost two weeks earlier, Rachel had rushed away from Portsmouth and now she felt as if she had done the same thing, just in the opposite direction. Joe looked at her from behind the counter, his face not seeming to register who she was.

'Is Gary here, Joe?' she asked.

'No. He's at home.'

Rachel turned and was out the door as quickly as she had been through it.

'Rachel, wait,' she heard Joe call out, but ignored him.

Later, Rachel would wonder what good grace of timing had made her arrive at Gary's house at the precise moment she did. In terms of the probability, given the distances and the time to travel them involved, Rachel was certain the chances of turning up at the moment she did were remote. Whatever the odds, she was thankful.

Rachel pulled onto Gary's street and neared his house just in time to see him standing on the porch, facing a woman and a small child in between the two of them. She parked the car against the kerb, several houses down, where she could watch. They would not have noticed her had she been closer, Rachel thought, as they seemed too involved in a conversation, their body language as aggressive as it could be in view of the young boy. Gary gave what seemed to be an exasperated wave of his hand and then there was a pause. He bent down and planted a kiss on the boy who threw his arms around the back of his neck. The child ran off down the steps ahead of the woman who turned and walked from Gary without so much as an acknowledgement. The boy bounded happily, most of his head obscured by an oversized hat with earflaps. Rachel waited until their car had disappeared from view before leaving her own and walking to Gary's.

Gary opened the door and looked as though he was expecting to see his ex and his son again, his face ready to be angry. It dissolved into confusion and surprise.

'Rachel. I thought you weren't coming until tomorrow night. You just missed Zak and Grace,' he said.

'I finished up business in New York sooner than I expected and I thought there was no sense hanging around there. I'm going to be spending enough time there as it is,' she replied.

'You're going to take the part in the play? That's great,' he said, a smile spreading and washing away any previous tension he had shown. Gary grabbed Rachel and gave her a tight squeeze. 'I am so glad you've decided that.'

'It's not going to be easy. The commute up here late Saturday nights will kill me once we're on Broadway,' she said.

'I told you, I can come down and spend a couple of nights. I already talked to Joe about it. I could even bring Zak if you want,' he said.

'Why not,' she said.

Gary took her hand and they went upstairs. They walked slowly and he gripped her hand tightly so Rachel felt the bones of her own fingers pushing against him.

In the bedroom, they fell against each other and kissed, long and deep, their tongues working at each other. There was neither rush nor restraint as they undressed, both of them comfortable and familiar enough with each other to take their time. Rachel let Gary unbutton her, removing her top clothing and leaving her in just underwear. Rachel responded in kind, removing Gary's shirt and helping him off with his boots before taking off his jeans.

Rachel stroked her own hands lightly over her bare breasts, feeling the tips of her nipples respond to the feathering motion. Gary watched her, the front of his underwear stretched by the erection. She looked down at him, staring at the fabric and trying to discern the outline of him beneath. The long shaft snaked away to the left, the ridge of his phallus plain to see against the white cotton. While she looked on, Gary gripped himself and squeezed, the crotch of his underwear forming around his shaft. As he exerted pressure on himself, Rachel saw it surge, filling with his blood as he prepared himself. She found herself staring, wanting to touch him, to stroke him and to feel him inside of her.

The front of her own underwear was already damp, the material feeling muggy against the bush of her pubic hair. Beneath, the lips of her vagina were inflated, sensitive and puffed, eager for his touch. Rachel slid both hands over the flat of her stomach and worked them under the sheer hemline of the panties. As soon as her fingers found the fringes of hair, Rachel closed her eyes and sighed with contentment. Even with her eyes open, she would not have been able to see what she was doing to herself, but with them closed, it made the act seem more secretive.

Rachel's fingers broached the border of her sex, coming to the top of her labia, where her clitoris was nestled. Gently, she agitated it between her index fingers, rolling the flesh around as though loosening the stressed bud. On she went, past the small point of so much potential excitement, and down into the depths of her labia, feeling the opening of her vagina. Not wanting to carry herself too quickly over the edge, she did not linger, merely touching herself as though checking she were ready for him. She was.

Opening her eyes, she could tell from his expression he had been watching her. In his eyes, she saw a hunger for her. Gary was still methodically manipulating himself with his hand. A small wet patch had appeared where the tip of his shaft made contact with the cloth. Rachel wanted to unclad him. Kneeling down, she pulled at the underwear, stretching it away from his body to get it over the protrusion of his cock. She left the underwear around his ankles and turned her attention to his member.

Rachel gazed at it intently, the stiff rod heavy, unwieldy almost, and yet capable of setting off such delicate desires in her. It was exciting to think of the brutal member buried in her soft sex as he heaved at her with a masculine passion. It would be so perfect to lay beneath him and cling on as he built up more and more fervour, the speed and depth becoming almost unbearable, the feelings of desperation and exhilaration as, in taking himself away, he took her with him.

Standing, Rachel slid her knickers down while Gary stepped free of his underwear. They had removed only the smallest amount of clothing, the last remnants of their dress, and yet for Rachel, the fact of being nude with him changed things in her mind. There was a myriad of things she could do with him, to him, or him to her. They were limited only by imagination or inhibition. Rachel did not find herself feeling inhibited with him and thought, at that moment, she might well have done anything with him and, because of the fact, wanted really to do only the simplest of things.

Rachel had lost count of the number of times they had kissed since she had seen him again for the first time. While they explored each other with eagerness, their bodies gravitated towards the bed, their joint weight toppling towards the mattress. Once there, they continued to use their mouths, their faces pressed together, skin against skin, bone against bone. They bit and nipped at each other, using the rough edges of teeth softly against each other. She lay back on the bed and let him lean over her, supporting himself on elbows and knees. Gary looked down at her and then stroked her hair with his hand, lifting the fringe with his fingers.

Before Rachel could kiss him again, he was gone, his head disappearing, his mouth lighting over her breasts and stomach as he made his way down to the source of her desire. Rachel stuck her hands in his hair and held his head in her hands as his tongue licked agonisingly along the fold of her sex. His mouth was adroit and she gasped as he moved around the small area of her vulva, finding new areas of it to excite and stimulate with his tongue. He licked her clitoris, teasing the sensitive point with light strokes of his tongue. Rachel clutched his head tighter when his mouth disappeared and she felt his thumbs carefully prying her apart, not so wide as to be a crude examination, but just enough to make her feel the stretch and the exposure of her vagina. Deep inside herself, Rachel felt an orgasm travelling through her with a fierce speed, ready to break free with only the minimum of aid from Gary.

The whole of his mouth seemed to be on her, opened wide and pressed onto her flesh. From its centre, his tongue pushed out of his jaws and into the passage of her sex. He was not able to get it very far into her, but it was enough, the point of it raspy and delightful in the slick channel of her vagina. She could feel the pressure of his chin as he compressed his face to her and she lifted her behind off the bed, bringing her groin up to meet him.

Rachel's legs quivered and her hips shook so much, he held them in his hands, steadying her. Rachel orgasmed convulsively against him, her body jarring in opposition to his mouth and the muscles that should have supported her giving way to the weakening effects of the climax. The pleasure of it flooded her and she felt light in his hands, as though he might be able to sweep her up with no effort at all. For almost a minute, she came in a relentless surge that spared no part of her and when she was done, she fell away from him and lay on the bed, resigned and unable to focus on anything.

Gary knelt up and took hold of Rachel's legs, pushing them tightly together. She was surprised by the action and the feeling it gave as her vulva was squeezed and felt narrower. He lay on her, with his legs on the outside of hers so he was almost straddling her. Once again he supported himself on his elbows and Rachel could feel his weight on her and the press of his erect cock against her wet sex. Down between her legs, where their bodies were pushing together, Rachel felt muggy and hot, aching for penetration.

Manoeuvring himself carefully, a hand reaching down between them to hold himself, Gary began to guide his cock towards her labia, which was compressed by her legs. At first, Rachel found it difficult to tell how far he had entered her or to what depth. The sensation was unusual and she could tell already she was going to enjoy taking him into her that way. She pushed her legs together, exerting pressure on her own as he carried on breaching the soft lips of her sex.

Rachel exhaled with a long and powerful breath, feeling the muscles in her back and shoulders relax as Gary leaned above her and moved his body closer and closer to hers, joining himself with her as he did so. His thighs were tensed from their position and the tendons in them stood proud and close to the surface of the skin. Rachel could feel their power and ran her hands over them and onto his equally strong back, the broad sweep of it divided into hard, well defined areas.

With a final push, almost a shove, his body made contact with hers and he was inside her. The angle was unusual, he sex pointing more forwards than it would have had she opened her legs, allowed him between them and wrapped them around him. Instead, he lay on top of her and rod

her, his firm legs clamping hers together and his long, hard
cock buried to the base in her sex.

His body was heavy on hers and Rachel felt smothered by
him, the masculine weight of his torso flattening her breasts
against her ribcage. Gently, Rachel stirred the muscles of
her pelvis and her sex moved around the intrusion, causing
Gary to let out a sigh. His head was on her shoulder and he
was planting small kisses on the bone where it was closest to
the surface, giving it the occasional nip between his teeth.
For a while, he seemed content to lay atop her and let
Rachel tease him with rhythmic contractions.

Gary used his legs to compress Rachel's which, in turn,
tightened her thighs and, ultimately, her sex. The smooth
insides of his thighs were rigid, easily strong enough to close
tightly against Rachel's legs. In her sex, the stiff length of
his cock was probing her at such a peculiar angle it was
overcoming. Rachel lay and let him set the pace, his body
bobbing up and down as he created motion with the opening and closing of his legs. The mattress moved noisily and
soon they were almost bouncing from the action of his limbs
against hers. As Rachel rebounded off the mattress upwards, he was there to meet her with a downward thrust
that caught her in space and held her still. For the barest
fraction of a second each time it happened, it was like being
suspended in mid-air as their bodies contacted and were
going neither up nor down, forwards or backwards.

She wondered how long he could keep up the exertion,
imagining that it must have been strenuous for him to
produce so much energy with such a tight movement of his
legs. Rachel's sex was alive with the friction afforded by the
tightness of her legs. Her labia splayed each time he
withdrew and Rachel could feel her lips trailing over the
outer edges of his swollen shaft, clinging onto him before
being rudely shoved aside when he plundered her once
again.

The earlier orgasm and his manipulation of her with his

mouth had been the perfect preparation for what he did now. What had previously been gentle and dainty, deft movements of his tongue in the sensitive area of her sex, was replaced by a rough thrusting which Rachel knew would produce a climax of almost unbearable intensity. It would be as though all the force expended up to that point, the propelling of body against body, had been stored up and ready to be released in one powerful burst, eventually seeping all through her.

Gary's efforts became more erratic, the carefully judged motion of his legs now echoed in his shoulders and arms, his whole body seized by the need for mobility. The orgasmic power she had imagined was already sweeping through Gary, the loss of control evident. Rachel squeezed Gary's rear and let her hands rest on it, feeling the rolling action of the muscles which made the buttocks shift from rounded to flat and hard with each savage lunge. Deep in her vagina was the end result of his efforts, his hard cock which delved and probed her. It was assailing, to be so dominated by his presence above her and inside her, and Rachel clung to him and let their bodies synchronise.

They thrashed around on the bed, her body more or less going in the direction Gary's took her, as though they were joined by some invisible force. Rachel felt completely sexually overcome by the act of their lovemaking, all her thoughts on hold as she forced all her energy into the sex.

Gary gave a low whine, starting so quietly it was hard to hear it at first. The noise level wound up in time with the increasing tenor of his body's movements. They looked at each other, faces running hot with sweat, passions burning their skin a mutual shade of crimson. Rachel felt hemmed in perfectly trapped beneath the heaving form of masculinity that was about to go into a dizzying freefall of passion. His weight sagged closer to her, his groin the only area of him that was jerking against her, their stomachs stuck together in perspiration and their arms groping frantically at each other

Throwing his head back, Gary let out a long howl and Rachel felt the sudden burst of semen into her, hot and hard as he threw himself into the release with all that he had. It was fast and verging on the unbearable, and yet so absolutely overwhelming that Rachel found herself coming somewhere in the middle of his orgasm, screaming out and joining him in the high pitched chorus of their sex. Rachel's sex snatched at Gary's cock, swallowing it and his seed in heavy palpitations. The hardness of Gary's cock in the muscular grip of her vagina was the perfect combination, creating a mixture of agony and ecstasy that seemed without end.

Gary was stroking her hair and they were relaxing towards sleep when he spoke.

'Are you sure you're not going to have any regrets about all this?' he asked.

Rachel answered without pause. 'Ask me in two months,' she said.

Chapter Thirty

Winter was over. The weather was still brisk as Rachel stood looking at the view of the Thames from Richmond Bridge, but the March sunshine was almost winning out over the breeze. Two children and a watchful parent were squatting by the river bank. The smallest of the two children, wrapped in a square blue duffel coat, was making his best attempt at hurling a pebble into the water.

Four days off, a break agreed well before the start of the sold-out Broadway run of *A Winter's Tale* by Carl Milken starring Rachel Franklin, were almost over. At the behest and generosity of her new best friends and patrons, Carl Milken and Blake Jordan, Rachel had rolled on and off Concorde and would soon be doing so again, the timing just tight enough to make the dash back to the theatre all the more glamorous. Being successful on Broadway, she had learned, was more of a phenomenon that it had been on the London stage. The buzz about the play was like chatter almost audible and thrumming positively through everything. In the nicest of ways, it really did feel as though the whole town was talking about her.

Right from the first full read through, during rehearsal and then the pre-New York run in Boston, Rachel knew it was going to be a hit. She was involved in a triumph. It was one of the rare occasions where everything fell into place and everyone involved knew it, all afraid to think too hard about what they were doing for fear of bursting the magic bubble. Already, Rachel knew in a year or two she would be looking back on the experience, trying to recapture the same rhythm. There was a connection between the principal elements that went far beyond the individual traits they brought to the table and, for Rachel at least, that was due to Milken, always a step or two ahead of her. When she was taking the characters off in a certain direction, she found Milken had already explored the territory, laid the ground for her. Rehearsals had been one of the happiest spells in her acting life.

A four day break was not long and while she was enjoying London, Rachel was already anxious to be back in New York, her temporary home from home. Her mother, who was still occupying most of her time oscillating between the houses in Kew and Oxford, was on good form, still full of long distance advice about what Rachel should and shouldn't be doing. Her mother coped fine without her and Rachel wondered why she had ever doubted the older, wiser woman would not. The biggest surprise of the run so far had been her mother turning up in New York for the show with Rachel's father in tow, who said he was in town on business in any case, although Rachel suspected he had been badgered into coming along. Whatever his real reasons, and they were always hard to fathom, Rachel enjoyed seeing him, not least because it had been amusing to accompany the ex-married couple around Bergdorf Goodman and watch her mother trounce her father's credit cards.

Another, more serious, aspect of her mother's visit was that it enabled Rachel to reintroduce her to Gary, the tension quickly rising to a head and then dissipating, a kind of silent peace established. One with which they could all live.

Once in a while, Rachel received a postcard from Prague, normally a lewd one Ollie had purchased in London prior to his temporary domicile. The words on the back were usually more risque than even the picture but less obviously so as they were encoded in the sort of language shared by intimate friends. In equal measure, Ollie was pressing on with his memoirs and his passions, one providing fuel for the other. He was being tempted back to the stage and there was even talk of a film role for him. Rachel had giggled when Liz Benton contacted her to say there were murmurs of interest in Rachel playing Ollie's daughter. 'Don't tell my mother,' was all she said in reply to Liz.

If, in friction, her relationship to Oliver might change from lover to daughter, then with Damien it had, in fact, turned into one of agony aunt. As far as Rachel could tell, Nikki Price was driving Damien to distraction and for the first time in his young life, he was obsessed with someone. For her part, Nikki seemed equally as taken with Damien and Rachel suspected there was enough nervous energy between the two of them to keep the fires burning. Sometimes, she wondered if she would still have the drive to keep up with a Damien, but mostly, Rachel was glad she no longer had to.

Later, she would call Gary in Portsmouth. The separation across the Atlantic was far worse than the one between New York and New Hampshire. There, at least, she felt on the same continent as him, only several hours from him. Rachel had decided that was to be her measure of the strength of her feelings towards any man. How much time and distance could she bear to put between the two of them. In their case, ten years and thousands of miles had been more than enough and Rachel did not want to go back to it.

A Winter's Tale was certain to transfer to the West End. It was simply a question of logistics, finding the right place and time. When it happened, Rachel knew it would be a triumphant return for her. In doing the play first and to such acclaim, she had forever made it her own, becoming the standard by which others would be judged. That put the pressure on anyone wanting to take over the role on Broadway when she left for England, a pressure obviously far too strenuous for the great Gloria Vaughan who had passed on the opportunity.

Would she bring Gary and Zak to London in the summer, when the transfer happened? They both seemed keen and his mother seemed to think it would do him good. In the shifting emotions of Gary, Zak and Zak's mother, Rachel had found a role that enabled her to flow easily between the three of them, fitting in and being accepted with greater readiness than she might have hoped for. Perhaps Gary, Zak and herself would set up camp in London. For once, the uncertainty of the future was an adventure rather than a source of dread.

Staring down at the river, watching the sleek water rush under her, Rachel looked on as the adult and two children wandered off down the towpath, small legs moving at double speed to keep up. Rachel raised her face up to the sky, squinting into the brightness. She took a deep breath and exhaled it vigorously. The air felt cleaner, vibrant and life-giving. Winter was behind her for another year and spring had taken hold.

The summer was not far away.

A Message from the Publisher

Headline Liaison is a new concept in erotic fiction: a list of books designed for the reading pleasure of both men and women, to be read alone – or together with your lover. As such, we would be most interested to hear from our readers.

Did you read the book with your partner? Did it fire your imagination? Did it turn you on – or off? Did you like the story, the characters, the setting? What did you think of the cover presentation? In short, what's your opinion? If you care to offer it, please write to:

> The Editor
> Headline Liaison
> 338 Euston Road
> London NW1 3BH

Or maybe you think you could do better if you wrote an erotic novel yourself. We are always on the look-out for new authors. If you'd like to try your hand at writing a book for possible inclusion in the Liaison list, here are our basic guidelines: We are looking for novels of approximately 80,000 words in which the erotic content should aim to please both men and women and should not describe illegal sexual activity (pedophilia, for example). The novel should contain sympathetic and interesting characters, pace, atmosphere and an intriguing plotline.

If you'd like to have a go, please submit to the Editor a sample of at least 10,000 words, clearly typed on one side of the paper only, together with a short resumé of the storyline. Should you wish your material returned to you please include a stamped addressed envelope. If we like it sufficiently, we will offer you a contract for publication.